'Terrific! Set in modern F
invigoratingly combines questions of identity,
shenanigans in the art world, love and murder'
MICHÈLE ROBERTS

'A breathtaking book confirming Claire Berest's
inexhaustible talent as a storyteller'
ELLE

'Deliciously unique and unpredictable . . . this novel
blossoms like a poisonous flower'
LE JOURNAL DU DIMANCHE

'An astonishing thriller'
LIBÉRATION

'A glowing, cinematic thriller, propelled throughout by
zippy, electric writing, which builds in pace and intensity
until reaching an ingenious, twisting finale'
BUZZ MAGAZINE

'A cleverly crafted novel made up of trompe l'oeil, red
herrings, and mistaken identities. Dreamlike and dark'
LE FIGARO

'An intense thriller where performance art intersects
with tragedy . . . brilliant and captivating'
LE PÈLERIN

CLAIRE BEREST is a writer from Paris. In 2019, her novel *Rien n'est noir* about the life of Frida Kahlo won Elle's Grand Prix des lectrices. With her sister Anne, she is also the author of *Gabriële*, a critically-acclaimed biography of her great-grandmother, Gabriële Buffet-Picabia, Marcel Duchamp's lover and muse. She is the great-granddaughter of the painter Francis Picabia.

SOPHIE LEWIS is a literary editor and translator from French and Portuguese into English. She has translated works by Jules Verne, Marcel Aymé, Violette Leduc, Leïla Slimani and João Gilberto Noll, among others. Her translations have been shortlisted for the Scott Moncrieff and Republic of Consciousness prizes, and longlisted for the International Booker Prize.

Claire Berest

ARTIFICE

Translated from the French by
Sophie Lewis

MLP

to Émilie, Laura,
Virginie and Anaïs,
who turned eighteen in the year 2000.

Our beating hearts.

'the imagination holds its own'
Journey to the End of the Night
Louis-Ferdinand Céline, translated by Ralph Manheim

'can only have been painted by a madman!'
Edvard Munch,
inscription hidden in his painting 'The Scream'

Abel

I

A fox, though young

Abel is numb, he can only see them falling to the ground, one after the other, unreal puppets killed off, men, women, in no order, he looks for Éric's face, and now Éric is turning to him with the same expression, the empty eyes always there in the middle of his face, the way you might decide to stick a flower in your buttonhole once and for all, by way of signature, or to wear a black jacket, always the same one, to fix all this shit of having to display your identity. Éric is staring calmly at the head of a woman who is still moving on the ground, terrified the way only imminent death can terrify, and he shoots the woman, without spite, in the middle of her forehead, to finish what he has begun. The woman dies and Abel wakes up.

Abel Bac woke up, his body gripped by the nightmare's immediacy, gasping for breath as if he had taken a lungful of seawater, bolt upright in the darkness of his room. He began to count backwards: ninety-three, ninety-two, ninety-one . . . Racing through the numbers at breakneck speed, like a deranged clock, then more slowly, trying to ease the familiar vice of the dream. You can have the same nightmare for twenty years and the terror is the same, as new, over the years the terror remains as fresh as ever. Abel went on counting . . . fifty-seven, fifty-six, fifty-five . . . when he heard a noise.

Abel heard a noise: scratchings on the woodwork, then the chinking of bracelets knocking together, a muffled bump, a rustle of things falling, stumbling footsteps. What was this racket? His eyes shocked wide in the half-light, Abel listened carefully to the unwonted commotion outside his front door. As if someone was fiddling with the keyhole. He got up and pulled on a pair of jeans. He reached the living room in five steps, the hall in three, he opened the door with a rough, ill-tempered pull, and a girl tumbled into him.

The girl tumbled into him. A dishevelled blonde, too much jewellery, boozy eyes, a reek of gin, he recognised his neighbour from upstairs. The one who had come by a few days ago to bother him with nebulous tales of recycling regulations in the building. 'I do separate the plastics,' he had repeated calmly, but without managing to stem her nervous chatter. So he had said nothing more until she stopped talking. Despite her apparent hopes, he had not invited her into his two-room apartment to continue their conversation on the importance of sorting the recycling. He had said goodbye.

This time, the girl was plastered. He looked at his watch: 2.27 a.m. He caught her just as she began to tip backwards. She could not stand up, was hardly on her feet at all. She muttered that her key wasn't working. 'Key . . . Don' work, key . . .' He glared at her from the height of his icy body. He righted her again and then propped her against the door frame, as he would a rickety piece of furniture awaiting repair. Abel gathered up the bothersome junk scattered from her bag and now strewn across his doorstep and stuffed it rapidly back into said handbag, which was hanging open and soaked through. 'Your bag is full of water,' he said.

'Key don' work,' she moaned again, more loudly.

'I realise. You're on the wrong floor.' He ran one arm under hers and gripped her firmly by the shoulder. 'Up we go, madame.'

'Madame? Madame?' she spluttered, in a fit of alcoholic hilarity. 'I'm a madame!' The laughter was too much for her and she pissed herself, literally, thus in her eyes compounding the comedy of the situation. 'Pissing myself!' Abel wondered exactly which circle of hell he had stumbled into.

They began to climb the sixteen steps to the building's top floor, to the row of former maids' rooms, doll's-house cells for living in. 'Which one is your studio?' She did not respond. Three doors. He took a punt on the furthest one, over which a charming garland of kraft-paper origami flowers dangled. 'Got to throw up,' she warned. 'That's not my problem,' he panted. Abel was hunting for the bunch of keys that had scraped at his door. Not here. Shit. With growing irritation, he propped his female parcel against the wall again. 'I'm coming back.' All the way down the sixteen steps, peering at the staircase, he spotted the keyring's gleam in a corner of the landing, grabbed it and ran back up, taking the steps four at a time. 'Got them now,' he muttered.

Abel found the young woman sunk into a foetal huddle on a flocked *Bienvenue!* doormat. Like a little kid, he thought. A naughty drunk kid. Third door, the garland, the key bit, bingo, at last he had it open, and a waft of jasmine enveloped him like a ghostly cough. He gripped the girl, took her bag too, and dropped the lot on the unmade bed.

Too much jasmine for seventeen square metres. Abel gagged.

He considered his charge and wondered if he ought to do something about her trousers, which were soaked. He weighed up his options. But the barely imaginable notion of approaching this woman's intimate regions forestalled his making any attempt.

He turned her head to the side, to stop her choking on vomit. Correct steps taken. *Au revoir.*

At 2.38, he went to get a bucket from his own apartment, filled it with three bleach tablets, two capfuls of white vinegar, and warm water, and armed himself with the mop. He buckled down to washing off the central stairs which were covered in pee. In his head, he was counting backwards again. To calm down.

2.53. Abel was back in bed, white sheet up to his chin, eyes wide open. He knew he would not be able to sleep again. He put on a T-shirt and a jumper – both clean. Not from the day before. Which day before, anyway? He tended to muddle his insomnias because the nightmares stopped him from dividing periods of time with any certainty.

He went out into the snow-white night of the Paris boulevards. He would go for a walk, as he usually did.

Abel Bac went out for a walk feeling as if he had lice, lice on his head. A colony of vermin to remind him of his body, to give him no peace. A stealthy but urgent itching. He scratched, a bit; the move opened the floodgates of an urge to scratch everywhere, to work his over-clipped nails into his scalp until it was raw. Now he dug deep, clawing himself, freely creating red furrows under his hair, out of sight. The satisfaction of scratching, the way we take pleasure in a soothing pain, pain in service of forgetting. Perhaps there really were lice living on his head. Lice caught through the inevitable bodily proximities, a professional hazard. Or were they literally *in* his head? Fabricated. The lice of his feelings.

Abel Bac stopped at the all-night pharmacy on place Clichy with its flashing green cross, siren song to the 18th arrondissement's local hoods. He did not join the queue, the pharmacist knew him. He was a good client.

'I'd like a headlice shampoo.'

'That'll be the third this month. You'll end up damaging your scalp.'

'And a pack of paracetamol.'

'Of course, as usual.'

'It's for my plants, not me.'

'Of course.'

The line of harrowed faces hoping for methadone or any kind of painkiller looked askance at Abel, not appreciating his circumvention of the queue. But no-one said a word. Abel frightened them. It wasn't his face but what they could not see. It wasn't that pair of faded blue eyes, high seas in prospect; it wasn't the still childish chin pressing full lips forward to match, nor the cheekbones razor-scraped in ice-cold water that alarmed them. No, it was the barely visible tension of his muscles, which vibrated like a red alert.

He put the shampoo and the pills in his backpack and adjusted the straps, feeling vaguely guilty for giving way to the impulse, then brushed aside his guilt with a sweep of his hand and stepped outside again. Back to his night-walk.

Abel entered his trance, step by step, finding the rhythm, so his body alone could choose its path; a touch too fast at first, he needed to taste the unfolding landscape, to let his brain capture the details, a shop window, a face, to let it record a burst of conversation, scraps of sounds, speech, music floating from the bars' half-closed doors, to find a point of balance amid this merry-go-round.

Nor must his trance move too slowly either, he let the drumming of his limbs beat the pavement, his feet shrug off their tingling, let the details gleaned around him become streaks, snags, to be forgotten before they were fully grasped, let his arms' swing match the pace of his steps, let the speed send a little sweat down his neck and warm his body. And, at last, he succeeded in getting lost. Which had become so difficult, and ever rarer.

Abel always knew where he was, he knew the city too well, his senses were sharp and would not let him lose track. A glance at a street sign, the familiar form of a square, an over-bright massage salon, a frustrated face: everything was information. Not to mention the smells. He predicted before even seeing them the restaurants, a bakery in a basement, the corner where vagrants would piss. Everything smelled. Everything leaked. Very occasionally he did manage to get lost. After an hour or two of walking to the automatic rhythm of his liberated limbs, his etherised head, suddenly he felt it, he was lost. And then the joy took hold. Not knowing where he was at all. Not even sure which neighbourhood he was in. To look around, serenely, at the unfamiliar windows, the unknown and dormant apartment blocks, and the few passersby with messageless faces. Everything settled inside him. The elation was worth the effort. The fleeting moment when he lost all sense of himself.

And then he could shake himself, deliberately discover where he had got to and start back, worn out and happy, the way tramps always end up returning to the fold when blue daybreak is safely moored to the sky.

He had set his quota at four night-walks per week. He forced himself to rest on the remaining nights, otherwise the lack of sleep became too much. When he slept, he dreamed about Éric, and he couldn't let himself wander too far that way. Tonight, he had not planned to walk. He had counted on some sleep. But the sozzled neighbour had messed with his schedule. She'd made him get up, so he didn't feel this incident need be classed as a failure of self-control.

*

Tonight, he did not get lost.

He knew the entire route he had taken. He had gone down the rue d'Amsterdam, turned off at rue de Liège, then taken rue Moncey, recognised the vintner with a promotion on natural wines, then Blanche, the dead flowers on rue de La Rochefoucauld, the Gustave Moreau museum, on as far as boulevard Haussmann, it was incredible all these maps in his head, the diagrams, the cut-throughs, shortcuts, landmarks, how could anyone tidy it all up . . .

He'd powered along rue Tiquetonne before heading back up boulevard de Sébastopol, had a moment's intoxication, a doubt, then recognised the maroon drapery of that restaurant on the rue des Vertus, the grey armature of some streetlights, the manhole cover. He had given up.

Back at his harbour, place Clichy, like a bull to his manger, where every alley was familiar, every skewed garden a memory, the sun was up now, and the Métro had opened, the *kiosquier* was bustling about, the early risers treating themselves to a croissant at the bistro to dip in their strong coffees. Abel stumped up to his apartment to change his T-shirt before going for a coffee at the Carolus. As he made his way up the four flights of his staircase, he remembered it was Thursday – his laundrette day. Then, at his own landing, he saw a newspaper on his doormat, probably a mistake, he left it there and went inside. It was as if the night air confined inside rushed out around him. In one movement he pulled off his T-shirt and flung it into the laundry basket to join a dozen identical white T-shirts. In fresh clothes, he did not linger but swung the door to behind him and came again to the newspaper lying folded on his mat. It was the *Parisien*, easily recognisable from its sky-blue banner stripe; he left it there and went down to the Carolus.

At the bar, the owner Ahmed automatically served Abel as soon as he stepped inside, a strong black coffee, a double, and called into the kitchen: 'Bread and butter!' This character moved through his early-morning routines: taking the tables outside, changing the binbags, turning on the machines, bringing in the day's papers, checking the approximate cleanliness of floors and tabletops, flicking the T.V. over to a rolling news channel.

And serving the cop's strong coffee, of course.

2

by no means raw

'Are you coming off shift or on, boss?'

'Leaving work.'

'Here's your bread and butter.'

'Thanks.'

A half-baguette cut longways, the two hulls of bread smothered in margarine. Abel was unwinding, his bodily exhaustion was acute, he gulped down the buttery spread.

'More butter.'

'On its way.'

The morning street life filtered in, lining up at the bar, they were almost all men, labourers, dustmen, local grandads already scratching at their lottery tickets, overgrown urban youth, the noise intensified as the men hailed each other and dug into their small talk. Abel could relax amid their exchanges, lose himself in the growing buzz, he was not alone here. He appreciated the regular racket of the coffee machine when Ahmed knocked the grounds out in its wooden drawer. Hammer. Metronome. That knock was squarer than the fragments of conversations swarming around him. There was still a mild whiff of rollies: Abel knew that, when the blinds went down, Ahmed would run lock-ins for the local Moroccans, they liked to play cards, and the old ashtrays would emerge from the cupboards again.

'Have you seen this, my boy? They're all out of ideas now, these artists.'

Ahmed held a newspaper out to him – he could keep up the chat with all his clients at once, he knew their professions, their rituals and tastes. Ahmed pronounced artists more like *aarrrgh-tistes*, and he washed his hands a lot, all the time actually.

Abel looked at the front page of the already crumpled *Parisien*, object of the proprietor's aspersions. In the journal's grainy central photograph he saw a white horse held at the harness by two policemen standing in front of the Pompidou Centre.

'They snuck a geegee into the gallery! The hack gotta be as lively as the art in there,' Ahmed said, pleased to have caught his customer's attention. 'Poor creature.' And he was off to wash his hands.

Abel focused on the photograph. He made a few slow circuits of the horse in his head. He was wondering what this horse reminded him of. It was there, but beyond his field of vision. He gave up, nodded in punctuation to Ahmed's gambits, but Ahmed was already lining up further coffees on the bar; Abel left a five-euro note on the counter by the row of white saucers, and made for the door. Then he paused and returned to snatch up the *Parisien*.

Ahmed saw but made no comment.

Back at his landing on the fourth floor, Abel noticed an earring stuck between the floorboards in front of his door: it was a little gold swan mounted on a ring. A souvenir from his inebriated neighbour. He pocketed it. The untouched, plastic-wrapped *Parisien* was still on the mat. He opened it: the same edition as the one swiped from Ahmed, with the white horse on the front page. He looked around, trying to penetrate the other doors on the floor, to guess which the paper ought to be addressed to. A name was indeed printed on the poor-quality plastic label that he'd torn apart, and the ink had leaked, blurring, bleeding through the addressee's name. He looked more closely and deciphered 'Abel Bac'. He had never subscribed to the *Parisien*.

He went inside and prepared the paracetamol bought the night before at the pharmacy: five pills dissolved in a large bottle of mineral water. And now he undertook to pour a little into each plant, avoiding watering them from above but instead topping up the water in the dish of pebbles beneath each one so it would rise naturally through the soil and up into the stems.

His bower of orchids.

He had ninety-three, scattered all over the living room. Covering the floor, perched on the few items of furniture, on the windowsills and in pots hanging from the ceiling. Soon to be a hundred. If none of them died.

Abel's floral surroundings were so foreign, so ecstatic, that they were never the same to him. They shifted, transformed. When he entered his apartment, he felt the opposite of habituality. His orchids provoked endless wonder, the way the moods of skies seen through a single window are infinitely volatile.

It was a field of faces, now calm, now all screaming mouths, from yellow to mauve, from white to pink.

He could go and wash.

Undressing, Abel felt the earring at the bottom of his pocket and put it in the top drawer along with the rest: the gleanings of his walks. He took some time over his ablutions, to regain some energy, access the strength not to sleep and make it to the evening. In the end he allowed himself to look at his watch, which lay on the bedside table: it was 8.10. He took a notebook from the pile next to the bed and, in his telegraphic style, noted his observations from this latest walk. The roads he had taken, the people encountered, any slight differences: some new graffiti, a broken window, a new billboard. Abel completed his lists. Next he went through the notebooks where his insomniac moments were set down: was it possible that he'd subscribed to the *Parisien*, one exhausted evening, in the grip of lord knew what obsession, and instantly forgotten? If so, it could only have happened recently. He found nothing of the kind mentioned in his tiny, precise, densely black-inked writing. He put the notebook back on the pile. Nice and straight.

At 8.30 he was seized with a panic over what to do with this day. What should one do when deprived of the logic of timetables so perfectly established until now? He was all at sea. His routine settled fifteen years earlier: precise time-keeping, Métro, cases, operations, hearings, paperwork, colleagues. The foundation structure obliterated. It was a week since he had been suspended from his role as police lieutenant in Paris's 1st district crime squad, D.P.J. 1. Thanks to a single snitch to the I.G.P.N., the national police inspectorate. But, dammit, who had gone digging up his past?

3

Had seen a horse

Camille Pierrat alternated between anxiety and irritation. That Abel had not replied to a single one of her messages was unsurprising, but that he had not even turned his phone on for a week was worrying. She had checked. In order to do so, she'd made a little systems tweak which was *never* O.K. and over which she risked getting into serious shit. She had requested authorisation for a live zero-six geolocation and had slipped Bac's phone number into the list. With the judge's authorisation and after the operator had connected it, she had deleted his number from the file. With a bit of luck, it would go off without a hitch. Situation to date: since Abel had been laid off, his phone had picked up no signals at all. It was simply off. Who turned off their phone for a whole week? She'd have to go and knock on his door. But she knew her colleague: he would never open it.

She was typing up a case that had been dragging on for months. A 52-year-old murdered, eighteen stab wounds. Felt like they'd reached the end of the road. The suspect list included everyone in the supermarket on a Saturday afternoon. Outwardly textbook ordinary guy, proprietor of a little bar, wife-and-two-kids-and-decent-neighbour, but he turned out to have had a whole party of skeletons in his cupboard. Tyrannical with his staff, withheld salaries, a string of mistresses. Not exactly a clean bill, but

Camille couldn't dig up anything that justified knifing someone eighteen times. Such vitriol; it was more like an exorcism. Everyone had said their piece. All the guy's papers, his computers, hard drives, his accounts: all sucked dry. Phone calls too. Alibis here, there and everywhere all cross-checked. The crime scene itself was a proper puzzle: the victim's body had been found in his study, doors and windows all wide open. They'd taken so many fingerprints, they'd nowhere left to file them. The weapon had vanished – weapons, rather. The depth and width of the wounds varied sufficiently to make it likely several knives had been used. But who stops in the middle of a frenzied stabbing to change weapons? It wasn't the kitchen at some trendy fucking restaurant.

Camille hated that moment in a case when all the stones had been turned and yet they were still on the starting blocks. It happened rarely. Life is not a crime novel. With most homicides, you soon got the measure of where it had all gone south, usually in the first few days. From there, the challenge was how to trap the rat, and that was the major part of her job: gathering evidence, getting a spotlight on the hotspot, setting a trap. And the best bit: making them talk.

There are two types of detective. Those who focus on the 'who': *who* had the resources, the opportunity and the availability to commit the act? There couldn't be thousands of them, all you needed was a bit of triage. And those who go for the 'why': *why*, in the case at hand, did someone feel the need to stick a knife in the podge of this unsavoury character eighteen times? Camille belonged to the 'who' contingent. It went with the 'how'. She was not there to run group therapy sessions. Once you'd patiently tallied up working schedules, connections to the victim, telephone records, disqualifying alibis, G.P.S. car locations and any likely witnesses, there weren't generally many lucky punters left. Straight maths. The 'why' was for the courts, for the public prosecutors and the lawyers. The stuff of books.

Abel Bac was one of the 'why tribe' – strictly a minority among cops – with their need to understand motivations and the origins of motivations, to put themselves in the shoes of both the crime's victim and its author, to plot each step of the road to ruin, to live it. Camille found all that exhausting; it took a lot of oxygen. But it was also why she liked working with Abel. As well as being exacting to the point of obsession, he had intuitions. Because you never got perfect answers to the why – you had to have imagination. Starting with the why, Abel sketched out ramifications that were invisible to the naked eye. His line was a 'Yes, Camille, but what if . . .?' And he came up with theories. Sometimes he'd sniff out an angle that didn't fit, a word, a detail that sounded the alarm. 'Yes, but what if . . .' was now their private joke, insofar as Abel Bac could be considered a humorist.

For example, the stabbing guy: Abel was sure it was the wife. From the outset. Except that nothing fitted. He'd come up with twenty theories: 'But what if . . . or what if . . .?' Abel the Saviour. At the supposed hour of the incident, the wife's phone registered a signal at the house of a friend she was visiting in an outer suburb. The friend had confirmed they were together. Her car's G.P.S. recorded the route she took to the friend's place, the lady was even snapped by speed cameras. A time-stamped speeding ticket stood as further back-up . . .

. . . but Abel would not be swayed. 'You'll see, Camille. It's warped, but it was her.'

It had been a week since Abel's suspension from work. He hadn't told a single colleague, either before or since. It had played out behind closed doors on the top floor. Camille had mentioned her surprise at his absence one morning and the boss had let her know, without further details. His number had been unreachable and still was. He had cut himself off. He would need to defend himself, to engage a lawyer while they carried out the formal investigation, prepare his own file, come up with a strategy, assert his rights. He'd have only a few months before being called in by the disciplinary board. They must have told him the reason, but as he'd said nothing to anyone, they were up shit creek without a paddle or even a telephone.

Camille didn't know Abel well. No-one in the force knew Abel Bac well. But they'd been working together for two years, and she'd picked up a few things about him. The humiliation of a disciplinary procedure would not blow over. He was out of his depth. Abel had always seemed made for this gig, to her: no personal life, hundred per cent living the job, doing far too much overtime for zilch and picking up the paperwork without complaint – one reason why he was well liked in the force. He worked like a convict and gave no-one any shit, because the truth is everyone thought he was a bit of an outlier and they always had.

This was one of the first things Camille was told when she joined: 'You'll see: Bac, he's a good worker, a good guy, but he's an *odd fish*,' the same way they warned her that the machine made vile coffee, that the boss was over-fond of his Bordeaux and that Francis was a randy bastard and borderline #metoo.

Since the announcement of his suspension, everyone had been freaking out. If Abel had committed some colossal act of idiocy, he could hardly be going down alone; other heads could well roll – hers, to start with. They had worked on the same cases. Although Camille couldn't see where they might have gone wrong. They might occasionally take a few shortcuts, or they would go a little nuts now and then out of fatigue. But a suspension meant something serious. He must have harassed a colleague or beaten up a kid in custody. She had called the union leaders. They didn't know anything and Abel hadn't been in touch with them. He lived alone, no partner or kids. Camille had no idea who to call to find out what was up. Here, everyone had their own shit: the trade was knackering, the data targets were a piss-take, there was home life to keep track of, the night-owl hours, the exhaustion, the frustration, the tension building with the public. It was weird: there had never been more crime series to stream, nor such a deep loathing for her profession.

No-one was friends with Abel. She was thinking in the past tense; a week is a long time when someone has disappeared. She tried it out in the present: *No-one is friends with Abel.* How about her?

Camille didn't keep up with that many friends, either. She was no it-girl with hundreds of followers on her Insta page. But it wasn't quite a desert either. She had mates from law school and police training, she went for evenings out with them. No particular boyfriend, but there had been relationships. No children, but she was only twenty-nine. She had a brother and parents, none of them particularly awful, nor especially cool. She did drinks with colleagues, remembered birthdays on time and generally brought a six-pack to house parties. She laughed at jokes, plus she could shut up when required: she could act the team player.

4

the first he ever saw

Elsa awoke the way you break free of a plague: with foghorns and cymbals. A rotting weight inside her skull and aching eyelids. She looked around, counted her ribs and ticked off her limbs. How had she got to bed? Her contact lenses had dried on her eyes and her feet still had shoes on. Heavy piss-up, and a heavy night. She sat up and the room spun. She stank. She stank a moderately pleasant mix of gin, sweat, saliva and debauchery. Automatically, she looked around: handbag? Phone? Wallet? Yes. Chaos under control. Joy of the chaos. She clutched at the black curtain of her night's last few hours, hunting for a way through to some memories. She'd come home on foot – uncertain. She'd definitely struggled over the entry code. She'd walked up the steps. Damn that stairwell without a lift. Threads of sensation: she still wasn't used to this minuscule apartment, the four walls like the insides of a box, a small box, a coffin apartment, a casket. Optical illusion.

She had pissed herself, what glory. Elsa peeled off the tight jeans sticking to her thighs and tossed them into a corner of the room along with the still-wet knickers tangled inside them. She stumbled into the bathroom to contemplate her degradation.

Leaning on the basin, she looked at her face. Traces of the night, black circles from the booze, a missing earring, just the one.

She washed her face with great splashes of water. Blurry mask, the last pastels of which slid down the plughole. She dumped the remnants of this body under a cold shower. A vision hit her as the water began to rinse away her excesses: an image.

It was him. She relaxed.

Thrilled.

It was him, the downstairs neighbour, he'd been there last night. She had gone to find him in the middle of the night, it was coming back. No, she hadn't! Yes, she had. Action missing. Flashes of him came back to her, him and his ice-cold presence. His aloofness.

Abel Bac.

Satisfied, she smiled.

5

'Ho! neighbour wolf,' said he

She had been buzzing for several minutes and now stood listening intently for the slightest movement to filter out from the other side. Nothing moved, but she sensed he was there. She waited long enough for him to think she had gone. In the dull air still this unblemished silence. Reaching her mouth up to the door frame, she declared: 'Bac, open this door or I'll put a bullet through your keyhole and I shan't be paying the locksmith. I'm counting to ten. One!'

Abruptly Abel opened the door.

A grey-faced Abel.

'Shit, you were right there.'

'Hello, Camille. I'd like to be left alone. Thanks. Bye, Camille.'

Camille held the door open just as Abel moved to close it, she demanded that he let her in; no reason he couldn't invite her in for a coffee, in his own place, the way normal people do, colleagues and friends. 'Abel, dammit, why not let me come in, this is stupid and annoying. You think it's fun for me? I've come all the way to place Clichy to see you, yes, I'm worried about you, is that so bad? No, I'm not going until we've had a coffee. I'm warning you, I have no intention of being sent on my way by you, Abel.'

The shamelessness of the situation horrified him. The use out loud of the word *friend*, the audible expression of anxiety, made

Abel feel as if his head were deep in honey, everything so sticky. He had not asked for anything from anyone.

Deep breath.

'Alright, Pierrat, a coffee; not here, downstairs, at the Carolus. I'll get changed and meet you there.' Camille withdrew her boot from the door frame – professional training – and shelved her irritation before this hard-won concession.

'If you're not there in five minutes, I'm coming back up and this time I'm shooting out your keyhole, no further warning.'

In two years, Camille had not once set foot in her colleague's apartment. The few beers shared at the end of a job had all been drunk in bars. Besides, Abel did not drink much, preferring to avoid intoxication. His drinking was purely form.

Sitting side by side on the Carolus' terrace, they might have been taken for tourists adrift at the seaside. The typical Parisian café terrace set-up – handkerchief-sized tables jammed together in rows across a minimal pavement area while maximising numbers of throats to feed and water – put paid to any kind of heart-to-heart.

'I hardly dare ask why they let you go, because I guess you'd rather not talk about it, but I'm asking anyway: Abel, what did you fuck up to land a suspension?'

'I don't want to talk about it.'

'D'you realise how serious this is? And why are you holing up in your apartment? You should tell the union right away, they're there to back you up. There's a bunch of steps to take, you've gotta defend yourself, you must hire a lawyer. You can't let them put a bomb under your whole career, just let it go like this – there must be some misunderstanding, right? You mustn't take the flak, you're one of the straightest cops I know. Frankly, you're obsessed with the rules. What did you do?'

The less Abel responded, the louder and faster Camille became. As is often the case when a man and a woman are talking. It's a historic leftover of women's oppression – they're trying to catch up.

Abel let himself be lulled by her noise, he didn't look at her, paid no attention to her expostulations, he was making the most of the distraction, sipping on her words. It had been a week since he'd talked to anyone, if you discounted the drunk blonde from upstairs and Ahmed. It was true: even he could do with another person's noise, now and then. Also filling his ears was Leonard Cohen, pouring his heart out to nobody inside the Carolus: *If you want another kind of love, I'll wear a mask for you. If you want a partner, take my hand . . . I'm your man.* What an odd word, 'partner', so ambiguous.

'Nothing, Pierrat. I didn't do anything.'

She set him going again. Put another coin in the jukebox. When Camille had started in the force, she had been so dogged, so anxious to do things right, to learn the codes and the jargon; something of a secret tomboy, she'd soon been on good terms with all the boys. Diligent and even-tempered, she had mastered the art of putting people in their place without raising hackles and had become hyper-tuned to the job. And she'd wanted to work with him, with Abel Bac. She must have been after a challenge, like so many women, Abel thought. He might have been unsophisticated, but he was no idiot.

'Why has your phone been locked all this week? Don't you have people to call? No Facebook friends? Are you playing the lonesome, misunderstood cowboy? You're what, maybe, forty-five, tops? Your life is not over, bro. It'll be at least as long and as bloody dull if you're holed up doing fuck all in your apartment.'

'Thirty-nine. I'm thirty-nine.'

'You look older. Sorry.'

'To answer your question: I don't know why I've been suspended. I think someone's made a complaint against me. I don't know what it's about. And I don't know of anyone with cause to complain about me for any reason. It's Byzantine.'

'Shit, these fancy words, you use. It's *Byzantine*! *Excuse me, ladies and gentlemen, but it's Byzantine!* That's exactly what we need those bastard lawyers for, to handle the Byzantine side of things. You get a lawyer so they can access the case, understand the situation, and prepare you for it. You don't have some ex with alimony you haven't paid?'

No, Abel had no ex-wife, nor a current one. Besides, unpaid alimony would not be sufficient reason for suspending a police officer. Camille knew it. She was trying to make him talk. He was impossible to read. Not a talker, he didn't make dirty jokes, he stayed shtum. So there were some rumours doing the rounds at work: he had a few screws loose, was into some twisted shit. Quite enough imagination there to make up for other people's silence.

Shortly after Camille's arrival in the force, one evening, there had been a very brief moment between them. An embrace, an awkwardness, an urge. *Almost* a moment. It hadn't changed anything. But perhaps, yes perhaps, that justified her. Awkward at first, discomfiting, clumsy. And then, forgotten. But she remembered it, that sweet second. The call of sex is practically nothing but it's a little less nothing than oblivion.

Abel's gaze again fell upon a *Parisien* lying on the next table. The same as this morning's copy, with the horse on the front, same as the one he'd nabbed from Ahmed's counter, same as the one left on his doorstep with his name on the plastic cover, the horse they had found in the Pompidou Centre.

'What's this murk, d'you know about it?'

Abel had the finicky habit of using the word *murk* at every juncture by way of saying shit, shitstorm, fuck-up or alien. Unsettling at first, old-fashioned and incongruous, but you got used to it. Camille glanced at the newspaper, she had caught something about it on the radio that morning and thought nothing of it. Somebody'd had a bit of fun slipping the animal into an art gallery at night. No vandalism, no theft, no damage.

No, she said, she had no idea. He asked if she would find out more, discover who exactly was looking after the case. She was happy to do that, but it was probably just drunken students fooling around.

'You think a drunk student can just stroll into an art gallery after dark like it's their living room? With a half-tonne animal on the end of a rope? There's C.C.T.V., guards, alarms; you know how many millions of paintings they're keeping cool in the Pompidou's basement? You really think people can just show up all butterwouldn't-melt and proceed to pull off a bunch of student pranks?'

'Steady on. Do you know much about art, yourself? Done any time inside a gallery?'

There's another odd expression, *butter wouldn't melt*, she thought. Typical Bac. She'd asked him one day where he'd got that word *murk* from, which he now used on all occasions. It was something his mother used to say, he'd replied, and that kind of word, it stays with you. 'What did your mother do?' Camille had asked. And Bac had left the office without answering.

Murk was graphic; it said chaos, shit, bad luck, bureaucracy, marriage, death, Sunday mass, the tax office, everything. Camille had adopted the word herself and it had become part of their jargon. The same way they'd established the ritual of one of them saying, after a particularly difficult case, 'It was a day like any other day,' to which the other would reply, 'Yes, it was a day like any other.'

She had found a Brigitte Bardot song that had that line for its title, it was on the soppy side but with a sexy finish. So Camille had sent it to Abel for a laugh (and then decided it was practically a come-on to send someone a song and she'd regretted it).

'I'll go and gen up on the Pompidou since you want to know, but right now I have work to do. So this is my advice, Abel: this evening, you go and get properly plastered, for once in your life. In the process, you find yourself a girl, and you take her to the next level. And after you've shown her that next level, you take her right up through all the heavens and make her squawk like a bird and beg you never to stop. The next day you serve her coffee in a pretty cup, you take her to the door and you say: "Bye, madame, thank you, madame," and go take a shower. And after that you call a lawyer.'

'I don't enjoy drinking.'

'Now's a good time to get into it.'

Before heading off, Camille, suddenly doubtful, told Abel they couldn't simply not notify him of the reason for his suspension. That would be illegal. Was there actually some problem? Abel didn't reply. He only shrugged.

> *C'est un jour comme un autre*
> *Et pourtant tu t'en vas,*
> *Et pourtant tu t'en vas.*

6

to one quite green

The author of the *Parisien* report did not have much to go on, but
he shaped his piece skilfully to squeeze as much firepower as possible from his under-stocked arsenal. The story had to be
sufficiently unusual – and the day's news sufficiently turgid – for
this old nag to snatch the front page. 'A very handsome horse,
white in colour and in fine fettle, was found in the early hours of
this morning, by cleaners, in one of the reading rooms of the gallery's library. Sadly the animal was found to have chewed upon
several works and to have relieved itself of a steaming dungheap
within the honourable establishment.' The journalist was clearly
having a day at the races, revelling in the absurdity. 'According to
an internal source, it would seem that our Bucephalus took a
shine to the seventeenth-century classics of our literature, and
that, having spared Racine, he made a superb meal out of Cor-
neille. Thereby resolving, by means of his equine appetite, one of
the greatest rivalries in the history of French literature. As the
great Racine wrote, "All invention consists in making something
out of nothing." Or in making a whodunnit out of a horse?'

Was all this tomfoolery for real or was the guy making things up
for the sake of some good copy, Bac wondered. He felt mysteri-
ously galvanised by this item. Everyone seemed to think it was
just a piece of fluff, whereas he thought you don't take the piss

out of Paris for nothing. And there was something off about that horse. A line from the article leaped out at him: 'All invention consists in making something out of nothing.' What on earth could that mean? Nothing was . . . a void, was it? The image was obscured by the poor-quality paper so he couldn't make out the details. There must be other articles about this, but in order to look online he'd have to turn on his phone, and he'd been appreciating the enforced silence since he'd turned the thing off. Bac had locked it in his bathroom drawer. He had first considered whether to shove it to the back of the fridge or the oven, but had changed his mind. It was too expensive. He'd put it away with the paracetamol, the shampoo and the cotton buds. He guessed Pierrat would be trying to pinpoint where he'd picked up a signal. She was breaking the code, should he have reminded her? You don't just put people's phones under surveillance, at the very least you need a formal letter of request. And he knew only too well the extent of what a telephone could reveal. He felt dizzy.

On the stairs in his building, before any visual cue, he smelled the scent of the previous night, frantic and heady, lingering in the air. Patently much cleaner, his neighbour sprang around a bend in the banister, as if summoned from nowhere. 'I was just looking for you!' she called, triumphant, with a joyous self-assurance that already had Abel bristling. 'Yes, I was looking for you,' she said again as if it were a music-hall routine. 'It was you who helped me to bed last night! I've been wanting to thank you!' And she launched herself towards him, while Bac froze, aghast at this irregular approach.

'At least you didn't rape me, right?'

Disconcerted, he thought she shouldn't be such a smartypants; he could show her a few rape victims, if she wanted to know. But instead of saying that and taking her down a peg, he muttered grouchily that it was nothing. He had only helped her up the stairs.

'Nothing? There's always something in nothing!'

'Why do you say there's always something in nothing?'

'You take everything so straight – and you're in a bad mood, too, am I right? Well, in French (and Catalan too!) the word for nothing, *rien* or *res*, comes from the Latin word for thing: *res*. It's a lovely paradox. Were you aware of it?'

She laughed. She let out a great guffaw of shameless laughter. Like the night before when she'd peed herself.

Who is this madwoman, he thought.

'Or perhaps you're always in a bad mood and this gloomy face is your regular facade? I know, I started it when I tried to get into your apartment. It turns out that your door has a disturbing similarity to mine, and also that I hadn't counted the floors. Can you forgive me? I woke you up, of course. Were you asleep? But perhaps you were in the middle of a nightmare and, from another point of view, I was actually saving you from a rather unpleasant five minutes?'

Abel was disarmed for a second, because he had indeed been having a nightmare when he was woken by this brazen girl. His nightmare, always and forever Éric coming after him . . . but what struck him was that this stranger seemed to know. Abel tried to escape by edging past her while muttering a *good day to you* intended to silence this crazy prattler.

'Oh, what a handsome Lusitano!'

'I beg your pardon?'

'There, in the photograph in your paper!'

'You are talking about the horse?'

'Yes.'

Abel stared at the photograph.

'A what?'

'Let me see . . . Yes, it's a Lusitano, a rather rare breed of horse. He's majestic, don't you think? It was the preferred breed of the Sun King. They have these dreamy light-blue eyes.'

'What's your job?'

'I'm writing an art history thesis.'

'What link is there with horses?'

'None. I used to love horses when I was little, you know it's a thing: girls like horses, Prince Charmings and too much gin and tonic. Do you like horses?'

'No. I mean, not particularly. This animal was discovered inside the Pompidou Centre.'

But why am I engaging in this discussion, he admonished himself. He had no wish to talk to her, and yet he stayed talking to her as if the girl were blocking his escape route.

'Really? Inside the gallery? That's a buzz. Was it a happening?'

'Which means . . .?'

'A kind of performance?'

'No, it's an offence.'

'Don't you know what performance art is? Haven't you heard of installations?'

'No.'

'Shall I explain?'

'No, thank you.'

Elsa looked back at Abel and closed her mouth. She leaned in towards him and gently examined him. She looked into Abel's eyes as if she might see right through them, into their depths. She lifted her fingers to his cheek, slowly, as people do when trying not to alarm a wild animal. He did not move as she picked an eyelash from his cheekbone.

'You had an eyelash on your cheek. They say you should eat it, for good luck. Would you like me to eat it – the eyelash?'

7

'A creature,

A Lusitano. That fruitcake had been right. Abel compared photographs of Lusitano horses online with the image in the newspaper. That was indeed what it was: a horse of Portuguese ancestry, prized by kings, notably by Louis XIV. Cremello was the name for this one's colour, and it was a rare one. And, whereas specimens from other breeds of horse were named after their personalities, the Lusitanos were named according to the year they were born. Now this one had even spent the night in an art gallery.

He knew this horse.

Abel knew this particular horse, but he could not put his finger on where from. As if it had been in another life.

A few newspapers had also covered the story online. The reporter for *Libération* mentioned a Greek artist, Jannis Kounellis, who had shown live horses as art in Rome in 1969, and hinted at this being a kind of illegal nocturnal homage to Kounellis, a pioneer in the Arte Povera movement. No-one had any more information, so the journalists were extrapolating wildly. Bac looked up Arte Povera. He read that it was art that 'opposed both the gloss of pop art and the neutrality of minimalism'. He wondered whether to look up pop art and minimalism but decided against.

When he had turned his phone on to go online, a clutch of messages had started blinking through, one after the other. Texts, voicemails, emails. He ignored them while doing his research. Now he took a look at the notifications. He deleted them all without reading them, the way you take steps against an allergy. He was afraid. Afraid of messages explaining why he'd been disposed of. Why they no longer required his services. Benched. Out of the game. Sidelined. Dead. He was equally afraid of an absence of messages: that the world might have no idea he'd gone. That Abel Bac was fading out. He felt the prick of panic. Alarm bells. Breathe. He went to the bathroom for his cotton buds. Hesitated, and filled a big glass of water. The room was spinning; the familiar beginnings of a panic attack. He started counting backwards in his head: ninety-three, ninety-two... Then, kneeling, he began to clean his orchids, dipping the tips of the cotton buds in the water and stroking their leaves from top to bottom, to clear the fine dust and moisten the plants' stems. For a few seconds, the water brought out the deep green of their thick, vibrant leaves, then it dried, so quickly that the green faded back to sleep. It calmed him. It made sense. He was regaining control. Forty-three, forty-two, forty-one...

Down to zero, he sat in the middle of the orchids and drank what was left of the water in the glass.

Abel called Camille, who pointed out, astonished, that he had, at last, rediscovered the use of his telephone. He asked if she could do him a favour and pick up some things he had left at the office. 'Discreetly,' he added. And he would rather she not discuss his situation with their colleagues. Really rather not. 'Relax, Bac, we have other things to discuss than your ugly mug.' She was trying to play it down, she could hear how tense he was. 'Do you know what a Lusitano is?' he asked, out of the blue. No, no idea. 'No matter. Did you find out about the horse?'

'Are you serious? You think I've nothing else to be getting on with besides this crap? In ten minutes I've a meeting with the brother of our knifed client, just off a plane from Canada, and he is one unhappy bunny.' He would like her to stop talking about work. 'I told you I'll do it. I think it's the 4th arrondissement station which has picked up the Pompidou file. I've a mate there, I'll drop him a line.' He thanked her. She replied that he was starting to lose it, and she'd recommend he get himself a date on Tinder. And she giggled, like an idiot. It was a joke in the force, Abel Bac and Tinder. Everyone gave him stick about it, because one day he had said about a case that the accused and the plaintiff appeared to have met at a bar called Tinder and he couldn't think where in Paris the bar was. Cue: hilarity. And it had stuck. Everyone competing to get their quips in: 'Abel, see you at the Tinder tonight, let's sink a few shots!'

Now Camille was proposing a deal, joking apart: if he truly *did* fix a date for this evening on Tinder, she would get all the dope on his art gallery story. *Quid pro quo.*

'You want me to make a fool of myself?'

'No, I want you to get out of your rut. And I require photographic evidence.'

Abel realised he had given Camille a good deal too much latitude in their friendship.

One evening, about a year earlier, they'd come out of a 48-hour interrogation with a paedophile. A guy who'd gone all the way with his niece. They had found a collection of porn photographs on his computer, a real upper-crust shop of horrors. And the guy had three kids of his own. The techies in the juvenile division who had dealt with most of the files, they had been co-submitting, but Abel had seen plenty of it.

Four of the officers had taken turns with the interrogation. Abel had not handled it well. The detainee was arrogant and refusing to respond. Above them all. One of those people who are perfectly aware of their *weaknesses*, but the awareness only gives them a greater sense of superiority, of their power. Which means they do not conceive their particular foible *as* a weakness. Instead they value it like some intriguing, even fabulous, secret garden. They have taken on board that their 'garden' is offensive to the majority, and are able to go on as good fathers and ideal husbands, *sine die*. What's more, they derive double satisfaction: from the pursuit of their personal inclinations and from the certainty of being the sole agents of their deviance, which they understand in the word's original sense, without moral judgment, as *that which takes a different course*.

Faced with this person, Abel could not be precise; he proceeded in chaotic fashion, did not maintain the correct distance, and, as he gradually lost control of the interrogation, he let himself be led even further off-course.

Pierrat had impressed him. Young as she was for a cop, she had calmly but decisively taken over the lead. She had steadily hemmed in the accused man, using reassurance and flattery, then led him with an iron grip all the way to confession. She had kept up an implacable pace to her questioning and suggestions, without overdoing it. Her knowledge of the case had been flawless. Abel had been struck by an obscure notion: Camille Pierrat was not working for her own amusement, nor was she displaying her balls for all to see in some ego-stroking session. She was dancing through this interrogation, meticulous in her execution of an essential, joyless choreography.

They had gone off-duty around midnight and, suddenly cheerful, Pierrat had suggested they go for a drink, to release the stress. He had accepted, it was what you did, the standard ritual. They had worked hard.

It was a day like any other, Bac.

Yes, Pierrat, *a day like any other.*

She had led him down to rue Daunou, into an all-night dive where she knew some people. A pianist was playing on auto-pilot, apparently exhausted by his own handsomeness. She ordered and ordered again for them both, and very soon Abel had drunk too much. Out of practice. But you don't drop a colleague after that kind of achievement – you just don't. That's how it is.

At one point, he'd gone to piss out his beers. And she had suddenly appeared there in the shabby corridor with its red drapery and holes in the plaster. A musical slurry suddenly hit them at full blast, the pretty-boy pianist must have taken a break. Abel had no idea where he was now. He was suddenly riven with anxiety that she had heard him pissing. Then Camille had pushed him against the wall without warning – and kissed him. She had taken the lead, as in her performance at the interrogation, with surprising strength for her size, and she had bitten him on the lip. This unexpected move was too fierce for Abel to do anything other than let her go on. He had therefore responded, as best he could, to his peer's expectations, her mammalian urgency. She had turned him round and pressed him against the corridor's other wall. It was too much. Suddenly unviable. He had peeled himself away without roughness, excused himself without looking at her, and left.

Before leaving the bar, Pierrat abandoned, Pierrat stuck in that old red corridor, he had paid for their drinks. Fifty-one euros.

Handsome and exhausted as ever, the pianist had meanwhile returned to his keyboard.

Abel had gone home on foot, taking detours, scratching the lice on his head, choosing streets at random; he had walked, his body relaxed, off-duty as if released from some long confinement, shaking out his limbs so that every heel-tap rang out, the strides loosening his muscles, the way Jews go to the mikvah, to be cleansed.

He had no bent for analysis, but thoughts are like bats, circling, whistling, crashing into each other in the belfries of our minds. He'd been caught off guard, he had accepted Camille's embrace. He couldn't work out whether he had, even fleetingly, felt some desire, or if he'd just had to go with it. Camille had bitten his lip and for an instant, a millisecond, the taste of blood had seemed natural. Invigorating.

This was not what Abel did. He did not pin women against walls in order to get hot and heavy with them. He allowed himself no such impulses. He could be moved by a person's beauty, by an easygoing grace, he could be aroused by a body, by the swing of a bottom, sweat dampening an armpit, a sensual neckline. He enjoyed flesh, like everyone else. But he was alarmed by desire, frightened by the complexity of the links required to connect. Even a desirable person appeared to him primarily as a series of pitfalls. Continents of booby-traps. As if these holes and throats that asked only to be filled were lit with neuroses in the dark.

He was not excited by a sordid encounter, nor by pre-coital manoeuvring. Prostitutes might have offered him a simple middle way but too many had passed through his case files: too young, too wasted, too exploited. Approaching a woman demanded a paradoxical combination of *savoir-faire* and letting go. He had never really got past his seventeen-year-old awkwardness. Something in him had come to a stop then and grown no further.

He was the poor fucker whose kind would die out in the natural course of evolution.

So he spent a long time analysing what had happened in that corridor with Camille Pierrat. That lone vampire kiss. The next day he had given her the cold shoulder – a very cold one. Quite naturally, not meanly.

She was intelligent. She understood.

Mila

8

in our meadows I have seen,

'You ought to write a short text for the catalogue to your Moscow exhibition.'

'I don't want to.'

'A few lines from you will make all the difference.'

'You can just use something from a piece I've already written.'

'It needs to be new. Have a think about it. Next, it seems there's a problem with authenticating one of your pieces that went on show at the J. Levy gallery in New York.'

'You'll deal with it.'

'I'd like to send you the photographs, at least.'

'No, I don't care if someone's trying to pass off a fake Mila. Besides, there are experts to look after that stuff. All my performances have been recorded.'

'O.K., Mila. Lastly, and I'm sorry to raise this again, but there's still a major problem in Lisbon, as you know, with the pro-lifers.'

Jérôme Masson was worried because one of Mila's pieces – from an older series first shown in 2010 and known as 'The Fires' – was looking likely to be excluded from an exhibition, thanks to a campaign against it by pro-life activists. He had made several attempts to negotiate with the curators but they were damned whichever way they jumped.

'They did choose a "Fire". Why are they so worked up? It's not as if I offered them a "Piss Christ".'

'You knew very well that dead foetuses tied with dog-chains to the models' heads would go down like a lead balloon over there. People fainted the first time it was shown. So, yes, they're damned whatever they do, because they can't take your piece out – that would cause a major shitstorm: censorship, freedom of expression and all that jazz. And they can't afford to be on the wrong side of public opinion. The Catholic community is influential in Portugal.'

'Well, they'll have to offend one of us. If you don't want to *upset people*, don't be a contemporary art curator.'

A rare occurrence in the art world: some artists were even calling for a boycott of her work. They were accusing her of 'lunacy and imperilling' (sic) – they envy my status, Mila thought – in a first, community-minded judgment. But she knew it went deeper than that. She was not one of them, and she never would be. She was the outsider who confirmed the rule of the inner circle. The anomaly.

'And the Manifesta Biennale's ethics committee is sending me email after email about irregularities in your status.'

'I don't give a shit.' Mila wrapped up her telephone call with Jérôme Masson, her lawyer, with her usual vulgarity. It was a daily event. He had been calling her at the same time, Sundays included, except in cases of *force majeure*, for nearly two decades now.

Mila disliked speaking on the telephone, but their physical meetings were strictly occasional: they could not be seen together. Jérôme was known to the public as Mila's agent and it was only by exercising great caution that they had preserved her anonymity from the very start of her career.

Mila was never bothered by the *turpitudes of doability*, as she called it; if she wanted to do something, she did, and so it went, end of. Which was one explanation for her success, Masson thought. She was an obsidian door without a keyhole. Whereas Masson . . . The lawyer cleared his throat and repeated that they were talking about a loss of several hundred thousand euros if it went to shit in Portugal. The show wasn't yet confirmed. He reminded Mila that her last installation had also prompted responses of repugnance.

'Sorry to be crude, but do you ever search for your name in social media these days?' he asked, suddenly acerbic.

'No, never.'

Masson went on: 'This kind of controversy is not a good sign, Mila. People don't think you're revolutionary anymore, they think you're gross, you see? You're not exactly Banksy. You're not building boats for refugees.'

'And you're not Emmanuel Perrotin, Jérôme, or the fucking Dalai Lama.'

But Masson wouldn't let go. He thought she should present a new image of herself, she should begin a fresh cycle, one that was more . . . Masson hunted for the right word . . . He tried: *ecumenical*?

'You mean, more consensual? That would be nuts. You've never had a problem before with the ones that misfired.'

Masson was getting annoyed. Collectors bought her work because of her haunting imagery and her established status; she was a safe bet. But even superstars lose their edge and start to disappoint, he warned. She observed that he was *doing a lot of thinking with that clever little head of his* and that if there truly were good and bad controversies, she would be *delighted* if he were to instruct her on the subject, for he seemed to have very enlightened opinions on everything. Masson replied that he wouldn't be drawn by her provocations today, he had no time for that. Although he didn't say so, he was worried. While Mila often veered between hostility and nonchalance, almost as a game between them, he sensed something else in their latest discussions, a weariness, a disturbing absence of joy. He ended the call with a reminder to think about the city she wanted to move to. Otherwise he would choose for her, if that would be easier. He took his leave.

'Speak tomorrow, six o'clock.'

'Yes, till then, till tomorrow.'

She hung up resentfully, slamming the phone down like in a bad film. But she knew it meant nothing, she was alone in the room with her telephone and no-one could see her, no-one was watching. In order to care, you needed to *see* the other person, didn't you?

No matter how irritating she found him, she would never break with Masson. Their connection was too deep. He was the only one who knew her true identity. It was their Faustian pact, *to the death*. Although the lawyer was bound by a battery of confidentiality clauses, it would still be unthinkable to leave him. They could easily be one of those old couples, soul twins, for whom divorce was not an option but an occasional fantasy. Masson was very efficient, no question. He knew every twist and turn of the art world and could exploit its legal loopholes like a skilled torero. He enjoyed the spotlight a bit too much, which was understandable; her fame had only become his responsibility through contamination. He represented her, and nobody else knew who she really was. Masson had to face the media frenzy engendered by the mystery of Mila. A mystery that had now lasted twenty years . . . It was a perfect system, a Hitchcockian MacGuffin – the director's device of selecting some crucial but impenetrable minor element to drive each of his plots. The classic example being the 'government secrets' in *North by Northwest*, about which the film's viewers never discover anything at all.

Would it make any difference to the value of her work if people knew who was hidden behind 'Mila'? Masson had often asked her this when she expressed misgivings about her secrecy. Would it interest anyone to know that she was an ordinary girl from an average small town between Paris and Orléans, who never went to art school and whose life changed tack at seventeen due to an utterly random roll of the dice? Over to Masson to turn that into some measly epitaph, she thought. Her anonymity was her MacGuffin, a hazy void to be filled in as required. She could be a man, a woman, a group; she had various nationalities; she was beautiful, disfigured or hidden behind some other celebrity; she was a political activist; she was black, she was white, a messiah and a prophet: all of it was possible. Anyone can project what they wish onto a MacGuffin, and everyone feeds the myth. It was Masson who had made the call on this, it had been his idea not to reveal her identity, and then, much too quickly, it had become too late, impossible to go back. Anonymity had become part of her creative method.

Mila's anonymity protected her, Masson insisted.

'Is this protection or prison?' she had begun to ask in return. 'What if I die suddenly, Jérôme, what would you do? Would you create another myth? Would you never reveal my identity? Would you make up some story – and make me more interesting than I am? Would it suit you if I died? You want me to jump out the window – right here and now? I'll do it, Jérôme, I'm jumping!

You'll have to put me in a common grave, on the sly. It won't cost much. Or perhaps you'll have me cremated and then you'll auction off my ashes! And my work will sell for even more – wow! It's a win-win-win-*win*!'

Mila would leave this kind of strident message on Masson's answerphone in the middle of the night. Sometimes her messages went on a long time; sometimes they became incoherent. She was scared of disappearing, of wandering in the darkness without a final resting place. She left him this kind of message when she'd been drinking by herself, ceremoniously, in the middle of her mirrors. Jérôme didn't worry unduly; he was used to it. These days, he kept his telephone turned off at night.

There's no bond like a secret.

9

Sleek, grand!

Mila looked down at the Thames through the bay window of her studio. It was an eagle's eyrie overlooking the bones of the city, impenetrable, fortified, but open to the winds thanks to the many windows piercing its walls like so many searching eyes. It was a wrench to think about leaving this place. But Jérôme was unmovable on this point: she had to go. The journalists of the tiny world of art were all betting she was in London. She had been there two years, the average period for her stays, for her dockings. Where to go after London? She had spent summers and winters in Brussels, Oslo, Berlin, Rome and Lisbon. She spoke the languages of all the places she had lived in – she had an ear. When you had mastered two or three, you could speak twelve, of course you could, the languages criss-crossed and fed into each other like living, interdependent beings.

She had thought, when she arrived, that she would not like London. It had been Masson's idea, 'The best hiding place is in full view of the world,' he had argued. And London was still the beating heart of contemporary art, along with New York, of course. As for Masson, he had set up his office in Paris, in the 6th, a *good address*. Her trusty right-hand man. Each believed that the other would be nothing without them. Mila was the artist, Masson the craftsman: two faces to the same Chimera, the monster milA, invisible queen of contemporary art. There were fewer than fifty of her kind in the world, whose works sold for millions at Christie's and Sotheby's, in their familiarly lawless 'second market'. Well, fewer than fifty who were still alive. She'd been one of them for some years now, no longer required to prove her worth in galleries. Her latest installations were often now sold straight into the market, a safe investment every time. The original photographs Mila had taken of her very first performances back in the 2000s had reached a record sale price of more than 120 million euros. 'milA' was now a brand of secondary merchandise and listed on the Paris stock exchange. With her name turned logo, recognisable as an haute couture brand: lowercase *m*, two strokes off-set, one short, one long, for the *i* and *l* – one aligned low like a root, the other an arrow to the heavens – and the capital *A*, the *A* that was now her coat of arms and her Mount Olympus. Everything was sold with her logo stamped on it, bags, mugs, vanity cases, caps, shoes. She was *too high to fall* . . .

Masson and she had written her story as a duo, combining her excess with his marketing genius. Two twisted kids with unlimited cash having the best fun setting their toybox on fire.

More than twenty years ago, Jérôme Masson had been Mila's friend. At the time he was just Jérôme. He wasn't a lawyer and she wasn't yet Mila. Masson and she, brought together by the odd fortune of having grown up in the same town and attended the same lycée. Vallé was a boring semi-genteel, semi-working-class town that sat snoring, sixty kilometres from the capital; nothing ever happened in Vallé.

Or almost nothing. The inhabitants had experienced one horrendous incident: a dozen residents had been killed in the street by a raving madman; it made the headlines of the national press and journalists had set up shop there for a few months, to sniff out the town's dirty underwear. Then they had gone again and the town had returned to its ontological silence. Of course, Vallé was the home town of Mila, the famous artist, but that the Vallois did not know.

Mila and Jérôme had been classmates at the lycée, meeting year after year in the same classes, having both made the unusual choice to study Russian. Their teacher was an unsettling babushka permanently wrapped in long fringed shawls and sporting absurd little pince-nez that she repeatedly lost in the classroom. Madame Bukobza. She insisted that her students choose a Russian name in their first year, which then followed them through to the final year, practically a baptism. Jérôme had opted for Anton, a dandyish choice in honour of Chekhov, whose 'The Cherry Orchard' he had put on in theatre club. And Mila who was not yet Mila, well, she had chosen Mila.

She liked the name's ambiguity, tipping into the intimacy of a diminutive. Mila . . . you could possess it. *Mi* you are my *la*. She liked its mingled heritage, the Slav, Spanish and German, its possible antecedence in Milena, 'people's beloved'. Mi-la, syllables that kept their languor no matter the accent they were spoken in. At the lycée she was neither eccentric nor anarchic but rather a reserved figure; she would have liked to be that, one day – to be beloved of the people; also to see what it was like to *surrender* herself. She proudly claimed she had chosen the name in honour of Mila Racine, a Jewish resistance fighter who died in the camp of Mauthausen. They had visited the camp on a school trip with their history teacher. That had made a deep impression on her. The bodies. She did not know any Jews. There were not many in Vallé, where she had been born and brought up. That name had stayed with her, Mila Racine, because it was the loveliest name she had heard in her life, and it seemed to resonate from very far away through an immense darkness. At the lycée Mila and Anton were certainly not as popular as the sports students, the skaters or the grungers – it was the Nineties. But the 'Russians', as they called themselves privately among the handful of their trusty comrades . . .

. . . the Russians, then, were happy with their literary aura and cool associations. They made up a clan that was broadly admired and feared amid the adolescent jungle, a tiny little group bound by a little-taught language which conferred an exotic and subtle flavour to them, overlaid by a certain savage energy.

Mila could not have dreamed, when she had chosen to study Russian, that this four-letter name would become the screen to her identity, her black hole, her artist name, swallowing up the person she had once been. Mi-La, two suspended notes, the title of her glory, her flashes of brilliance and her whims. Her real name was long gone; even Masson no longer used it.

10

I seem to see him yet,

The first time she had needed legal representation, because she was in a tight spot, she had been twenty-three and she had called her one lawyer friend. She and Jérôme had stayed in touch after school, thanks to parties thrown by ex-lycée students – nights when everyone drank too much and analysed their peers' futures in frustration and concupiscence. There were some who would do well enough, some who would shoot to the top, and some who would get stuck knocking at the wrong doors. Their futures seemed already plotted out and foreseeable in the still gangly bodies of these young people imperceptibly metamorphosing into adults. Mila was somewhat isolated, because of what had happened to her. There was no ill will, but her outsider status seemed to seep from her skin and kept easy relations out of her reach. She had come adrift. She had crossed a line and become someone else. People did not know how to react: with scepticism or laurels?

When Mila got into trouble with her artistic initiatives (she was arrested and detained at a police station for damage to public property), she knew that Jérôme Masson had been called to the bar. He was in pupillage at a big chambers of business lawyers, slogging away to make the grade, refining his address book, working all hours and taking on every task for his bosses in the single-minded hope of one day being exactly like them. He did not know it then but Mila was to be his golden-egg layer. How could Jérôme have imagined what would come next? Mila herself would never have believed it.

Besides, she was far from claiming her 'actions' were some kind of *artistic intervention*. She had no context or reference. She was making it up as she went along, without theory or education. One art critic would later compare her to the young Arthur Rimbaud starting out in Charleville, but even Rimbaud had read the great poets before he arrived in Paris, an education that allowed him then to shit on the rest of them. Mila had neither seen nor read anything of the scene she would be breaking into, except for one piece by Marina Abramović which she had come across the very day her life had been shattered. Do we remain locked into the day our traumas occur? Does some part of us cease to grow upon meeting a horror that is too much? The soul's depths imprinted like film with everything that happened that day.

the finest beast I ever met

To make the move to London two years earlier, Mila had had to leave Lisbon, to tear herself away. She had missed the energising flights of steps that carried you down into the lower city, and the little train that wound along the coast, through Belém and Cascais, missed her dips into the Portuguese sea, always so cold and exhilarating, missed her Lisboa where love was essentially tragic, the ceilings falling apart and the night unsilent. Leaving. Breaking the hourglass of her few habits. The same palaver in reverse. When she'd settled in London, she had been working on her 'Martyrs' series. This was a series of effigies of famous martyrs that she suspended from various monuments, hanging them as if from a fantasia of gallows. She had started with the Christian martyrs: Saint Sebastian a pincushion of arrows, Saint George holding his sliced-off head, Saint Blandine . . .

Blandine had been a real headache. Mila had been determined to stick her on the obelisk at place de la Concorde in Paris. The action had gone wrong: she and her team had narrowly escaped discovery. They had run away, with the Saint Blandine doll tucked under their arms, as it were. Masson had been furious; she was taking too many risks. She had felt giddy. Eventually she had attached her Lyonnaise saint to an ornament on the Saint-Jacques tower in Paris, this time by bribing the necessary officials to look the other way. Next she had hung Georges Danton on a church in the suburbs of Milan, Olympe de Gouges from the Little Mermaid in Copenhagen, Louis XVI from a window at the National Assembly President's second home, Alfred Dreyfus in Geneva and Jean Moulin from the sails of the Moulin Rouge. Not to mention Lionel Jospin at Métro Solférino – you had to have a giggle sometimes.

Each time the life-size dolls were furnished with radios in their pockets, all playing the blues beats of the Rolling Stones' 'I've Got a Witness'. *Witness* – that other word for a martyr: he who sees.

Jospin had objected. Masson had sorted it out.

People had got talking far beyond the tiny circle of contemporary art. Thinking they were witnessing actual hangings, flaneurs and bystanders had screamed and gone into fits on the ground. Who would dare make light of death, etc, etc. She had not felt obliged to listen to their preaching; death was her business and Mila did whatever she wished. She had, though, sent a bunch of flowers to Jospin with an apologetic note. Red roses, of course. Mila would have liked to keep some of the dolls, she had spent time with each of them, sewing their clothes, refining their features, the nails and teeth, sticking their eyelashes on one by one, working on their wrinkles and their turpitudes. They were her children. Impassive and objectified children. In order to shape them to perfection she had undertaken serious training with a sculptor from the Grévin waxworks museum. She had given herself a watertight yet entirely false C.V., and the guy had never made the link between his hard-working if unforthcoming intern and the artist Mila's 'Martyrs', when the latter made the headlines. Some of these dolls were now in galleries (in the Tate, the Pompidou, the Guggenheim in Bilbao) or in private collections. Others had been placed under seal and formally confiscated. Mila had planned a burglary to get them back; they were her children, after all. Masson had pulled the plug on that. For ten years, the money she earned allowed her to create ever more sophisticated installations. And yet she felt as if she were running low on ideas. More and more often her pieces depended on visual puns or provocations, and less often on necessity. It was strange to be so famous and never to be recognised in the street. She used to love wandering around the biennales, at the F.I.A.C. and other giant trade fairs for contemporary art, and feeling invisible and omnipresent.

Like God.

She was thirty-nine now. She wanted to know people and for people to know her. She wanted to decide where she would set up home and be in control of her own space and time. That was what she had done with her various installations and performances for more than fifteen years: she'd disrupted, bent and twisted space and time. Her art was made up of events in series, like heartbeats. The whole of it performative, as when you conjugate the verb to die: ungraspable and brutal. A poltergeist.

Her art took place within the extreme fragility of the gaze. It was in the first moment of the encounter that it took on all its meaning. Afterwards, what was left was like scalps and stripped hides that could be recomposed on demand, fetishes and trinkets that cost their collectors dear, which could be reinstalled to show what had taken place. They were dead images. Souvenirs.

Mila's studio walls were crowded with drawings and mirrors of all sizes and shapes. She collected them. She had some rare pieces: a mirror from the Hall of Mirrors at Versailles, bought at auction; an asymmetrical mirror signed by Line Vautrin; a sixteenth-century tortoiseshell found in an antiques shop in Venice . . . They accompanied her through all her moves and were the first to be unpacked whenever she moved somewhere new: her army of mirrors. Everywhere, wherever she stood, she could see her slightest movement, she who was only a name, whom no-one was allowed to see. She who was unseen.

Staring at the black and blue Thames, which looked as cold as the sharpest metal, she really did feel like throwing herself out of the window, like keeping the promise of her nocturnal answerphone messages to Jérôme, giving in to that odd, morbid impulse which is the attraction to the void. To see what he – Masson – would do with her damaged body; to see what it was like to be dead.

But without really dying, because, of course, Mila could never die.

Abel

12

Is he a stouter one than we?

Faced with a mobile phone screen, Abel Bac could not shake the sensation he was being filmed. Being examined, befuddled, mocked. It was not natural to spend so much time in collusion with a screen made of glass, plastic, cobalt and carbon. He installed the Tinder app. Which took him a good while, since he had no idea how to install an app. He watched online tutorials, read discussions in forums, and in the end took the correct steps. He thought of the many cases in which suspects had been betrayed by their telephones. Hubris. Police inquiries had been turned on their heads by the advent of the smartphone. And hard drives. It was staggering. But why do people entrust their secret gardens to these bits of cobalt? When their minds are all they need?

He had to create his profile. Keep it simple. He would rather not lie. Putting 'I'm a copper' would be a big admission, he thought. He didn't want to attract losers looking for a buzz. How do you feel when you see a dead body? I don't feel anything and that's the truth. He was after something more *passe-partout*. He put 'consultant'. He had never understood what that actually meant. It had the perfect degree of vagueness. He put his age. He added that he liked music and films. It was something to put in the boxes and would not put anyone off. He wanted to be Monsieur Nobody, or rather, *Everybody*: all the bodies at once.

The most painful bit was the visual aspect of the process. He considered digging out the photograph from his employment file. But he had been almost twenty years younger when that was taken. That would be weird. He realised he did not possess a recent photograph. Then straight away moved to block the nasty lurch towards bat-thoughts prompted by this realisation. He took the bull by the horns and switched his phone into selfie mode, raised it as high as he could and tried to take one of himself. He thought: *attractive*. He rattled off a dozen clicks, phone outstretched, then bent over it to discover the results, the way you take a cake out of the oven.

To see his square head flattened, without a hint of a smile, his eyes bleached, was unbearable. He deleted every picture. He took more. He tried adding a bit of shadow in order to camouflage one side, for a touch of style, a hint of mystery. He tried it nearer, and further away. He angled the phone, to cover up. That was worse. The man he saw looked as friendly as a serial killer. It was rising in him: the fury. The temptation of the mockery that was hollowing out his every gesture, stripping bare his most ordinary inclinations. He'd be too ridiculous, would he? Everyone hassling him with their Tinder jokes. He'd had enough now. Didn't he too have a right to do this normal thing?

13

the wolf demanded, eagerly

The girl was there.

Upon his first 'match' in the app, he had engaged in conversation with the candidate. Minimal, the bare bones. Hi / Hi / Smiley / You're not busy / No / Another smiley. He hadn't bothered with small talk; he didn't know how to send smileys. She had agreed to meet that evening. She had asked where. He had replied: at the Carolus, place Clichy. 8.30. It seemed like an appropriate hour for a date. True, it was a weak move – lacking imagination; his comfort zone; panic.

She is there.

He knows her name is Anna.

She is blonde, short on confidence, plump, over-dressed, has a nail-biting issue, lots of beauty spots, nervous, audible breathing, rather deep dimples, a slight squint, soft hair from this distance, well washed, a free hand with the perfume, feminine, awkward.

Count down, ninety-three, ninety-two . . .

All the drama of isolation increased by a factor of ten. He is ordering a bottle of wine at the bar. At the Carolus! Ahmed gives him a searching look, he's never seen the cop come in with a chick, he's ready to play his part, servant at the ready, curious and vaguely uneasy. What else should he do?

What should he do – order white or order red? He'll die of shame. What possessed him to suggest meeting here? He should have gone three arrondissements away, somewhere posh, look as though he knows the score, project an air of self-confidence, let himself be someone else, just for a minute, for a second, he is very hot. He has taken two showers today. He still feels unclean. He thinks his odour might upset her – upset this woman, this chubby blonde with her deep dimples. She is talking, he hears nothing, he tries, there's interference on the line, the strain is too much. He tries some close focuses: on her nails, on her hair, on her damn dimples.

She's wearing a flashy, tight-fitting top made of silk. Violet silk, or mauve.

He imagines her lying on the ground.

Square top, triangle bum. The images are coming together too fast. He tries to concentrate. She's speaking. Speaking to him. This is not a screen, she's not made of carbon. Already she has too much history, too much bosom, too much silk. She is here. She's not dead. He has autopsy images in his head. He pictures Éric, raising his gun head-high.

Breathe.

Abel had been surprised by the technology's implacability. Only just installed and the murk had got going. And this girl had *matched* him. To what command was he responding by joining in this game? It wasn't clear. He was unmoved by his colleague Pierrat's needling. But the sudden withering of his life since his expulsion was chafing at his insomniac mind. And when he did sleep, the dream of Éric kept playing over and over. Éric killing people without turning a hair, handsome Éric killing people he didn't know. He had dreamed about this constantly, since turning twenty. But not so often. For a week, now, the dream had been coming to him all the time, it was gaining colour, growing clearer. He was embarrassed now, too, thinking about the last time he had made love with a woman. It was a long time ago, foreign. All those years, he hadn't had time, the occasion, the simplicity. He couldn't have.

He had had so little opportunity, in his life, to go to bed with a woman. Time had gone by and the dormant nerve had only seized up further. So why not? Why not do the *normal* thing again?

'Well, I haven't been on Tinder very long, have you? It's kind of dumb.' Anna laughs, embarrassed. 'Well, I guess it isn't dumb, it's good people can meet new people, right? Perhaps our screens really do make invisible connections between people.' She laughs again, the same laugh which dies instantly before it can break out, a laugh to paper over the silence, forced from her throat, a defensive laugh, a tic. 'Bit of a cliché, what I'm saying . . . Actually, one of my friends made me sign up. She even helped me to set up my profile, you see.'

Anna goes quiet and looks at him, she's asking for his help. Abel says nothing. He pours more white wine into both glasses, although Anna has hardly touched hers. She says chin-chin, then, 'You should look at each other when you drink,' and Abel wishes he could die on the spot.

'How old are you?' he asks. He's said something, anything, the first thing that came into his head, to stop the onward tick of this silence. A first push to get the canoe off the rocks.

'Right. Well, I'm thirty-one, it's in my profile,' Anna says, marginally deepening the line across her forehead.

He hasn't looked at her profile. She matched him, he had logged as much without registering anything further. This was an apparently ordinary woman who was consenting to engage in conversation. That was all he had thought.

Anna remains silent, she doesn't drink, doesn't shift; a very slight movement of her chest indicates to Abel that she's still alive. She is breathing.

'You think I'm too old, that's what it is,' she resolves to say, without the throat laugh.

No, Anna, truly I do not, Anna, you're young. I just wish you would disappear, I want to be sitting in the dark of my living room, listening to my orchids, I wish you weren't here at all, it's not personal, Abel thinks.

'Do you think you look old?' he tries.

Anna is crushed. She takes a little sip very slowly, takes this time to gather her courage, to really taste the wine, which is not very good but not terrible – Ahmed has tried to uncork one that won't give them stomach cramps.

'I don't know, Abel. That's a strange question.'

'What I mean, Anna, is that compared to a twenty-year-old, you're old, but compared to a forty-year-old woman, you're not old. That's all.'

Anna drops down another two circles. She says, 'Sorry, I'll be back, I'll just pop to the loo, 'scuse me, I'm coming back.' She stands, very aware of her body, it's torture getting up from this table elegantly and walking away without showing the strain.

Abel knows it's all going to shit. He catches Ahmed's eye, triggering a thumbs-up and a wide smile.

Anna comes back, her eyes glistening. Abel thinks it might be anger, or that she's wiped away a brief tear in the ladies, and what's left is dazzling her vision. But her make-up is still immaculate.

Anna sits down again, energy renewed, paralysis shed, fresh zeal in her head's slightly jerky bobbing.

'Excuse me, Abel. We began badly, I think. You haven't said a thing, right from the start, I feel so uncomfortable. You seem, I don't know how to put it, stiff, let's say. So I'm coming out with boring small talk, but I'm the only one making an effort. The truth is I've been dumped by a guy I was with for seven years, a classic move, apparently. I'm at the end of my tether, I work all hours, all my friends are in couples and the idea of flirting with a man – even, to be honest, the idea of sleeping with any man who isn't Paul – seems unimaginable, so I signed up to this shitty app two days ago, I "liked" you because you seemed, I don't know . . . normal? And now you're here you look as though you've a great broom up your arse, this dive is a shithole, the wine is disgusting and now you're saying that I'm old compared to a girl who's twenty, and you're quite right, of course it's true, but I got together with Paul when I was twenty-four, so I was young then, and when I see a photograph I don't think I've changed that much, but I'm not going to pretend life hasn't happened, and you won't say a word, and you want to know why I "liked" you, truly? Because, on my walk to work this morning, I took an extra loop so I could go past my ex's building, to make myself suffer, probably, to see if everything was going on as before in the neighbourhood, which I know like the back of my hand because I was with Paul for seven years and he spent all seven years living in that damn building, and I spent three years there too, cos I moved in with him and we shared the cost of doing it up fifty-fifty of course, and when he dumped me I had to leave because it was his apartment first, and so I went past it this morning, I saw the tobacconist's on the ground floor, the same guy who's always begging in the same place, the newspaper kiosk, and there was some graffiti on the building which wasn't there before, a huge bit of graffiti, it was a shock.'

Anna stops talking, as if to contemplate the fog created by her words in the air around her. She catches her breath.

'It was a shock, that graffiti, time's passed, that's what I thought, something has happened, before there was nothing there and the nothing had gone, so I decided I have to stop taking these loops in the mornings to go by Paul's place, because it's been six months that I've been getting up an hour earlier, now, to add in that loop, and this morning, this morning, the graffiti, it was horrendous, it must have happened in the night because I came by yesterday morning and it wasn't there, and I don't know, it seemed *unfair*, it was *unbearable*, so then I liked the first just-about acceptable guy on Tinder, so I could stop doing this damn loop before going to work in the morning because, you know, I'm exhausted.'

'What's the graffiti of?'

'A horse. It's a big white horse.'

'And it appeared this morning?'

'Yes, I think so.'

'What part of town does your friend live in?'

Anna is now sinking to rock bottom, but she replies out of politeness:

'Paul lives on rue du Faubourg Poissonnière.'

'Do you know what breed of horse it was? Do you know much about horses?'

'Seriously? I'm going to go now, Abel, O.K.?'

'Of course, Anna, certainly.'

'So I'll let you pay for that horrible bottle of wine?'

'Quite alright, Anna.'

'Goodbye, Abel.'

Anna gets up, pulls on her jacket, one sleeve then the other, she takes her time to do up three buttons, forgetting that her body exists in space, her movements are automatic, protective, the night is cool, she walks away; and Abel thinks he could perhaps have slept with her, that this is really stupid, they had compatible agendas, each to use the other in good faith like a towel to wipe off dust accumulated on the crockery, that he should go after her and say: I'm an idiot, please forget how we kicked off, come to bed with me, because my scalp is driving me mad and you're also scratching your itches and you don't look old, Anna, you look truly lovable. And Abel sees Ahmed, who has not followed the debacle and is looking at him with his thumb held high, still smiling at his brother-in-arms.

14

Some picture of him

He had done nothing wrong. He'd pursued the thing from start to finish. Invited a free woman to have a drink with him and followed the business through to its conclusion. Or rather, he had followed their shared intention as far as possible, to the point that one of the two protagonists preferred to terminate the aforementioned shared intention. The outcome had not been gratifying. But it had happened. Something had happened. He was not at home tonight, he was out of his rut. It was difficult for Abel to conceive another person as anything besides the protagonist of some sleazy and exotic story, unless that character took part in his daily life for long enough that, by natural progression, they became a person. Anna was both too much and too little. He almost wished he could examine her under the microscope, or on the coroner's bench.

A thought struck Abel: he was just around the corner from the graffiti, yes, it was only ten minutes' walk away. If he headed up to Pigalle and took the rue de Dunkerque, he'd practically be there. The rue du Faubourg-Poissonnière was a long one but it wasn't rue de Vaugirard for all that, he could walk its length without spending the whole night on it. The worry was that she might, in fact, have meant to say the boulevard Poissonnière, that would indeed be a murk, but frankly, who confuses the rue du Faubourg-Poissonnière with the boulevard Poissonnière?

'Everyone,' Pierrat would have shot back, 'except for you,' but he drove the thought away. He hadn't taken a photograph to send her the proof of his technological encounter, but how could he have blithely asked the girl, asked Anna, if it wouldn't bother her to adopt the pose required for a selfie alongside him? *It's to show my colleague, proof that I really had a date.* She'd have thought he was sick in the head. He waved to Ahmed to bring him the bill; the latter having understood the situation now adopted a wonky three-quarters smile of solicitude. Some people in our lives do not need words.

Abel knew the time without looking at his watch: the Anna fiasco had taken about forty-five minutes, he had been early, she on time, but he had taken a position on the pavement opposite the Carolus in order to let her arrive first and watch her sit down before he arrived. It must therefore be 9.15, he calculated.

Abel left the Carolus and swung into step, immediately achieving a steady, rapid and harmonious pace. The boulevard de Clichy, to his left the Moulin Rouge with its doors as ever flanked by bouncers in cheaply made tailcoats and visible headsets, an outdated goldfish bowl for monied tourists; he powered on, leaving the winking clusters of fatuous sex shops behind, the Bouillon Pigalle was all steamed up, on the boulevard Marguerite de Rochechouart he kept up a metronomic rhythm, he knew his muscles, focused on the obstacles to avoid, he saw men alone like himself, girls still under-age with their hair over-straightened, miniature handbags and no coats hunting for welcoming night-clubs where by dint of having frozen their arses off they would skip the cloakroom fee, thereafter to hook some idiots who would keep them in cheap bubbly all night; soon he could see Dunker-que, but before the turn-off he changed his mind, instead of going right, he went straight on towards Barbès, that way he could take the rue du Faubourg-Poissonnière from the top down and not risk missing something.

He had arrived. He waited for his heart to slow, he felt like spitting on the ground but didn't dare. He put the little Café Barbès behind him, with its red awning and couscous, not to be confused with its identically named sibling, a temple of gentrification in this neighbourhood which was still dodgy for night-time strolls, and he headed on down the road. All along this narrow artery, he was able to take in the facades on both odd and even sides. He passed fabric shops casually displaying saris next to kaftans next to white viscose wedding dresses with badly sewn buttons, and continued down to the junction with Dunkerque: nothing. His detour had proven needless, but Abel had never regretted a methodical approach. He crossed at the junction and continued his quest for a horse, *a big white horse*, Anna had said. He peered, looked up, made sure, all without checking his pace, suddenly he spotted a tobacconist, a newspaper kiosk, he defined a zone, focused in and saw it.

He saw it above the little local butcher's shop with its rotisserie washed down for the night: his horse. He felt a satisfaction very close to that familiar one generated by his work as an investigating officer. The tickle of elation when an anecdotal detail offered a moment's illumination, and then that unexpected gleam allowed the rest to fall into place. He went and stood directly opposite the image painted on the wall, to appreciate the object of his distraction: an impressive white horse, gleaming white, stencilled and still fresh, one of its hooves apparently about to knock on the panes of a first-floor window. A Lusitano. He took a photograph of the horse and sent it without comment to Camille Pierrat.

It *was* a Lusitano, Anna, he thought, and only then did Abel pause to consider the detour she inflicted on herself every morning, going to meet her past; to consider this time stolen from the start of her day, in which blonde Anna went back over the barren field of her old habits the way you might secretly visit a graveyard whose only existence is now in your mind.

Each to their own ghosts.

Mila

15

let me see.

Mila had not been one of those teenagers who are committed to art from high school, who claim they can't help it, parade a precocious talent and look down on everything else with the incandescent pride of youth – for if youth is humble, it's not youth. No, a detailed analysis of Mila's girlhood revealed no hint of what she would become, except by extrapolation that she was already *in camouflage.*

She had been a studious child whose gaiety sat easily with a natural inclination to make friends; and her middle-class parents nurtured her, their only child, with a light hand. Her early artistic passions had flourished amid Klimt's kisses and Schiele's bony bodies, adventuring among Basquiat's precocious scrawls. Like most of her peers, she happened randomly on images that gripped her, and pushed her personal rebellion as far as blacklisting Leo Tolstoy after reading his little essay on art, because the great Russian writer seemed to equate Beauty with God and to rate Baudelaire and Verlaine so poorly as to eject them from the canon. That had shocked her.

Mila was a good student. With no parental pressure, she had chosen Russian as her main foreign language, Latin for her optional class and the piano for her spare time, with the curiosity of a serene and well-to-do child. Labelled exceptional, as far as that went for an adjective that had long ago lost its glitter and become a cliché, she was exceptional in that her successes always seemed to come easily. Her adolescent flirtations with the wild side followed the usual pattern of hormonal crises and the shrill objections emitted by a body undergoing transformation on the double. No more, no less.

And Mila, who had not changed her name (except in Russian class), had thought that after her baccalaureate she might work towards a first year of médicine, because she was good at science and it was vaguely romantic to become a doctor, just as her comrade Jérôme had law in his sights, because you did have to choose your path through the relative calm of a late-Nineties world in which memories of war were reduced to fading postcards and which hadn't yet felt the whipcrack impact of two planes upon its Twin Towers. It was a world still dreaming of the new millennium.

She still was not yet Mila.

The idea of contemporary art was as good as alien to her, except in the literal sense. Based on the little she knew, she imagined that there were still painters and sculptors, as there had been in every period since the caves of Lascaux. But that contemporary art could be a market for some practitioners and a field of signs for others; that in its name the Pont Neuf had been wrapped in fabric and eggs been distributed stamped with the artist's thumbprint – none of that had yet reached Vallé, or not as far as Mila.

Thanks to a school trip to Paris with Monsieur Verdier, who was keen to 'widen their horizons' as he liked to proclaim, Mila's encounter with an exhibition of Arman's work at the Musée du Jeu de Paume had left her speechless, or at very least bemused before what appeared to be transparent cubes filled with rubbish. But she had at least known, thanks to the formidable art teacher's horizon-widening, that there could be no question of derision, so legendary was his 'fascism': at the end of each lesson the teacher would look over the students' work and pick out four or five examples. 'The worst of all your dross,' he would say, his lips tightly compressed. Then he would rub out each effort with a damp sponge. Returning each sheet of paper to its owner, he always pronounced the same sentence: 'You will do me the kindness of using this to begin again. We shall not go wasting paper on such incompetents. It's a costly commodity.' Mila's attempts regularly ended being wiped out by Monsieur Verdier, and she had sometimes felt a twinge at seeing a piece of work in which she had invested something of herself, even something still undefined, drain away with the water.

Of her outing to the Arman exhibition, Mila had retained the joyful surprise that something so strange could be put in such a beautiful gallery – the Jeu de Paume being like a modern steel-and-glass cathedral within a royal garden. Had she some inkling then that art might be a troubling of the senses, a different experience of time, space or matter? Back then, the idea that the body itself could be a medium for expression meant nothing to Mila except her adolescent zigzagging, which addressed the same instinctive lines of enquiry: where do the boundaries lie?

Mila who was not yet Mila had grown up in Vallé, a town almost without history apart from one grim news item. But that, just then, she could not foresee. A town that was neither near nor far, neither big nor little. Once she had her baccalaureate she would leave for Paris to start her medical studies: it was an avenue to elsewhere.

And then both her parents died:

Out of the blue, by a bullet to the brain, in the same instant.

16

If I could paint

Mila, who wasn't yet called Mila, was reluctant to do what she was going to do: give her folks the slip. She and all the other aspiring school leavers in France had got their results a week earlier, announced by means of Bible-thin pages stuck with substandard glue to the walls of courtyards emptied by the approaching holidays. All the Russians had their baccalaureate; Mila didn't know anyone who was doing retakes.

Smiles were exchanged. They would from now on always be graduates of the class of 2000, young people leaving childhood behind and attaining their majority along with the sacrosanct qualification in the last year of a century at the dawn of a new millennium. It was joyous, and more than that, even: they were intoxicated by the luck of the calendar.

Parties were thrown in friends' gardens, they moved from one to the next as proud as peacocks, counting on satisfied parents to bring the good champagne from their cellars, the bottles awaiting this kind of occasion, for the patriarchs to pop corks and quench all thirsts. Mila had followed the dancing until late every night, she had drunk a good deal too much, these things had never happened to her before.

She could feel her heart beating with Rimbaud's *scent of the lime trees on the fine June evenings*, his wafts of beer and his unlucky stars, Rimbaud who she'd revised for the bac, not entirely sure she understood his genius but making as if she did, and seeking kinship with this boy who had been her age at the precise moment he was writing these words, as well as some interesting coprophiliac sonnets in which he was definitely talking about his arsehole.

She had never had problems with her parents, she was used to obeying them without complaint – their demands were fair and appropriate. Neither dominating nor negligent, they had never let a spark grow into a conflagration, and Mila almost regretted this when she heard some of her friends mouthing off, handsome in their teenage furies, handsome in their wars of liberation. Mila's relationship with her parents was ridiculously good; they had given her everything without losing sight of who they were: a well-balanced couple. What a feat such balance was. A couple who upheld their three commandments of respect, goodwill and independence, She a violinist in a good orchestra, He a senior official at E.D.F. Energy, they managed to combine an interest in culture, the security of their property, financial moderation and an essential dash of fun.

But on this new day of sap and champagne, Mila could taste a parting of the ways. The summer holidays were to begin with a trip to Brittany with her parents. As they did every year when school finished, they tidied the house and packed suitcases to take with the three of them in the car, in the very well-maintained white Renault 21, though it was showing signs of age and 'we ought to get a new model' as He, her father, used to say to Her, her mother.

It was a drive of five hours and forty minutes, with stops at the same two service stations as always; they would picnic at the first one and have a coffee on the grass at the second one. Mila would buy her magazines there and a particular kind of biscuit that she never bought at any other time of year: they were *the biscuits that she bought at the service station on the way to Brittany,* and it would have been unthinkable to eat them other than freighted with the taste of going on their summer holiday.

Her parents would take three weeks off work in order to go to the little family house, inherited from his parents and which lay empty the rest of the year, for the grandparents were dead and Mila's family was unusual in that the two parents were themselves also only children. Mila had no cousins or siblings, and had dispelled this primal solitude through the bonds she had made with her schoolfriends. She did not imagine that this pro-creation in perfect proportion with their own family scale had been a deliberate choice but rather the result of difficulty the women of the family had in falling pregnant. Mila was not, at that point, especially bothered by this, and she would not have time to raise the question with her mother. We learn these things to our cost, that certain questions must not wait to be asked, because later it is too late and people can no longer give the answers. So she had not asked her mother; and for herself, she who would later be Mila would choose not to have children.

But that year, Mila had come to the end of school and she did not want to go to Brittany with her parents. She wanted to keep on enjoying the fun that was being plotted everywhere she looked, parties and gatherings of young people impatient to live.

'I'll stay here a few days and then I'll join you!' she said vehe-mently, poised for battle, to her annoyingly fair parents who were shocked at this last-minute desertion. 'I'll catch a train and you can pick me up at the station.' Of course her parents were not against the idea, but, really, why had she not suggested it before, instead of on the very day of their departure. They would have organised it, bought her a train ticket, done some shopping so she wasn't left with an empty fridge.

'I didn't think of it before. And it's fucking irritating the way you need to plan everything all the time!'

Her use of the word *fucking* was the high-water mark of her adolescent rebellion.

In fact, she was meant to meet the group of Russians and go to Paris with them. Thomas had his licence, Jérôme had borrowed his brother's car, Rose and Julie would squash onto the back seat with her, and they would drive to meet the rest of the group, who were heading straight there by train.

The whole story was this: her escape had in fact been planned. Her father was a little put out at being presented with the situation: that a plot had been laid a good while earlier for their getaway. 'Besides,' Mila added, 'the Russians are coming to pick me up in five minutes.'

He said nothing more, but suddenly She, Mila's mother, made that indescribable noise which is the silent sound of a smile blooming in the midst of a tense discussion, and then she told her daughter that she was right, that she could have told them about it earlier, and it didn't matter. And then Mila could say that very strange thing to say to her parents: that she had been afraid of hurting them by not coming straight to Brittany.

So while She, Mila's mother, was defusing the situation, He, her father, had the brand-new sensation of seeing a young woman here who had been afraid of *hurting him*, and, looking at his daughter, he realised he had never had this feeling before because, until now, it was he who had done his best to prevent his daughter ever being hurt.

He felt old.

said fox

She and He were to leave that day. They had decided that they had to go on July 14, Bastille Day, that's what the traffic alerts had decreed. She and He were to take the autoroute, He at the wheel for the first leg, a route so familiar, taken so many times, that they no longer needed a map; then He would cede the wheel to Her, his wife, at the first stop, so that neither would be too tired while driving. After twenty years they knew the score. And He, Mila's father, decided He would buy his daughter her biscuits at the service station anyway, for he was attached to the rituals and he loved his daughter.

Mila whose name was not yet Mila stood on the pavement outside the house to kiss her parents and thank them once more for their permission, and all three waited for her friends to come and collect her, and when the promised lift had come and set off for Paris, the Great Elsewhere, Mila's parents stayed, arms aloft, to salute the young people's departure, arms still waving goodbye long after it had become impossible for the car's occupants to see them. They had agreed that Mila would join them by train five days later. She and He had given her money and emergency telephone numbers, and her father had even entrusted his own mobile phone to his daughter, who didn't have one. 'Just in case,' he said several times. 'If you need to reach us, you can call your mother's number.' Her father never let the thing out of his sight, so this struck Mila as strange. 'I really don't need it, Papa.' 'But take it, go on, you never know . . .' She, Mila's mother, had taken off her favourite silk scarf which she wore round her neck every day of the year except in extreme heatwaves – but you don't get heat-waves in Brittany – and had tucked it into Mila's pocket, to leave a part of herself with her daughter, a token of her softness. The scarf was heavily impregnated with Chanel No. 5, the only per-fume Mila associated with her mother, one of those unchanging totems that are not to be questioned. And Mila had been troubled by these almost superstitious gestures. *Bon voyage* to you, Mila thought. Thanks for going without me. And *Bon voyage* to me too, left alone without a safety net for the first time in my life. When at last she stopped staring back through the rear wind-screen, she was able to look forward,

at her route;

and the sensation of all her desires floated, suspended inside the car the way water lilies idle on a pond. Lilies that seem so strangely exalted.

The promise of Rimbaud's 'loud, blinding cafés', only two hours' drive from Vallé. They had planned to get to an arthouse cinema in the Latin Quarter where at 8 p.m. they were premier-ing an amateur documentary about a Serbian artist Mila hadn't heard of. The Unknown! They would speak with liberated tongues, of things shocking and ungraspable. After that they would go out to drink and dance like young savages. And Mila knew she would feel this body, her body, as languid as a water lily, as intoxicated as a day of doubt. The capital city was theirs and it was the evening of a national holiday; they would join the celebrations. They had the keys of a distant aunt of Rose who was away for the month of July, in whose apartment they would all crash. Theirs were the waves and reefs. At the tops of their voices and head-to-tail. They would sleep on the living room sofas or they might not sleep at all. Mila would not wash again, would consider nothing but understand everything, her uneventful education making her charming adult life so urgent she could touch it.

Mila had negotiated five days.

At least, that's what she thought then, with the deceptive and paradoxical ease of certainties we think are carved in stone.

Abel

18

I should delight

Elsa, his neighbour, had suggested they take the Métro or a taxi but he would not countenance it; Abel wanted to go on foot. She pointed out that it would take a long time and that was when he said that he had at no point requested her company and, all things considered, Elsa doubtless had better things to do.

When Abel happened to notice her in front of their building, Elsa had commented that they were bumping into each other rather often recently, and it surely meant something. He had replied that, living in the same block, the probability of unplanned encounters was high. 'Yes, but I've been living here a year, Abel, and we never used to bump into each other before.' Now she knew his first name. She had begun by saying quite out of the blue: 'Ah there you are, hello again, and I still don't even know your name . . . !' and at the same time asking what he was doing just then.

'What are you up to today? You seem to go round and round almost as if you were imprisoned in our building. Like a fairy-tale character, you know?'

'No, I don't know. I was just going out.'

'Where to?'

'I'm going to the Pompidou Centre. Are you interrogating me?'

'You're going to see where the Lusitano was found, right?'

'Yes.'

'Can I come too?'

'No, I prefer to go alone and I feel sure you have better things to do.'

'I am very discreet. And I've nothing better to do just now. Please, let me come with you!'

'You don't seem at all like a discreet woman.'

Elsa let rip with that powerful laugh that he had heard her give before, a laugh that welled up from her gut and burst out shamelessly, as if seeking to spatter everyone in the vicinity, to contaminate them. This woman doesn't respect the rules of personal space most people tacitly observe, Abel thought. That was when she had suggested they go by Métro or in a taxi, taking firm control of the expedition in full Girl Guide mode, and Abel had said that he wished to go there on foot. Their route to the gallery would take an hour. Then Elsa had asked her neighbour if he had a problem with public transport.

'I like walking. It helps my insomnia.'

Generally speaking, roaming for some time with a vague destination is like writing a thesis, Elsa said, this being her own occupation for the last three years – not that she could claim to be even halfway to the end, she added for Abel's benefit, although the latter had asked her no questions thus far.

'So all this seems rather a coherent little jaunt, even though I don't have quite the shoes for it.'

'You talk a great deal.'

'And you hardly at all. I compensate, don't you think? You don't ask questions. You don't digress. It's as if your empathy mechanism has gone rusty, Abel.'

'Talking the way you do, without any filter, is a bit aggressive.'

'Why do you let me go on, then? Why are you letting me come with you? You could send me packing.'

'I believe I'm attempting to be polite. But you are . . .'

'I'm what?'

'You see, Elsa, you don't give me a moment to consider, to find the right words, even to finish my sentences. You seem perfectly at ease.'

'True. Then why are you going to the Pompidou Centre to see where the horse was found?'

'Why would someone put a horse in an art gallery?'

'Why would anyone shit in a tin?'

'Excuse me?'

'You haven't heard of that piece? *Artist's Shit*. An artist packed his faeces in tin cans and sold them for their weight in gold. And that's not just a manner of speaking; he indexed their weight in grammes to the actual market price of gold.'

'Who would do a thing like that?'

'An Italian artist called Piero Manzoni, back in the Sixties.'

'How could people be sure it was his faeces in the tins?'

'They couldn't. It was hermetically sealed, like tinned peas. You had to take the artist's word, he signed the tins and wrote on them in several languages that they contained his shit. Having said that, it seems a few of them did start leaking and they smelled rather nasty. He may have done it after all.'

'And did people buy his shit?'

'At first not really, but these days they're worth a lot. Much more than their weight in gold, actually. A few years ago, one of them sold at auction for more than two hundred thousand euros.'

'Is this what your thesis is about?'

'No. I'm writing . . . well, you could say that I'm looking at the invisible architecture of spaces of freedom created by activists in contemporary art. They're also known as "artivists".'

'That's a bit vague.'

'It isn't, but your reaction is what I'm expecting from the majority of readers: incomprehension leading to rejection. Don't worry, your denial is part of the process.'

'My denial? I only said that it was vague; you're going a bit far now.'

'Not at all, I'm just being an educator. Besides, you're a crucial link for the artivists.'

'I am?'

'Yes: you're the potential viewer. The viewer faces irruption into a realm coded by an exogenous element – call it an external element, if you prefer – and then reacts. Their reaction constitutes the very vitality of the gesture offered by the maker. In other words, that's what brings it to life. The existence of the artist's gesture is dependent upon the viewer's gaze, to put it another way. Just as the Jew exists in the eyes of the anti-Semite, according to Sartre – but that's another story. So, the work of art exists through the viewer's gaze and, more than that, through their subsequent action, be it rejection, destruction, sublimation, preservation or anything else.'

'And are you earning a living with this thesis?'

'Hahaha, the return to capitalist roots. Do I look like someone who's earning a living? I think you saw my apartment . . .'

'You seem to have a good deal too much free time. Are you coming with me because my horse in the Pompidou Centre fits with your writing murk and you've become interested in it?'

'Or could it be you I'm interested in, Abel? Does what I'm saying upset you? You look a bit troubled.'

'No, I'm not upset. Do stop commenting on my reactions.'

'Putting a live horse inside an art gallery is as incongruous as putting shit in a tin, isn't it? I don't know you, this is the second time you've mentioned this horse, and you said "my horse" as if it belonged to you, as if it's become your horse. It was you who put it in the gallery – go on, confess!'

'This tin of faeces gains a meaning solely through someone buying it, correct?'

'Or by making us talk.'

'You have talked about it to me. I was doing perfectly well until then. It's strange how artists think people who aren't interested in art are lost in some kind of desert. And how writers think people who don't read don't know which way is up.'

'People who don't read do not know which way is up.'

'You see?'

'Who said I was an artist? I said I was writing a thesis.'

'It's the same murk.'

'You use that word *murk* a lot, if you don't mind my saying.'

'If that Italian artist of yours wants to warn us that we're buying a load of shit, I think he's chosen a rather lightweight target.'

'What *was* Manzoni's intention? That's a huge question. He was having fun with the art market. "Buy my shit! You're gagging for it, you bunch of idiots!" And then, they weren't tins with ring-pulls, they were sealed. It's interesting to think about the contents of a box that's inaccessible, isn't it? Buying that box means buying a mirage, an idea . . . a talisman. And then, too, it's funny to publicise a tin of shit. What are you – a Calvinist? People don't make art solely in order to shoot something down, Abel. Where did you get that idea? Do you think your horse was meant to expose something in particular?'

'The Italian went to a lot of trouble to do something that's no use to anyone . . .'

'Well, what use are you? You're not working – are you unemployed? It's three o'clock in the afternoon in the middle of the week. Most people are at work. You look too old to be a student. Why are you so interested in this bit of news?'

'It's not a bit of news.'

'It is, quite literally, if you think about the words. It made the news, that's for sure. And then, putting a horse in a gallery is genuinely new, quite unheard-of, isn't it?'

'Is that what you call an *art performance*?'

'Ah, you see, you *are* interested – at last! It's one step at a time with you on the case.'

'Don't talk about me as if you know me. You don't know me.'

Elsa lost her smile. She turned to stand squarely before Abel, laid a hand on each of his shoulders and gave him a push, the way a boxer might provoke an adversary in an impromptu street fight. Abel stopped dead, speechless. He was much taller than her and more solidly built – it was as if an angry hummingbird had given him a peck.

'Abel, I understand your whole shtick, this not trusting anyone and being rough and ready, fine, I've got it. You brush me off every two minutes and I let it go, because, probably, you think I'm soft in the head: people who're a bit . . . *you* know, you can be *direct* with them. No, I don't know you, and I don't claim to know you. Calm down for a minute, will you? When I say, *it's one step at a time with you*, it's a way of saying that I'm concerned, that I'm interested in you, it's what people do when they meet, alright? What rock have you emerged from? Don't you meet new people in your life? And when it happens, don't you try to be friendly and conspiratorial with them? Do you see what I mean by conspiratorial? It isn't a bad thing.'

Caught off guard and stung by this woman, Abel felt as confused and awkward as an adolescent. Out of nowhere, he admitted to Elsa that, well, he'd signed up to Tinder, so now he *could* actually meet people.

'You signed up to Tinder? When?'

'Two days ago.'

'That's a riot. And have you slept with someone?'

'No. Not yet. Almost,' Abel said, vexed by the turn the conversation had taken, thanks to his admission.

'Almost? You're some kind of genius.'

'I have another date this evening.' Why did he go on saying these things, he admonished himself privately.

'I doff my hat to you, Abel. But let's get back to business, or rather to art; why does this horse matter so much to you? You haven't answered that yet.'

'You are impossible.'

'There, you're being unpleasant again. You haven't even asked my name, whereas I asked for yours.'

'I know your name. You are Elsa.'

'How do you know?'

'I looked at your letter box this morning.'

'Well I never: another box with a name on it, like Manzoni's tins of shit! And there I was thinking you didn't care since you hadn't asked me in return.'

'You don't interest me. You're making my head spin.'

Elsa and Abel went on with their walk, Abel setting the pace. He walked fast; he was feeling ridiculous, humiliated; he was angry. She noted the physical effort required for her to remain at his side, to match his pace. He moved smoothly and Elsa followed. She mapped his thigh muscles as if they were traced in ink beneath his cotton trousers. She smiled.

And for once said nothing. She had him cornered, she could wait.

And then Abel blurted:

'I say "my horse" because I've been seeing it everywhere for the last two days, as if it were seeking me out. I didn't ask anything of it. I say "*my* horse" because I don't feel neutral about it. Because it reminds me of something I can't quite remember. Do you see? An unpleasant recollection.'

'Has it shocked you?'

'Well, yes. Yes, it has shocked me.'

'Like the tins of shit. It is shocking. That was the point, or part of it. D'you agree? Once we've been shocked there is a trace of it left over, and that remaining trace is what it stimulates in you: nothing major, a tiny jolt. It's made you move forward, it sets you going. Hence we've been walking for half an hour, trying to pick up the trail of your horse. Why does that make you angry?'

'Who are you – the local shrink?'

'You say we haven't met before although I've been living in the building for a year. But I've crossed your path many times, and you didn't see me, Abel, you weren't seeing anything around you. Perhaps you and I have known each other for years. Your eyes seem dull. Why are you now looking around you again? Why have you signed up to Tinder?'

Abel muttered that she couldn't possibly have been there a year, of course he would have noticed her, then suddenly he tensed. On high alert, like a startled animal, he snatched at Elsa's jumper sleeve and yanked her towards him; pulled off-balance, she clung to him and, knocked backwards, Abel fell full-length across the pavement with a smack, a shock, the instant that a grey car flashed past them going much too fast.

He said: 'You don't rate looking around when you're crossing the road?'

She had grazed her elbows, his body was held down by hers

and Elsa said he'd scared her when he pulled her arm. She was shaken. She murmured, 'I was going to say . . . ', trying to get her breath back while her heart beat a fast military retreat. 'I was going to ask you to say my name aloud. Could you do that? Say "Elsa" . . .?'

19

T'anticipate

Her name is Michelle, the woman he's waiting for, and Abel has not invited her to the Carolus.

He had asked Elsa where in their neighbourhood he should invite a woman to meet him, somewhere not too far away. Elsa had said that the Avenir Bleu was a good place for a first date. Why, he had asked. She answered something like: 'Feels like a boutique vintner's, has natural wines, it's cool, not too expensive, and the waiters get you to taste the wines at the drop of a hat, so without any dodgy dealing you can get drunk practically on the house, there are candles on bookshelves, the books are fake but you can't tell, the lighting is soft so no-one gets stressed, and they've a short menu, but all the dishes have odd names, good conversation starters, and the tables are well spaced so you can try out a little flirty move without feeling watched, and the best of all is there's a way out via the loos, so if you realise your date is Magda Goebbels and you need to reverse at speed, you can!'

This was too much input in one go. Abel had picked one item from the slew and asked, 'A flirty move?'

'Getting close and touching her!' Elsa had almost shrieked, and from her small mouth that had sounded so natural and delectable that Abel let it go.

This evening's woman is Michelle and Abel has invited her to meet him at the Avenir Bleu.

He had thought when she matched with him on Tinder: Michelle, that sounds like a fake name. Or perhaps she's over fifty – which wouldn't in itself be a problem. He doesn't really have criteria, isn't motivated by any particular requirements. He doesn't know if he'd prefer a blonde or a brunette, a white woman or a black one, a young one or older. That's not where he's at. Or rather, that is where he's at: not knowing. So he lets the system decide for him. He doesn't look at the photographs except when he gets a match.

Why had he brought up Tinder with Elsa again? She is working her way into his life with all her questions, all her insinuations. Her presence overwhelms him . . . he's becoming disorientated. She had stayed with him all day, full of herself and crazy, she'd started singing as they walked, he was ashamed, but not really for being with her – only at having no control over her.

Ashamed of not knowing the song she was singing. He wasn't altogether sure it was legal to sing like that, so loudly, in a public place. And she, at the top of her lungs: 'Take me to the ends of the Earth.' It was a sailors' chanson, about harbours and languishing girls and the past, one he didn't know. He asked her if she knew a song called 'It's a day like any other'. She said, 'Of course, that's Bardot! Why? Do you like it?' And Bac had answered, somewhat limply, that a colleague had talked about it. 'A colleague? What's your line of work?' Bac did not reply. Elsa had begun singing it, just like that, from memory:

It's a day like any other
And yet you're leaving
You're leaving for someone else
Without one word to me
And I don't understand, don't understand!

Abel Bac felt he had been stripped bare. Bare and bereft.

This woman he didn't even know.

He had mentioned that he didn't know where to take her, his date for that evening, from Tinder. So Elsa had done her pitch for the Avenir Bleu, which would be perfect for a first date, where Abel was now waiting for Michelle.

After the Pompidou, he had gone back to his apartment, leaving Elsa on the staircase, after she had thanked him for the walk and wished him a pleasant evening. He had wanted to ask what she was doing that evening but had held back. He was about to go inside when he jumped: the *Parisien*, a new one, plastic-wrapped, had been left on his doorstep.

Again – the same edition – with the horse.

He had turned around to check if anyone was watching. But there was no-one, and Elsa had already disappeared up to her floor, leaving traces of her perfume in the air. Automatically he picked up the paper and, closing the door behind him, laid it on top of the first plastic-wrapped copy and the one stolen from the Carolus. Neatly stacked one on top of the other, three identical copies of the newspaper. Abel had stared at them, in the hope that something would happen, maybe that the papers would catch fire, or come to life? Abel could almost glimpse what the horse was reminding him of, but he refused to go down that path, he barred the route. Next he hesitated over setting down his findings from the day's walk in one of his notebooks; he would do it later. It had to be done but it could wait. Then he washed, twice.

At the Pompidou Centre that afternoon with the insinuating Elsa, he had felt bewildered by the uselessness of what he was doing. The gallery showed no signs of what had taken place inside it.

Besides, what *had* taken place? And why did he feel the need to see for himself something that wouldn't have left any trace? There was no stripy tape, no off-limits triangle, no C.S.E. (crime scene examiner) . . . In fact, there was no crime scene.

Abel Bac was good at what he did. He had been a policeman for almost twenty years, he had a reliable memory and was meticulous in every task; he was the best in his team at writing reports, he checked the spelling and syntax and never used a word randomly but selected each one for its precise nuance. A mud track was not a footpath, which wasn't a road, which wasn't a hiking trail, which wasn't an alley, which wasn't a backstreet. A circle was not a roundel, which wasn't a sphere. Everything counted. Devoted to his work, he had never begrudged the unpaid overtime, the shitty stakeouts, spending nights in cars that stank of kebabs and hormones. He spoke appropriately to people, to witnesses, lawyers and victims, the authors of the events. All were *people* and, until each case was closed, they deserved equal politeness.

Abel had never felt the need to be wealthier, to buy himself certain clothes in aid of a look, to move out and get a bigger apartment; he had been renting the same place for twenty years, since he left the army, in fact. He had never even felt the need to rise up the ranks, except by the natural steps conferred by length of service. He did not bet or smoke or take drugs. He only rarely and almost unintentionally slept with women, generally because he had not said no and the women seemed to want to. For a few seconds every day, he managed to feel like a normal man.

Abel was reflecting on this while gazing at the facade of the Pompidou Centre, a gallery he had never been inside. He was sensitive as a child. That's what his mother used to say. He used to listen to music, and to read old copies of the magazine *Historia* that had belonged to the dour man who had sold them the house – his mother was proud to be a home-owner and it was a small source of pride to him too. This gentleman had left a few green, mould-edged cardboard boxes in the attic, from which Abel had extracted piles of *Historia* and old school readers of classic texts. Abel even used to write. No-one would think it these days. Bac the war machine. Bac the misfit. He used to write little stories, short poems with rhymes and metaphors. He knew what a metaphor was. He had been a good student at his lycée for bumpkins. In his town, there had been two worlds whose paths never crossed. There was the upper town – and they called it *the upper town* even though that didn't really fit in any topographical sense, for the town was flat, but perhaps it hadn't always been so, the land had perhaps been deeply eroded and levelled out, for all he knew. The upper town was quite middle-class, with its clusters of pretty houses with chimneys and plaster mouldings, quiet neighbourhoods, an over-subscribed lycée, enticing and expensive shops. Not too many blacks or Arabs. The lower part of town, known as Les Rancinières, was semi-rural, semi-commuterville. There was even a big psychiatric hospital around which clustered its share of oddballs and lost souls, inhabiting the streets. There was a vocational lycée in Les Rancinières – his lycée. You could be trained in metallurgy or construction engineering, or in childcare, for the girls, and they had black people and Arabs there. The French teacher at the lycée had been cleverer than most. Madame Colombier. Abel knew her first name was Françoise, but he had only ever called her Madame Colombier. She used to talk to Abel sometimes, after class. She lent him books. The schools of the Republic were more than misty ideals; there would always be teachers in them who bent over backwards for the kids on the bottom rung.

Standing before the great art gallery, Elsa had said: 'Right,

shall we go in? We're not going to hang around out here . . .?'
Stressed, Abel realised for the first time since his suspension that
he no longer had his police I.D., a weapon, or any legitimate
claim to automatic entrance. That was what being suspended
meant, above all: the humiliation of giving up the attributes of his
trade, of his identity, almost.

This wasn't even a case, just a few pages of news in a newspaper that had triggered his reaction. And, yes, that horse. The
horse was a physical sign to him almost like a greeting. How
could he explain this to Elsa? How to admit to her that there
were too many blank zones in his head, regions where nobody
ventured; that they gaped open, haunted, and that he felt the
horse was tormenting him from his past. He could not tell her
about Éric, couldn't say that, twenty years later, he was still
dreaming about what Éric did. That he found it crazy he couldn't
shake it off, and yet he never dreamed about his mother. Why
him and not her? He had a notion that Elsa would have an answer
for that, that she would understand.

Faced with Abel's inertia, Elsa said she would investigate. If he
didn't want to move, she could try to find out, *for him*. He didn't
budge. He stared straight at the Pompidou Centre, that impossible, altogether ugly creation, a gutted cruise liner, mourning for
an ocean it would never see.

But strangely handsome even so.

Elsa went off towards the visitors' entrance. When she returned
thirty-two minutes later, Abel seemed still to be in precisely the
same spot, rooted next to the monumental gold flowerpot that
stood in the gallery's great paved forecourt.

'You haven't moved?'

'What is this thing?' he said, instead, indicating the gold-
coloured object.

'A gold flowerpot, fairly self-evident, don't you think? Have you never stopped in this forecourt before?'

'I never noticed it before. What's it meant to represent?'

'Nothing but what it is: a manufactured object, precisely the same as a million others, chosen to be shown as a work of art. If you like, we could take down all our statues and put up flowerpots instead . . . You never heard of Marcel Duchamp and the urinal he exhibited in a New York gallery?'

'No.'

'Shall I tell you?'

'No. Why are there no flowers in this pot?'

'Perhaps putting flowers in it would have given it some unique beauty. Flowers are beautiful, they're alive, they have flaws, whereas, as it is, it remains nothing but a pot, identical to other flowerpots.'

'I have orchids at home, lots of them. I've never really paid attention to their pots.'

'Would you show me your orchids?'

'I don't think so, no. No-one comes to my place. So, did you speak to someone?'

'It's not easy to get into the library, there's a queue that takes several hours. I told the guard at the entrance a little white lie, saying I'd been there yesterday and left my glasses behind. He let me through. Once I was in, I played the curious student and managed to speak to one of the librarians. He seemed upset by the story, he clearly hadn't seen the horse, but he heard about it when he came in the next day. He did confirm, though, that all the staff were talking about it. And he saw no way anyone could have got the horse into the building, through security, at night, without breaking anything or setting off alarms. He said no-one has investigated. The police came to pick up the horse and that was all.'

'No-one's investigating?'

'That's what he told me. I did some flirting and got his number. Just in case.'

'You flirt with people like that, just in case?'

'Anything wrong with that, Abel? We spent an hour and a half walking over here and you won't even go inside. You seem very tense.'

'This flowerpot without any flowers, I don't understand it. Just . . . I don't understand.'

This was not true. Abel had done some snooping around the gallery, but he didn't wish to share that information with Elsa. He'd walked all the way round the thing to get a handle on the crime scene. On rue du Renard, right behind the building, he'd noticed two well-dressed men smoking cigarettes outside an emergency exit. He'd scabbed one off them and borrowed a light, looking unconcerned, he had got chatting, just like that, a guy among guys, pretending he knew how to smoke, no sweat. The two cool cats were already talking about the horse. Abel played ignorant. What's this story about a horse? Play-acting, a standard cop move. Once more he felt in full possession of the situation, in control. Purposeful. For a moment he could forget he was out of circulation. The two men worked in the gallery, they brought him up to speed, roped Abel into the conversation, *random dudes smoking a cigarette*: very strange story, that, impossible to break in without leaving some trace, it doesn't add up, could be something fixed by the gallery's management, one of the pair proposed. A bit of manufactured hype. Abel asked questions, like butter wouldn't melt.

'Hype – really? But why? Who would do something like this?'

'It's a set-up, like a Maurizio Cattelan piece.'

'Who's that – Maurizio Cattelan?'

'A super-famous Italian artist. He's the one who created that statue of John Paul II floored by a meteorite, do you know it?' Guy 1 asked.

'And the hundred-and-twenty-thousand-dollar banana at Art Basel in Miami Beach,' Guy 2 added, as if that clinched it.

No, Abel Bac did not know at all, but he nodded. Conspiratorial. Yes, sure, the Pope taken out by a meteorite and that banana. Thinking over his recent conversation with Elsa, about the tins of shit, he wondered: what's with all these Italians making such preposterous things?

How about this Maurizio Cattelan, then?

Guy 2 said it's true, it looks like his work, with his fetish for horse taxidermy, could be something he'd do. And fag break was over for the sharp-suited dudes.

Abel didn't push it any further. He'd gone docilely back to wait for his neighbour beside the golden flowerpot without a flower.

20

your pleasure

Back home, Abel washed, twice. First on auto-pilot, Abel soaped his whole body, especially the armpits, quite hairy, then his crotch, while scolding himself: what had he honestly hoped to achieve with all that? He also soaped hard at his penis, bum crack and feet, then rinsed with scalding water. Drying off, he was frustrated for the first time since he'd moved in by the lack of a mirror in the bathroom. The lack of a mirror anywhere in his apartment. He would have liked to confirm the validity of his body as a man, not find himself in the risky scenario of falling short with respect to the other person, should Michelle ever present the possibility that he bare his body before her.

But he'd never had a mirror at home.

After the first shower, completely naked, he watered his orchids, allowing himself to be touched, inadvertently, by a petal, a leaf, a stem, as he made his way among them, so that each could drink, each have its fill of water and attention.

He felt bad, and went to wash again. But he rinsed with cold water, this time, to wake himself up, arouse his skin, feel his strength. And didn't go back over his privates, which were already clean. Abel was afraid of losing his grip on his habits, he had a fresh panic to tame every time, and nothing about today had made sense.

For the last week, some outside force seemed to have broken

into his life and washed away every one of the sea walls he'd built up over the last twenty years. First the call from the anonymous informer, which had cost him his job. He could not believe any internal investigation would work out for him, that they might disentangle what happened to him and rule in his favour. There wouldn't be any close examination; he was rotten by contamination. And then the horse. Now he remembered where he'd seen it before. And those copies of the *Parisien* addressed to him, on his doorstep. Who had subscribed on his behalf? The same person who had snitched to the police inspectorate? Whoever it was wanted to be sure he didn't miss the horse. He felt observed by an enemy. His head itched. Suddenly he was consumed with itching. He hunted for the headlice lotion and applied it. Spreading the product evenly throughout and right down to the roots, until all the hair was coated, plastered, so they would all be killed. Now to wait for twenty minutes.

His third shower.

Abel would meet Michelle at the Avenir Bleu that evening.

at the sight;

Michelle is very late.

She hasn't sent any message to apologise or explain. Rather annoyed, Abel has already drunk two glasses of wine while waiting. Two whole glasses. Of an 'organic, punchy, elevating tonic of a wine', as the gushy waitress described it. Abel had nodded, making an effort to look interested, to look *informed*. It is so rare for him to drink alone, and the situation is eating at him. Everything inside is loosening. He can only contemplate himself sitting nice and straight in this trendy restaurant, freshly shaved, waiting for a girl furnished by the internet, drinking by himself. But if he concentrates, perhaps he can identify a very new sensation, a prickling wavelet of electricity running up his spine and tickling his muscles, the glad bite of being out, seeing himself emerge from his rut. He is ever more attached to the wild beauty of his orchids, which are always on his mind. They are what he will never be.

At last Michelle arrives. She is forty-six – according to her profile; this time Abel checked beforehand. He didn't want to put his foot in it. She has very long hair, he guesses, for she has stacked it all up in an ingenious chignon of several levels, from which a few wild and elegant strands have rakishly escaped. Like stems without corollae. Michelle apologises for her lateness, speaking rapidly and with an elaborate ballet of hand gestures;

she seems torn between explaining by way of many digressions or perhaps taking the simple decision to move on, pronto, to alleviate this awkward moment of their encounter. Dithering, she mumbles bits of information, not completing a single sentence or casting any light, and ends up just sitting down. She seems a touch theatrical, Abel thinks. She talks loudly, he observes, embarrassed. Now sitting opposite him, breathless from running, her unfinished sentences still fluttering in the air like headless birds, Michelle asks Abel if she might take a sip from his glass (which must therefore be his third) as she is thirsty, and, upon his nod of assent, she drains the glass in one draught. He thinks of her saliva all over the vessel. Putting down the empty glass, she catches Abel's stunned expression and responds that she's nervous and that she'll order another for him right away of course, *Éric*.

The name rends the air between them.

Abel stiffens as if he's been struck, like a whip crack across his neck, and he whispers through almost closed lips that that's not his name, Éric.

'Éric is not my name.'

The woman opens her eyes wide and apologises right away, the truth is she can't remember his name at all. She laughs to cover her embarrassment.

'Excuse me, I can't think of your name anymore! I am a silly. I'm so sorry!'

'But why did you call me that?' he enquires with unwarranted fierceness.

This forty-something is starting to panic. She tries to explain herself, palms rising and falling parallel to the table in the classic gesture of pacification: it's just that she goes on lots of Tinder dates, she sometimes gets in a muddle, she'd actually forgotten about their date – there, if he'd rather she were completely honest, hence why she was late and actually she almost stood him up, only, realising she didn't have his number to call, she'd made herself rush over, dumping two girlfriends with whom she had, if he wanted the whole story, already begun an aperitif. But Abel will not let go, he's enraged and he asks again why Michelle called him Éric. Why that name? Her eyebrows at their furthest arch, the woman apologises again.

'I made a mistake.'

She'd neither noted down their date nor remembered his name. She has no idea what he's called, but it's no big deal, is it? As they don't really know each other. Abel growls that his name is Abel. Not Éric.

Michelle has got it now. 'I've got it now, Abel,' – and she tries to make a joke about these dates you set up online that cause all kinds of misunderstandings, hahaha, but Abel cannot relax, his face is closed off, Michelle's voice coming from further and further away, as if someone were talking at very low volume, only a few of the vowels are registering now, he is retreating into himself, a free dive down into a world of water that warps his perceptions of space, of time, the weight of his body. He focuses on the shape of that name, Éric, as if it were not a four-letter word but a form, a liquid, an animal to be stroked or feared. Now he can see the bodies on the ground, some seemingly beheaded by the bullets' point-blank impact, executed bodies, furious bodies, he sees an eye sucked from its socket, then he sees the horse, hears it neigh, the great horse, its white coat flecked with red streaks, spatters of blood. A church organ plays, towering, each note seems to rise from the cries of the bodies felled as they're murdered, as if each cry were sealed into an organ pipe and a madman were pumping the bellows. Women's cries. Animal howls. And the horse is transfixed with fear, he twists and bucks.

A hand on his shoulder, shaking him. 'Monsieur? Monsieur?' Abel looks around, the diners at their tables, the waiters rushing about, arms laden with plates standing to attention, green, red, white bottles, pockets sprouting pens and corkscrews.

'Are you alright, monsieur?' enquires the waitress who shook his shoulder.

Abel says yes, of course, he's quite alright; his hand is still gripping his empty glass, opposite the chair is starkly empty. 'Would you like me to call a doctor, monsieur?' Why, he thinks, why is this girl talking as if he's sick, but he can no longer make himself reply, his mouth has gone numb. People at the other tables are discreetly and less discreetly turning round to look, happy to dip their legitimate curiosity in another's misfortune. 'You are very pale,' the waitress insists. He's looking for things to hold on to, he sees a plate full of food in front of him, and dozens of bits of bread scattered all around it. A man approaches. 'I'm a doctor,' he proclaims, happy to be useful, to play a role in this *incident*. 'Where is the woman who was here with me?' Bac whispers. He is surprised by his feeble voice, his breathlessness; he is struggling to breathe. 'Where is the woman?' No-one is listening, no-one hears him, now everyone in the restaurant is bustling and buzzing around him.

Abel would like to get up and leave but he can't, he is now lying on the ground, his legs in the air, resting on an upturned chair, he's still gripping his empty glass, he can't seem to let it go. He orders his body to let this useless empty glass go, his hand is hurting, but nothing happens. He looks around for the waitress. 'Mademoiselle, mademoiselle . . .' he calls. He's so frustrated he feels like crying, at last he catches her eye, the eyes of the friendly waitress, she leans over and reassures him, you'll be alright, an ambulance is on its way, everything will be alright, can you hear me, monsieur?'

He would like to sink into her, to curl up in her solicitude and rub himself out.

'You fell, monsieur, you had a fit. Do you think you could let go of that glass? You're going to give yourself a nasty cut.' Abel looks at his hand, which is gripping a bouquet of spears of broken glass, his hand covered in blood.

'The woman who was with me?' he repeats.

'She left, monsieur.'

'When?'

'At least an hour ago . . .'

Mila

22

But come

Mila was thirty-nine. It was a figure, an abstraction. Mila wasn't afraid of getting wrinkles or of suddenly losing a reassuring sexiness, but it was the idea of a cycle that bothered her, a cycle that, sooner or later, would have to end. For a long time she had worked through rage, she had devised actions intended to exhaust this rage and so live in her solitude, and in this she had let herself be led by intuition.

At eighteen nothing remained of what Mila had been before, so she could act without premeditation. She had no more parents and nothing left of her superego. She had done what she wanted, she had gone rogue, she had treated this reality as a realm of signs that she must penetrate and force others to penetrate. And luck had played its part. That journalist from *Le Monde* who'd turned up out of nowhere, who'd taken a shine to her and her hijackings of Parisian statues, and who, thanks to an inquisitive article, had pushed her out into the world. And Masson, who had brought Mila about by becoming her mouthpiece, who had brazenly gone knocking on the door of the biggest modern-art gallerist in Paris, Antoine Spuillier, and asked him to represent her. Masson had decided to camouflage her, to create her, to bet on her, she who no longer slept at night, who went out looking for objects to tamper with, to transfigure, without any specific intention, and she had found herself a cover girl for *Beaux-Arts* magazine in

2006 – well, not her but a photograph of one of her witching-hour happenings – and then everything had categorically changed. Her success had been as unexpected as it was all-consuming, she so much an outsider, who'd never set foot in Central Saint Martin's or any other incubator for this hermetic milieu, a bubble inside a bubble; Mila who'd never cultivated any network or alliances, a chemically pure exogenous element uncontaminated by the contemporary art scene, who had blundered in with the subtlety of Leatherface setting about his massacre with the nearest chainsaw. But a self-made success, living by her own means, alien to the woman she had been; she was a senseless success in the image of her own inner world where she thrashed and fought. The rage at her back, she had worked with assurance. She had learned to create her art pieces while also creating Mila, and with the confidence of her status she had gone to town, she could do anything. She found herself able to think at great scale, like the Mexican painters who painted thousands of square metres of public buildings in the Thirties. But Mila's pieces were monumental in their mix of intangibility and bravado. They came to life through the unwary gaze of their inadvertent beholders. They were received like a rapture of the everyday. Mila imposed no limits on herself: everything was allowed.

She would soon be forty and she was living for the sake of her incarnation – the other her, Mila. Could anyone fall in love with a woman who didn't exist? She couldn't give a shit about being desirable. That kind of power was a faded wallpaper. She slept with people – plenty of them, men and women. She was accessible. For she had the self-assurance and the money to be welcome anywhere, *dearie*. She had an 'open sesame' to every cave. She had become a Gatsby. Everything is much simpler when you don't really exist. Eccentricity becomes an inevitable accessory.

No, the problem was that she no longer had either the rage or the certainty. And this had hit her without warning. She was sad, just sad; sad from morning to night. What could you do with that? When the chemicals and the pills don't even begin to relieve the dead weight in your belly from the first coffee? She needed to be reborn, to revive the person she had been before Mila.

So she had to kill off Mila. It was crystal-clear, and at Mila's funeral there would have to be a performance the like of which no-one had ever, *ever* dreamed. Her firework finale.

For that was how everything had begun. But for once she wanted more than one spectator – more than millions of spectators! She wanted a partner. Someone who would be at the heart of the piece without knowing it, yet who would be there alongside her, body and soul.

An accomplice.

23

who knows?

That night in London she made her decision. She would fight her final round, and that would be the end of Mila. She hadn't left the studio, but she felt as though she had been on an all-night bender, alone with her thoughts. All night long, she had agonised over her next piece; it would be the last product of her anonymity, her grand finale. How could she represent the time before and the turning point of her life? How to distil her backstory into a performance that was ephemeral yet so powerful it would hit the viewer like a punch in the teeth? She would go back to her beginnings, recreate her trauma, but this time she would be the instigator, she would be in charge. So many ideas clamoured at her; it was a paroxysmal night of creation. She meant to stage an exorcism.

Mila sketched some designs, got some key words down on a board which she then stared at until they started to melt together: *Vallé*, *lights*, *red*, so the words would come alive, overflow her and show her a way forward. Mila called on everything she'd produced in her life as an artist in order now to surpass it all, to sweep it all away.

She had glimpsed the shape of her great project. She had noted down a few instructions for Masson. This was her warning to him: from now on she would be focused on her next piece.

She had no interest in discussing anything else: not current exhibitions, nor potential invitations, nor any new hitches. This marked the end of their daily telephone calls; Mila required silence so she could concentrate. She would send him guidance on the project as and when: there would be research to carry out (a private investigator would be required) and she would need a new team of assistants. And she would be moving to Paris in the end, for it was there that everything would take place. Therefore she would need French assistants and a Parisian network. Further, Mila informed Masson that she required direct communication with certain art galleries and also with a popular daily newspaper – *Le Parisien* would be ideal. All would be invited to contribute to aspects of her unprecedented next piece. She was thinking of the Pompidou Centre, for now; other partners would be required too.

Mila's piece would take place on three occasions and at three locations, like a triptych, and all in a very restricted timeframe. It would be a nocturnal performance series that would unfold in bursts, forming a puzzle for the viewer to 'piece' together. It would be unnerving: a cathedral; a Bosch painting; a map of the moon.

A key to myself.

Masson was used to the state of hyper-excitement that gripped Mila when she threw herself into a brand-new idea. He would not be surprised.

'These are the most urgent points, in this order: you need to find me a studio in Paris as soon as possible; moving my things from London can wait. Set up meetings with the gallery directors, starting with the Pompidou. And, so we don't forget, I will need a live horse to begin the installation.'

Claire Berest

Not just any horse –
a Lusitano.
He would see why later.

And for once in their lives,
everything would make sense.
She promised.

Abel

24

perhaps it is a prey

A young doctor with an expression of virtuous exhaustion silently knotted the last few sutures across his right hand. Abel decided that the young man was able both to maintain this focus and to be elsewhere entirely, deep in his task and already out of the door, a tall, put-upon kid. 'Wait here. The duty psychiatrist will come and see you,' he said to Abel tersely, a man with no time to waste, meanwhile packing up his tiny, fiddly instruments. He walked away. Their eyes had not once met. Abel was in no pain, but he felt the weight of his fatigue. His seized-up hand showed several deep lacerations, he'd driven the slices of broken glass in with every ounce of his strength, although he couldn't remember it. He decided seconds too late to make himself scarce; the shrink was already strolling in, eyes focused on his patient. 'Monsieur, please come with me.' He was gesturing to a corridor. Abel hesitated.

'Were you heading out?'

'No.'

'Yes, you were. It's what most people who should urgently be seeing a psychiatrist do: they cut and run. So I like to see how many I can catch before they get away. Like going after butterflies with a net, d'you see?'

Doctor Guérin, according to the name written on his breast pocket, wanted him to describe what he remembered from before he was admitted. Guérin was a short, thin gentleman with spectacles dangling at his neck, five o'clock shadow showing early and a general aura of freshness. As if he'd only just applied left and right spritzes of aftershave. He was waiting, apparently in no hurry at all.

Abel cooperated, limply, describing the restaurant, the heat, the wine he had drunk. 'Were you alone?' Not at first, Abel said, but even so he had been, in a way: he'd been with a woman he didn't know and who had arrived very late.

'What state of mind were you in?'

'None,' Abel replied.

'Well now, monsieur, it's a difficult thing to be in no state of mind at all. Although you could have been dead.'

Abel did not respond, he didn't smile, he froze.

'Do you often go to restaurants?'

'No.'

'Do you often meet women you don't know?'

'No.'

'How much do you drink?'

'Rarely. Very little.'

'Can you tell me what day it is?'

Silence from Abel. He cast his mind back. It was hazy. It was mad that it seemed hazy. Whatever the circumstances, Abel knew who he was, where he was going and the day of the week. He tried to work it out, in relation to the day before, or the next day. But what day was yesterday? 'No, I'm not sure,' he ended by answering, reluctantly.

'Do you work?'

'Not at the moment.'

'Meaning?'

'I'm on a sort of break.'

'Are you on holiday?'

'No. I'm waiting . . . I'm waiting to go back to work.'

'To do what?'

'My job . . . my profession.'

'Why did your job stop?'

'I don't want to talk about it.'

'Do you take any medication?'

'No.'

'Had you taken any drugs this evening?'

'No. You should know I am a police officer.'

'Ah I see. But that's not impossible – you are also a man.'

'No, it is impossible.'

'Alright. How do you sleep at the moment?'

'Badly.'

'What is the last thing you remember of this evening, before you reached the hospital?'

'I would like to leave now.'

'Is that the last thing you remember?'

'No. I would like to leave this place, right now.'

'Of course, monsieur, you may leave. I am not detaining you, only talking with you.'

Abel snatched up his coat and rose. The doctor said: 'In a way, this is what happened at the restaurant, you know. You *needed* to leave – and so you left. You fainted. You switched yourself off.'

Abel sighed and sat down again.

'The waitress who helped you told the paramedics. You were sitting by yourself for quite a while, after the lady who was with you had left, and when the waitress asked you some questions, you didn't answer, you were staring into space, she said. After that, you experienced, I believe, a panic attack.'

'And so?'

'Has this ever happened to you before?'

'No.'

'Right. That makes it an unanticipated attack.'

'Of course it was unanticipated. I didn't go out in order to have an attack.'

'No, what I mean is that you have no known trigger nor any identified phobia that tends to cause you stress.'

'No.'

Abel was aware he was lying, which put him on edge.

'How old are you?'

'Thirty-nine.'

'You look older.'

Abel narrowed his eyes.

Guérin explained: 'No, you are healthy for your age, you're robust. It's your face. You might have come straight out of a refugee camp.'

'I beg your pardon?'

'Which doesn't make you ugly, I should point out. You just have a terrorised expression. Alright, back to the matter at hand. Something must have happened in this restaurant, perhaps something quite tiny, which triggered a short-circuit and plunged you into a state of fear. Do you recall being frightened?'

'No.'

'Any dizziness? A feeling of suffocation?'

Abel made an effort. He closed his eyes and let his mind sink into the sensations of this body of his, so firmly locked against the world. Into the ruts and ridges of the shreds of the last few hours. He opened them again to find himself staring into Guérin's eyes.

'She got my name wrong.'

'Meaning?'

'I remember that the girl who was with me used a different name for me, not my name.'

'O.K. Did that anger you? Were you humiliated?'

'No, it's just it was a name that reminded me of someone . . .'

'O.K. And what was *her* name?'

'I can't remember,' Abel said.

25

By fortune offer'd in our way.

To help him sleep, the medic gave Abel some Xanax, under the counter, as it were, without a prescription, the way you share a secret or proffer a favour. And he recommended that he 'see' someone.

He had kept Abel from leaving one more time, this skinny little man, holding him by the sleeve for a last word. 'Do it. See someone. This will happen again, for sure – and worse.' And Guérin went on smiling vaguely, as if ready to execute a neat click of his heels upon the tiles of the emergency section, a final flourish to his injunction.

Good to have this Xanax, Abel thought, he could give it to his orchids.

Then he had a go at finding in his mobile the number of the woman from his date. He found nothing, neither messages nor any digital trail. But he saw several missed calls from Camille Pierrat, who, tired of the run-around, had now texted: 'I'm waiting at your place, I have news.' His heart began to race, she would be more than capable of breaking into his place, he tried to think, but his head felt so scattered, so lumpen. He called Pierrat, or tried to call her, but it was as if he'd forgotten quite how his telephone worked. After several tries, the thing began to ring. Abel asked his colleague where she was. Camille was waiting at the Carolus, below his place; in fact she was in the middle of a little *tête-à-tête* with Ahmed, the proprietor . . .

'You know Ahmed, his chat is as picturesque as yours. Know what he just told me? I was taking him through one of my homicide jobs. And he said: "Pah! Worth his weight in nutty slack." Crackers, don't you think? What can that even mean, nutty slack? Anyway. Where are you? Get your arse over here, bruv.'

Abel asked her what day it was.

'Thursday. Why? You sound knackered out. You're talking like someone on day release, Bac, are you panting?'

And Abel, as he made his way stiffly back to his place Clichy, intoned:

'It is Thursday, Thursday, Thursday, Thursday, Thursday, Thursday, Thursday, Thursday, Thursday . . .'

But in the streets his fellow night-owls heard: '. . . her say, her say, her say . . .'

Mila

26

They went

A handsome grey wolf with pearly green eyes raised a champagne flute in his paw, and the rapidly ascending bubbles glittered in his eyes. He wore evening dress: a narrow black tie that matched the lapels of his dinner jacket. He was poised, leaning over, as if caught mid-conversation with a she-wolf who was flirtatiously showing off her violet pearl necklace and expertly knotted Hermès scarf. She too had a flute of champagne, set down beside her on a small Empire-style table. Seated on a deep, blue-velvet sofa, she was surrounded by others of her species, all in evening attire, in this elegant salon with its ceiling draped in hundreds of garlands, like some monstrous flower of shimmering streamers, a wild extravaganza of

blue, white and red.

. . . Together the garlands formed an explosion of France's colours, of her brash red and her tender blue, united by a white highlighted by regal glints of gold, and all lit by hundreds of tea lights which lent this salon the intimacy of a candlelit supper, marred only by the fervour of a nocturnal revolutionary gathering with its thousands of tiny French flags tucked into gaps between walls and furnishings, pinned to windows and fluttering (though actually perfectly stationary) from the paw of one of the wolves, who held his pennant aloft.

As if elated, fevered, already drunk.

A drunken wolf.

On the tables, on fine porcelain plates, waited still-hot fries and sausages, pots of red ketchup, bottles of champagne and mountainous stacks of cakes. A tape recorder was playing a retro sound, joyous old provincial hits. You could easily picture one of the wolves leaping nimbly with all four legs out of his armchair to join the dance, a satanic salsa.

Mila surveyed her *tableau vivant* with satisfaction. The effect was eye-catching, morbid, disturbing. She also savoured the muffled atmosphere peculiar to this kind of grand private mansion, where you felt as though all of civilisation had been consigned to a distant star. The walls' thickness weighed on the senses. The black and white checked tiles in the hallway showed in brief flashes amid the darkness, under the sweep of Mila's assistants' headlamps as they parcelled up the last bits and pieces. Impeccable ants. She had hired pros and they were silent, efficient, focused. They were carrying out her plan and were well paid for it. They'd no need even to speak: everything had been anticipated down to the tiniest details; they hadn't heard the sound of her voice nor seen the cast of her face, hidden behind a black anorak. She paid lavishly for their discretion and for their subsequent return to the void.

The floor made her think of piano keys appearing and disappearing, or of scattered dominos. Mila took in the scene for one last time so as not to forget it. She had taken hundreds of photographs, of course, with a Leica Compact as well as her Polaroid instants. These images were as important to her as the installation itself. This was her story, the traces of which would once more become invisible. The photographs said *this happened*. They were highly prized among collectors. From the first, Mila had insisted the photographs she herself took of the process were an essential facet of her performances.

For now, she was determined to remember the physical effect created by her staging. She looked her fill. When she left the museum, that would be it, the first and last time she would see it; all she would have left would be the images. And it was soothing to know she was all-powerful in the midst of this party, to look on it from above, and from outside the reach of time – immortal. She seized a glass of champagne from a pedestal table and, without bumping anything, leaned in to raise a toast with the green-eyed wolf.

No, it wasn't dominos she had in mind. Black and white – it was a chessboard. She was at the heart of her work.

The Queen.

Abel

27

The horse,

Camille Pierrat, her tough, wiry little body perched on a leather-ette stool, seemed to have found her berth at Ahmed's bar, and she broke into a big smile at Abel's arrival at the Carolus. For Abel, she stuck out like a parrot in a flock of pigeons. It wasn't that her clothes were particularly colourful, more that she was intruding on territory that was his. Abel nodded to Ahmed. 'Get me a coffee?' Ahmed smiled by way of a yes.

'You're ordering coffees at midnight now?' she began.

'I need to clear my head.'

'Why don't you ever invite me to your place, Bac? What are you hiding – a body? Your strap-on collection?'

And her laugh,

Pierrat's laugh, so different from Elsa's, a cascade like the resounding tumble of wooden balls inside an old-fashioned toy. Impenetrable, Abel unbuttoned his coat. He'd left the hospital at too rapid a clip, like a junkie, and he was exhausted.

'You know the other thing he came out with, Ahmed, while I was waiting for you? I was talking about a defendant, saying we couldn't get anything to stick to him, you know. I said: *'This was one guy with a real Teflon slick to him . . .'* And Ahmed said: 'Out of the fryer and down the pan . . .' Who says that? D'you get it? Like out of the pan and into the fire but . . . d'you get it?'

'I understand it fine.'

'I see. Did we happen to get up on the wrong side this morning?'

'I'm tired. But I've a question. Do you think I look terrorised?'

Surprised, Camille had not answered when Ahmed returned to announce: 'A short black for the sarge!' Camille observed her colleague, who did indeed look as though he'd seen a ghost. But Bac always appeared to have half his mind elsewhere. On the other hand, it was rare for him to ask such a question. Ordinarily Bac was more the lips-sealed type.

'You just seem quite tired, Bac. What did you get up to the other night? Where did that horse graffiti you sent me come from?'

'You could have called me to ask that – why have you turned up at my place at this time of night?'

'I did call, you bastard, I called three times. You didn't pick up. I was worried you'd gone and strung yourself up. So, like the good girl I am, I brought my ladder along to check on you.'

'I had a drink with a girl the evening I took that photograph. A girl I found on Tinder.'

'I don't believe a word of that – not one! Abel Bac on Tinder – hahaha. I'll have to tell the division. Ahmed, champagne, please! This is the best thing I've heard all year. So did she do a good job on your baton?'

'We didn't . . .'

'S'O.K., I was just having a giggle. Well, what's this to do with the horse?'

'It's complicated, but, in short, she's the one who told me about the graffiti. I sent you that horse because it's the same as the one they found in the Pompidou Centre. And the paint was fresh. I found it on the rue du Faubourg Poissonnière. It's superb. Must be the same joker who goes strolling round our galleries at night.'

'Shit, my friend, you're onto something.'

Ahmed brought champagne. Camille fell quiet, and pensively sank two good glugs from her flute as if for fuel. Only then did she confide to Abel that his case had taken a new turn. It seemed their comedian had reoffended, but the news was still under wraps, otherwise the press would be all over it and make a proper media circus out of their case.

'What's happened?' Abel pressed her. 'Another Lusitano?'

'Lusitano? Come again? Listen, I came to see you because you wanted me to update you on the Pompidou horse and then you send me this picture of the horse graffiti, which nobody knows about. It's amazing that you found it . . . Were you just taking a walk that way? A romantic stroll with your Tinder date?'

'Let it go, Pierrat. What's happened?'

'Another gallery has had a night-time break-in. It's a crazy story. I hadn't even heard of the place: the Museum of Hunting and Nature. It's a small one on rue des Archives, with lots of weapons, tapestries and stuffed animals. That kind of thing. A kid, or a few kids, if you want my take, went on a bit of a spree: they got in without leaving any marks, nothing was stolen or damaged, as at the Pompidou. But in one of the rooms, the burglars went for a complete refurb . . . There's . . . well . . . I can't even describe it. It's as if you're looking at a painting but you're inside it, or as if you've walked into one of Aesop's fables, with the animals dressed like humans, everything in there like it's a fairy tale . . . And the animals look as if they're dancing and singing, celebrating something. But nothing moves. It's gorgeous, but it's also . . . upsetting, if you know what I mean?'

'What kind of animals are in there?'

'The people who constructed this bazaar, seems they found some stuffed wolves elsewhere in the museum – just the wolves – and set them up *together* like this. They dressed them in fancy clothes and positioned all the wolves as if they were . . . having a party. See?'

Worried, Abel was on the point of answering no, he couldn't really picture what she was describing, but Camille cut in and continued:

'Look, none of it looked too bad, at first sight. Nobody was hurt, nothing was damaged. Like with the horse in the Pompidou. Though no doubt some top execs won't appreciate that jokers are coming and going in our public institutions as if they were railway junctions. Where it goes really nuts is that all the pretty decorations, the trinkets, armchairs, glassware – none of that came from the museum. The wolves did, but the rest didn't . . . Wanna guess where that came from?'

'No.'

'From François Pinault's home!'

'The businessman?'

'Yup. He's a massive arts benefactor and billionaire . . . Major art collector, too, it looks like.'

'How did his furniture turn up in a museum on rue des Archives?'

'His Paris apartment was burgled – that same night. Pinault wasn't there, he was travelling. All of it belongs to him. And the cherry on the cake is they even nicked one of his paintings, a Picasso maybe, something of that sort. The guys did a kind of wholesale removal on his living room.'

'So to be completely clear: some guy robbed François Pinault of his furnishings, took them to the hunting museum and arranged them again in there?' Abel said, brows furrowed in perplexity.

'That's it. And he went and sat the stuffed wolves on Pinault's peerless selection of chairs, very prettily kitted out in clothes also borrowed from Pinault. One of the wolves is wearing his flannel tie. And the x-million-dollar painting that vanished from his living room wall, well that's now hanging, sweet as you please, in the Museum of Hunting and Nature.'

'What's in the painting?'

'I don't remember. I wrote it down somewhere, I'll dig it out.'

'And what are they doing?'

'Who d'you mean, they?'

'The wolves!' Abel snapped irritably.

'Right, well, they seem to be enjoying a drink, a glass of champagne and best-quality bubbles too, all courtesy of Pinault's cellar, I should add . . . Not like Ahmed's fizz. They're partying. It's weird. No, you'll see . . . I took some pictures.'

Camille picked up her mobile and sent some images rolling rapidly over the screen, then she stopped and held the object out to Abel. 'Go on, look.' Abel stared back at her shots of wolves dressed to the nines, the flags and tinsel. Pierrat's words clattered around his head like squash balls in a glass cage. 'But what the hell are they celebrating . . . Bastille Day?' he muttered. Camille guffawed heartily, all her teeth on show.

'Yes, I guess so! I forgot to say – but I remember now: the stolen painting, that's what's in it . . . It's a Bastille Day scene. Look, you can see it in this photograph, at the back . . .' Camille hunted through the notes in her phone. 'Here it is: a painting by Van Gogh. It's called 'The Fourteenth of July in Paris'. This, my friend, is worth its weight in nutty slack, as Ahmed would say. In fact, our wolves are patriots,' Camille said, and considerately drained the last drops of her champagne before attacking Abel Bac's untouched glass.

Mila

28

turn'd loose to graze

Of that Paris night, snatched from her parents as they left for Brittany, Mila would retain only ambiguous fragments that hovered between joy and nausea. She had tossed caution to the winds. At first it had been *the best night of her life*, as teenagers say seriously when they have brand-new sensations. Mila would keep it pinned up like a mental postcard as her last happy memory from a life cut short.

The film the Russians saw at the little cinema called Le Champo was an analysis of an artwork by Marina Abramović, a performance called 'Rhythm 0'. Mila had not known people did things like this. She wouldn't have been able to imagine it, she felt as if she were discovering a new planet. This woman, Marina Abramović, seemed to be a famous artist who used her body as the material of her art. 'Rhythm 0' was one of the experiments she'd carried out in the 1970s, the last in a series of performances that had begun with 'Rhythm 10', then 'Rhythm 9', 'Rhythm 8', and so on down to nought.

Now, thirty years after those performances, Mila felt she had emerged from Vallé a true greenhorn, seventeen years old and seventeen thousand miles behind in everything. She knew that she knew nothing. But *rien* comes from the Latin word for *thing* as Monsieur Verdier had loved to repeat, and the quip had become a running joke in his class. And there breathed inside her that evening, as she emerged from the Parisian cinema, the urgent new sensation that life was racing at top speed, and curiosity presenting fresh heights and giddy new views. As if the desperation of adolescent bodies to collide and experience each other would reach its apogee in this night of escape.

Inside the Studio Morra art gallery, in Naples in 1974, Marina Abramović stood in the middle of the room. She had arranged seventy-two objects on a table. There were all kinds of things on it: flowers, a feather, lipstick, paints, perfume, a fork, matches, wine, a saw, soap, cake, grapes, a hammer, honey, scissors, alcohol, a razor, a hat, a whip . . . even a pistol loaded with a single genuine bullet. On a welcome sign at the door, her visitors read:

> *Performance*
> *I am the object.*
> *During this period I take full responsibility.*

The viewers had six hours ahead of them, between 8 p.m. and 2 a.m., to do what they wanted with the artist. They could use anything on the table and they had access to her body. No matter what happened, Abramović would not react. Everything was allowed.

What do you do when you have total freedom?

As they all left the cinema, the Russians' excitement was electric. They had talked more and more loudly and all night, from bistro to bistro, *quick quick* – as *bistro* means in Russian – they had talked of the tomorrows they would build, of their avid bodies, of her – Abramović – of Gogol, Bulgakov and Dostoyevsky . . . and of art. But my god, what was art? Inspired and shocked by the film about the Yugoslav artist, their impressions, questions and consternations had fed their mouths as much as the warm blond beers and the cold vodka that finally enveloped their night.

Vodka!

They had sung in the streets, they'd embraced out of sheer exhilaration that July night in 2000, when you still paid in francs and smoked inside cafes until your lips bled. They had managed to climb the spear-tipped railings of the Luxembourg gardens, it was quite a feat, but nothing could stop them that night, not the wrought-iron spikes nor their fears, and the young people had strolled arm-in-arm under the consoling trees, their bodies white-hot, like that statue of an unruly faun they found in the garden, which seemed to invite Mila to take off all her clothes and join the dance. An effervescent melee of friends seeking to grow closer, to string themselves like pearls along the ribbon of a single passion, in this Paris booming with horns replaying a victory filled with guillotines and glittering tomorrows. And fired-up Mila had decided, whatever transpired, to finish the night with Paul, whose Russian name was Fyodor and whom vodka had rendered irresistible; this would be her ultimate fanfare. Fyodor, with his wrongly buttoned shirt and his manly facial down, the very shape of a desire. *I am the object.* And the horrifying images of Abramović's performance throbbed in her eyeballs like the drug of a fallen paradise.

Mila was a virgin. Her sex life had stuttered from furtive fingers to encouraging sighs, she was only seventeen, but she realised that some nights demanded breakthroughs, and so, on with the dance!

And for now she thought this Paris moment might never end, her freshly graduated friends and she could stay together and never grow old. Trapped amid the Bastille Day trumpets and the cheap champagne passersby were drinking out of flutes, in the streets of Paris. As if pinned within the perfection of a work of art.

As if they were, in fact, unwittingly, all puppets in a sophisticated performance, and the true challenge was how to recognise real life.

Abel

29

Not liking much

Abel had left rather suddenly. All but fled. He could not share with Camille his distress at seeing her pictures of the vandalism scene in the museum. This, after the horse? The grotesque tableau with those dolled-up animals! But worst of all: on Bastille Day. At that Abel had wobbled, seeing the images with all those symbols of the patriotic festival. A Bastille Day – of course. He wasn't mad. Now he understood perfectly why the horse in the Pompidou had seemed familiar, everything was coming together. But who could be doing this? Who was doing this to *him*? The *Parisien* on his doormat was no accident. Someone was playing hide-and-seek with him. He knew that if he shared with Camille his sense of being connected to these *things*, these 'installations' as his neighbour Elsa would say, he would look completely paranoid. But it was eating him, like the lice on his head: every inch of him was in their sights, he was being drawn into it; and the person who was playing Chinatown in the art galleries every night was doing it to push him over the edge. It was knowing, deliberate . . .

. . . meticulous.

How could he tell Camille? How do you tell a story? He couldn't. He'd said only that he was exhausted, he had to go to bed, he had had enough. He had left her at the Carolus. He had not said he had just come from the hospital, that he had had a kind of blackout or a fit, he didn't know how to describe what had happened.

He did not confide. Abel confided in nobody, and that was how he'd been throughout his adult life. He had built his own cage and barricaded himself in. People's propensity to tell the world about themselves, to be forever excavating themselves, both fascinated and repelled him. The repulsion was not a judgment: he did not think ill of people for opening up to all and sundry, for the benefit of their best friends or indeed to strangers beside them on the bus, certainly not, but it did repel him, it sent an icy shiver down his spine. Unease. People who told you about their everyday hassles: the delayed train, the broken boiler, the noisy neighbour; people who importuned you over their health troubles, shared with you their problems with their skin, their teeth, their hair; people who scattered around them fistfuls of data about their sex lives like rice at a wedding, who paraded their conquests, talking about cocks and asses and pussies, from in front, from behind or standing up; people who talked about their net worth, their holidays, their cars, their menstrual cups; people who talked about their child-hoods, who told of bereavements they had endured; people who said things like 'As for me, it broke my heart' and who talked about shame, anxiety, bipolar disorder and burnout.

People were becoming *functions*.

All the same, what strength it took. It had been so many years since Abel had allowed anyone to get close to him. He said noth-ing, revealed nothing. And nothing meant *nothing*. He had no close friends. What for? He could discuss the cases he was work-ing on with Camille, he could smile at his colleagues' anecdotes or sympathise when the anecdotes were gloomy. He could say that he'd been in the army before joining the police. He could say that he lived in Paris, on place Clichy, on the fourth floor.

He could not say that he liked orchids, that he was insomniac or that he hardly managed to sleep with women anymore. He could not recount his nightmares, which were always the same and poisoned his nights. That he felt spied on. He could not say that Éric waited for him in his dreams, that Éric was hiding at the edges of all his nights, lying in wait.

The last woman he had slept with – really slept with, after undressing and foreplay, through to penetration and night-night, be seeing you – was back when . . . He did some calculations, tried to recall some points of reference, and so began to revisit the cases he had worked on. These were his waymarkers. Back when . . . he was on the case of the woman defenestrated by her spouse on the rue de Clignancourt. From the fifth floor, three years ago. It was then that he'd slept with a colleague from the narc squad after some leaving drinks. She had made the first move. He had followed, he had gone to her place. She had shared custody of her two children, a boy and a girl, he remembered, and that night they were with their father, as she had explained. Her apartment had been a real mess; she was going through a bit of an unhinged time in her life, she had also told him, in those exact words, and he had thought: 'Stop the chat, so we can get the job done.' He'd been tempted to cut and run, he was ill at ease. But he'd had to go through with it, to make the moves: the hands, the arms, the lips, the expected things, to get the job done. So he had done it almost as if holding his breath. She had been pretty, or at least what you would call a good-looking woman, and she was patient.

An attractive orchid only somewhat unhinged.

So he had undone the buttons at the top of her white shirt and she had ripped off the lower ones in one go, he'd pressed himself against her narrow, spiky body, she was a little too thin and angular, but he'd gone on pressing until he got an erection, then he'd licked her neck which had tasted salty, and he'd decided he would lick her armpits, and on doing so had discovered fine little hairs she didn't shave, and suddenly he had liked that, he was into it. So he had licked her fine little hairs and his excitement had precipitated execution.

Leaving her place in the morning (escaping?), he had felt proud and sad. As if he had passed an exam, but in a compulsory subject he would not have chosen.

With whom could he have shared such intimate things – Camille? That he lived with the sensation of having such an infestation on his head that he used a toxic shampoo every week? That his scalp was flaking off because of it?

Yes, he was fascinated by what people went on revealing of themselves as if yelling through loudhailers. Fascinated by the social networks with their long tunnels of set lines and clichés, dazzling like streetlights inside a black box; pictures of yourself everywhere like dangling mirrors instead of foliage. He was floored by the selfies which forced you to look at yourself, making everyone active spectators of their imperfection, selfies which demanded gentleness, self-forgiveness, selfies which told of absence, of dissolution of the heartland. How many must he, Abel, have analysed in the course of investigations? Other people's selfies, their telephones full of them like sweetly rotten eggs, full of secrets and little deals, full of suspicion and immodesty.

He would so have liked to do that, to take a photograph of himself at arm's length, to sink his gaze, through the blank lens, into the eyes of some other person who would want to look at him, who would be intrigued by his gesture, someone who would look at his photograph.

30

their looks or ways,

Abel was exhausted but he knew he would not get to sleep, because Éric had him in his crosshairs. He would have to wash himself, at length, let the hot water do its work of numbing, breaking him down. Softly, softly he climbed the steps to his apartment, without turning the lights on, as if afraid his neighbour might jump out; she seemed to pop up all the time like some mad puppet on springs that had escaped its box. He was now climbing so slowly, perhaps he could get there by moving backwards.

He saw his landing. His orchids were waiting. The thought of his plants soothed him. Like the thought of huddling under a blanket on a cold night.

He anticipated each movement he would make, the way you go through each step of an escape plan. He would enter his apartment, close the door, check the little cupboard on the right was properly locked (he kept his police gun there and, although he didn't have it at the moment – he had been compelled to return it as part of the suspension – he knew he would check that padlock because he had done so every day since almost forever), he would greet all his plants with his gaze, he would get undressed . . . Stepping through the door, Abel saw that a letter had been slipped under it to await him inside. A white envelope addressed to him. No stamp, no address; it had been posted through the gap by its sender. On it was inscribed *Abel Bac*, beautifully executed, like . . .

what was it? Yes, like calligraphy. It was done in blue pen, fountain pen, its dark blue inescapably recalling the exercise books of his childhood. Abel never received letters, apart from electricity statements and maintenance bills for the building. The letter had scotched the reassuring chain of steps he'd meant to execute when he reached home. Flustered, he opened it, like that, without ceremony, there in the doorway which opened directly into his living room, where his orchids lived. He unfolded a page covered with the same old-fashioned handwriting. And began to read:

> *A fox, though young, by no means raw,*
> *Had seen a horse, the first he ever saw:*
>
> *'Ho! neighbour wolf,' said he to one quite green,*
> *'A creature in our meadow I have seen, –*
> *Sleek, grand! I seem to see him yet, –*
> *The finest beast I ever met.'*
>
> *'Is he a stouter one than we?'*
> *The wolf demanded, eagerly;*
> *'Some picture of him let me see.'*
>
> *'If I could paint,' said fox, I should delight*
> *To anticipate your pleasure at the sight;*
> *But come; who knows? perhaps it is a prey*
> *By fortune offer'd in our way.'*
>
> *They went. The horse, turn'd loose to graze,*
> *Not liking much their looks or ways . . .*

The fable played out, unconcerned. The page was unsigned.

31

Was just

Very gently Abel folded the letter again and put it in his pocket with care, then with equal care looked behind him. There was nothing there, nothing apart from the cupboards of his kitchen which opened onto the living room, the spotless work surface; there was no-one there. He almost expected someone to appear, to have broken into his home, the person who was playing with him: his mother back from the dead, or Éric and his gun, he too returned from the shades, why not? The state he was in, he could even entertain the irrational.

But no, of course, there was no-one in his kitchen, nothing alive except for a few orchids perched on the shelves, rehoused there when they had become so numerous he had had to let them colonise the whole space. There was nothing human here apart from him.

And Abel knew that this poem slipped under his door – this fable, rather – was connected to what had happened in the Pompidou Centre, to the horse and the dressed-up wolves at that weird museum on rue des Archives. He knew. Someone was winking at him, sending him a twisted sign, a kind of path to follow. And all his plants, so beautiful and exalted, seemed to be spying on him too. As if every one of his orchids had little button eyes, thousands of eyes, perverse watchers, wondering if Abel was going to react, if he would break with the passivity. But Abel was eighteen years old again and so clumsy. Perhaps he had never stopped being eighteen, he had been stuck at that day, that place, and life had gone on without him. He did not undress with a view to showering as he had planned; he gave his plants a mental nod and left his apartment once more, still calm, his back to the door, his steps careful, the way we instinctively move to avoid antagonising an animal opponent awaiting our first misstep. Flight of stairs, he did not even think; how new it was for him to do something without thinking it through. He climbed without pausing, all the way to Elsa's door.

He knocked hard.

'It's the middle of the night. Did you get the wrong floor too?' she asked, opening the door wide to Abel. She seemed hardly surprised. Her pyjamas were too big for her, making her look like a small, lunatic dictator. 'If I may, your face is practically Munch's "The Scream",' she added, letting him in, without either one needing to say: *May I come in? – Yes, do come in.*

'I can make you a tea,' Elsa suggested, 'or we could do some rum shots . . .'

'Tea, please,' Abel said as he sat or rather fell into a deep, once-elegant and once leather-covered armchair, now more a heap of sack-cloth, straw and loose springs.

'That's less fun,' Elsa said, hunting around her tiny galley kitchen to dig up a teabag from somewhere and a couple of mugs. 'Do you know Munch's "The Scream?"' she asked, head inside a cupboard.

'No.'

'Well, you do, actually, it's one of the most famous paintings in the world. You'll have seen it on posters, in films, you simply didn't know you knew it, alright?'

'Alright.'

'Do you know the horror film "Scream"?'

'Yes.'

'O.K. The killer's mask, which became so iconic, do you remember that? It's inspired by Munch's "The Scream".'

'And I look like that?'

'Yes.'

She burst into laughter, her high-pitched, gushing laugh that was starting to sound to Abel like something familiar, a reassuring noise: Elsa's laugh.

He had a notion that he was surrounded by laughing women.

Elsa was energetically dunking an unlabelled teabag in one mug of warm water then the other, after which she handed one to Abel. She apologised for being without a kettle: she'd used hot water straight from the tap. 'It won't be amazing,' she added, 'but it was you who wanted tea.' She told Abel that Munch was a Norwegian painter, and 'The Scream' was the title of one of his paintings, a good, unpretentious name for a painting, even if he in fact actually painted five versions of the same subject, so that made five 'Screams'. 'It's as if Da Vinci painted five "Mona Lisas", you know? In the painting you see a man yelling and holding his head in his hands. He looks more like a ghost than a man – or like a skull. He's got no hair and his eyes are popping out. He's standing in front of a stretch of water, on a jetty with a railing. They say it's the Oslo Fjord behind him, but I've always thought he was on the deck of a boat. Above him there's a crimson sky, a wild sky, almost marbled with blood. Munch said he painted it after a walk with friends when all of a sudden he'd heard, or at least felt, a great shout, as if Nature herself were bellowing, and then he was gripped with an appalling fear ... So, yes, Abel, you do look like someone in the grip of a great anxiety, if you don't mind my saying, and you also look wiped out. How long has it been since you slept?'

'Have you seen the actual painting?' Abel answered softly, for in comparison Elsa seemed very loud.

'Yes, I have. Funny you ask, because just now, when I was describing it, I'd forgotten that I'd already seen it live somewhere not just in books. It's so well known that I managed to overlook my own personal experience. Am I making sense?'

'I don't know.'

'Quickly then, I'm talking too much ... In Paris, when I was a teenager, I saw the painting. It was the end of the Nineties, I don't know which year exactly. There was a show at the Museum of Modern Art, I think, on Scandinavian painters, it was called something like 'The Northern Light', something like that. It was appealing, a nice name for an exhibition, pretty but acute too. I went with my art class and our teacher. And Munch's "The Scream" was there. That was the first time I saw it. As it happened, very shortly before it was stolen.'

'Someone stole it?'

'Yes, at the beginning of the 2000s, along with another very dark and beautiful Munch painting called "Madonna". They thought the paintings had been destroyed. I remember, when I read about it in the papers, I felt as though by stealing this painting which had so dazzled me as a teenager they'd somehow robbed me, personally. As though it was a personal insult. I was furious. I wanted to kick their heads in.'

'And were the paintings saved?'

'It's funny, you talk as if they were people. Let's use *tu* for each other, don't you think? We said we would ... Yes, they were found a few years later. And we still have them. Munch was quite a desperate guy, see, ill and depressive. The railing in the painting is the barrier to stop the man leaping into the void. He was awkward around women. He even wanted to shoot one of his lovers.

Towards the end he shot himself. You could have investigated his case if you'd been around then! In fact he only injured his hand, which is telling for a painter! Well, this tea is gross. It's like I'm sipping water from the lav. I'm getting the rum out, sorry. I also have gin.'

Abel was feeling good. He was at rest in this uncomfortable but enveloping armchair amid the fuss of this woman talking nonstop about distant things, about painters and tenebrous paintings, without even asking why he had knocked on her door in the middle of the night.

As if being civilised meant precisely not asking someone why they dared to interrupt our sleep, but rather to drink tea that tasted of old boots with consummate ease at three in the morning. He felt good because being in Elsa's apartment seemed to keep all that was happening outside and troubling him at arm's length: the letter in his pocket, Camille who kept hassling him, his disastrous Tinder dates, his suspension from the police. The wolves celebrating Bastille Day . . .

His panic.

Nothing panicked him in Elsa's place, inside this minuscule apartment that looked like a film set, where most of the furniture seemed to be a form of trompe l'oeil, and he allowed her to pour some rum directly into his tea, the alcohol mixing with the lukewarm water, and now a sip of the pungent poison at last sucked him down into the drowse of a hunted animal for a moment in a place of safety.

Mila

32

about to

With Fyodor's industrious though fumbling assistance, Mila made short work of her burdensome hymen that night. It was July 14, 2000, Mila was in Paris and she was seventeen. All the words she thought of were Russian and came with the tragic piquancy of a Barbara chanson. For her, this was something like a remake of Sade's *The 120 Days of Sodom*. She was triumphant, she was free, she was reborn. It had taken fifteen minutes and fewer than ten fevered thrusts from her accomplice's hips, so sweetly swaddled in awkwardness. But their combined breath: *tovarisch!* This was the wind of the open ocean.

She had sat up, goddess in full awareness of her powers, and left Fyodor to his drowsing to go and smoke a cigarette on Rose's aunt's balcony, Mila who never smoked. Mila who had just made love for the first time.

She felt this was now the only appropriate thing to do: have a smoke. She had found half a pack of Lucky Strikes on the floor, lying open and inviting, as she stepped over the adolescent bodies scattered around this stranger's perfect apartment, like an arrested tableau of the calm after a bacchanal. On the balcony, she had focused on operating the lighter, taking it slowly; and, breathing in the harsh smoke, she had examined and enjoyed her naked body, her desired, disquieting, entrancing body, a disturbing double to the abused body of the artist Marina Abramović.

At the beginning of Abramović's performance, for the first three hours, the viewers are intimidated and amused. Well meaning and curious, they give Marina A. a rose, just to see. They kiss her on the cheek, they clasp her in their arms. They grow mildly bolder, like harmless sparrows heedless of how keen their pecks may feel. Delighted by this passive living doll, they give her hugs and keep it gentle, still tamed by the pact of civilisation. It takes them fully three hours.

Time does its work and now Abramović's performance goes off the rails. She doesn't react, truly, not at all. As she promised. All well and good. The viewers cut her clothes with the scissors and her bare breasts appear like beacons, or like Rimbaud's 'dazzling lamps' in the light of the Neapolitan gallery. They cut her neck and one man drinks her blood, actually sucking at her skin. They manipulate her and shake her, lay her out on the table with her legs apart. A man sinks the knife into the table between her legs, close to her pubis. They cover her in food. The keyed-up viewers form two camps, as instinctively as in any war: those who want to protect her and those who want to abuse her.

They – for in that moment they are a formless *they*, the same crowd of people that watches hangings or shaves women's heads, a pronoun into which we dissolve – they write *END* on her forehead with the lipstick. What end? When a viewer grabs the pistol and points it at Marina's temple, holding the artist's finger on the trigger,

... only then does the gallerist intervene: he dashes forward, pushes the man away, snatches the gun and throws it out of the window. He had promised Marina not to step in during the six hours of the performance. Some promises are unsustainable.

Mila, who has just made love for the first time, runs through these images in her mind, over and over. This is what we really are, this herd. It's true and brutal, disturbing. She feels awakened, changed, watchful. She has just made love and her skin is sweating manic droplets.

Six hours have passed and the performance is concluding. Abramović emerges from her catatonia covered in blood and in the food spread over her by others, her eyes filled with tears. She moves towards her viewers in order to speak to them, to make contact – and they flee. Unable to see her living, too ashamed to accept a face-to-face encounter.

Mila slipped into Marina's place, imagining herself being manipulated, her legs parted. She was sullied and all-powerful, because she would have written the Tablets of the Law herself. She wanted to change everything, to understand everything. She wanted to revel and to condemn.

She was seventeen.

She lit another cigarette, proudly, then noticed that her phone was blinking (the one entrusted to her by her father). And showing ten missed calls. It was 4.10 in the morning. A vague alarm spread through her.

She did not recognise the number. She called back despite the time. She heard three beeps as the call went through. 'Hello, Vallé police station . . .'

They had died instantly.

She and He.

The officer did not hesitate once Mila had given proof of her identity on the telephone. He asked only if she was alone, and she had replied, 'I'm with some friends.' Then he had told her quickly and plainly. There is no call for suspense when relaying a death to a relative.

They, *She and He*, wouldn't have had time to grasp anything at all. She understood: they did not realise they were dying. But what was there to understand? A man had shot her parents during the Bastille Day celebration in Vallé. They were not the only casualties. The officer had wanted to let Mila know as rapidly as possible, before she found out from the headlines the next day. Mila, who was not yet known as Mila. The policeman expressed his condolences.

But at that moment, Mila wasn't listening to the details, she was repeating: 'No, it can't be. No, it can't be true.' Faster and faster and louder and louder. Until the bodies of the Russians scattered around Rose's aunt's apartment awoke, and rose and gathered around her scream; until they formed an ancient chorus around her, a solid net of their outstretched arms. And Mila, who was not yet Mila, explained nothing to her comrades, only yelled: 'Where's my scarf? I want my scarf!'

And, sober now, Paul who was Fyodor in Russian class, who had just made love with Mila, hunted and found by digging through her bag a scarf which he brought to her, a scarf impregnated with Chanel No. 5, the scarf left by her mother; Paul who had just made love for the first time in his life with the body of this girl, who was now howling like a madwoman, the scarf pressed to her nose.

When Marina Abramović got back to her hotel in Naples, that night, after her performance of 'Rhythm 0', she looked at herself in a mirror, she at all of twenty-eight, she saw that a whole section of her black hair had turned white in the course of the performance.

The stress.

Abel

33

gallop off

'The rum is better than the tea, though, don't you think?' Abel
says nothing. He seemed to be dozing in the armchair, like an
injured cat; Elsa thought he looked a fright, and she felt guilty.

He looked like someone who could never go home again. He
had run aground at her place, his last redoubt. She felt they
ought to talk *genuinely*, without pretence or euphemism. And
she remembered the hackneyed line: *We really need to talk.*
The cliché leaned on by couples or families in crisis who, by
invoking it, were hoping to trigger a shake-up, a change of
scene or mood. As if everyday talk were *false*. As if to talk with
care, gauging the other's vulnerability and taking the measure
of their blind spots and their narcissistic weaknesses, were to
talk falsely. She suddenly thought, before this dormant Abel,
that the cliché was brutal – or perhaps that reality was brutal.
She wanted to shake Abel. Then just as she was preparing to
kick down some of the barriers between them (a kiss or a slap?
Or why not tell him everything?), Abel sprang bolt upright as if
suddenly awoken and said, out of nowhere, that he'd been suspended from his job.

'I was suspended from work. It's been about a week and I don't
understand why. I mean, I know why, but I don't understand who
is trying to get rid of me. Since then, everything's been changing
around me. I wasn't sleeping much before, but now I can't sleep

at all, so I'm wondering if maybe I'm imagining all of this? Maybe I'm going mad?'

'What's your work?' Elsa asked him gently.

'I'm a policeman. Been a policeman for nearly twenty years. I was in the army when I was young, then I took the police college exam.'

'And where do you work?' she went on, because that's the kind of question you were meant to ask, she thought.

'At D.P.J. 1, the lead crime squad in Paris. I'm a detective. I thought I might soon make Captain. Not that that would have mattered much to me, but it would've been something real. It made some kind of sense, linear progress. You see?'

'Yes, I see. A kind of sense.'

'Now, everything's stopped.'

'Why were you suspended?' Elsa asked, reasonably. She felt bad asking him all these questions, she was physically discomfited at delving into his life, even though she didn't do embarrassment, but it was too late now, she had to go on. Abel explained that it was hard for him to discuss. But he had a go. He described how his management had received an anonymous call about him, a malicious call that revealed he had lied in his original application. He had then been brusquely informed that checks were in progress and that, for the duration of the inquiry, he was suspended.

'And you see, suspended – that's exactly how I feel. As though I'm dangling, unable to touch the ground anymore. I can't get a grip on things. It's as though I'm being hanged with a slow knot, strangling without dying.'

'What are you expecting, Abel? Is there nothing you can do?'

'I received a summons for first thing on Monday. I'll be interviewed. I should go with a lawyer – at least, that's the procedure.'

'Have you instructed a lawyer?'

'No.'

'Why not?'

'I don't know. That's what my colleague Camille Pierrat wants me to do: get a lawyer and get my arse in gear, as she says. She likes swearing. She swears all the time.'

'She sounds like a good person, your colleague . . .' Elsa said. 'Have you any idea of the identity of the person who could have made that telephone call?'

'No, no idea.'

'Sorry to be blunt, but *did* you lie in your application, Abel?'

Instead of answering, Abel said he had found a strange letter slipped under his front door. Just now. And he'd come to see her after finding it. Because he wanted to be sure that what he was living through was actually happening; because, it was hard to explain, he felt he needed a witness. And he said aloud, though as if to himself: 'Funny, I'm the detective, and now I'm the one being investigated.' He took the letter from his pocket and held it out. Elsa opened it and read. 'Is that all? Just that? Nothing else in the envelope?' Abel shook his head.

'But it's one of Aesop's fables!' Elsa said.

'So the letter's real? I'm not dreaming?' Abel said, rendered suddenly childish by his distress, Elsa thought.

'Of course it's real. It's here in my hands.'

'Right,' Abel said. 'Yes. It's a fable. "The Fox, the Wolf and the Horse".' He rose from his self-protective slump in Elsa's dis-embowelled armchair. And repeated: ' "The Fox, the Wolf and the Horse." '

'What's the matter?' Elsa asked anxiously.

'Nothing. Only . . . how to explain? There was the horse at the Pompidou and . . .'

'And what?'

'Let's just say that someone mentioned wolves to me this evening, but I can't go into the details. It's worrying.'

'Do you think it's a game? A riddle, maybe?'

'It could be that someone is playing games with me. Or perhaps I'm losing the plot . . . And there's no fox.'

'Wait, Abel . . . Do you know the road the Pompidou abuts, the one that runs behind it?' Elsa asked, flushed with excitement, her shoulders thrown back and her fine, long neck reaching out to him.

Abel looked at Elsa's eyes, which seemed to sparkle with a troubling intensity.

'Yes, I know it,' he said.

He paused.

'It's the rue du Renard.'

34

Sir

The words floated in the air between them, Abel and Elsa, words of foreboding, full of mirrors in which reflections fluttered, ambiguous glimmers of silence, of things unsaid, of maybes. Abel missed the wellbeing that had filled him when he took refuge with his neighbour, but the spell was broken. Elsa now seemed rather frightening. He could not have said what had happened between them just then, or since he had come in, to make him feel threatened once more. Perhaps it was simply because he had confided in her, and with every piece of himself that he let go, he was further stripped and eroded.

He wondered how old Elsa was; she might be one of those women who look younger than they really are. Women in whose faces a mask of freshness overlays a perceptibly older presence.

She did seem double. He ought to go right now, go back down the few steps to his apartment, where he could dispose of the anonymous letter with its ridiculous fable.

Elsa reminded him of a woman from one of his cases some years before. It had followed a school's report on a six-year-old pupil, raising suspicions of abuse. The case should have been taken to the juvenile division but, after some witching-hour disagreements, it had washed up with his division, on Abel Bac's desk.

The little girl had been puny but fantastically graceful, she seemed to float over the ground, an ethereal presence, making no noise and leaving no trace of her passing. The concerns focused on the father, concerns about inappropriate touching and other abusive behaviours, for the child was repeatedly ill, she had lost weight and was forever being rushed to hospital, yet the doctors never found anything. It was that troubling absence of illness that had haunted Bac. The doctors had discussed some psychological cause, psychosomatic reactions, perhaps, and the father had been strange: evasive and distracted.

The mother, on the other hand, was really something.

She too had been indescribably graceful, an overwhelming beauty, which made it hard to look her in the eye. In contrast with her stunning physique, she was gentle, deeply caring, concerned and horrified by her daughter's malaise; she had seemed even more distressed than the girl. When Bac suggested the possibility of inappropriate behaviour by the father, he had expected an absolute refusal, that she would perhaps walk out in indignation, for that was often what happened in this kind of scenario. But this mother had seemed relieved, as if Abel had extracted some appalling thorn from her life. She must have known something.

Abel had put a lot of work into that case – too much. It was a bad sign, one he ought not to have ignored, when he named one of his orchids after her – the very graceful mother.

He had even given her his personal mobile number, so she could call him at any time, should she anticipate some danger for herself or her daughter. The father had been hermetic: he'd revealed nothing under interrogation. He grew angry, but it was as if he had just touched down from another planet. And the more loudly he proclaimed his outrage and his innocence, the less readable Abel found him, the less he made sense.

Elsa reminded him of that woman, not because Elsa was

spectacularly beautiful like the girl's mother, but because they were both the kind of woman who changes the shade of a room on stepping into it, because even before they spoke, the air particles seemed to pause in anticipation of the star turn. The kind of people you met by chance, without warning, who knocked you off your feet and thereafter never left you in peace. And you knew it straight away, but it was too late, you hesitated to shield yourself, uncertain whether to get out while you could or, instead, to welcome the whirlwind, for there was nothing like it.

Elsa and her outsize laugh, Elsa and her scent that followed you everywhere, Elsa who knew everything about everything, who seemed to find fun in every situation like a mischievous kid, Elsa who seemed almost unreal.

When Abel said yes, he knew that street behind the Pompidou, said calmly but with a sense of physical occasion that it was the rue du Renard, Elsa was delighted and appeared about to say something important, he saw the intensity in her eyes, the tension in her arms and at her delicate collarbone where it showed above her oversized men's pyjamas, and then the phone rang, Elsa's phone.

Like a bad ad break, which nonetheless gave Abel time to wonder who could be calling at this hour, in the middle of the night? Although he had himself shown up without warning at an inopportune hour.

Elsa appeared to panic, she answered the phone and with a few brief words dismissed her caller; she seemed to know exactly who was calling and why. She said she was busy and would call back tomorrow. Putting the phone down too vigorously, she knocked Abel's mug (half-full of terrible tea and decent rum), which wobbled, then fell into his lap. Elsa scrambled to *do something* (catch the mug? clean him up?), suddenly she was touching

Abel, she shivered at the contact, she lifted his shirt a bit to stop the liquid from spreading further but her move misfired, he blanched, she was practically on top of him, as if astride a horse, she was invading him, he couldn't breathe, he said too loudly and quickly: 'It's O.K.! It's O.K.! I'm fine!'

But Elsa was everywhere, like a sticky liqueur, the viscous scarlet of a nail polish.

So Abel stood and took his leave, just as he had fled Pierrat at the Carolus bar an hour earlier, and his Tinder date, Michelle – now he remembered, her name was Michelle, that girl! He wished he could tell Doctor Guérin in the emergency department: 'I've remembered her name!'

He excused himself, said: 'I'm going home to change, uh, I mean, to go to bed, I'm sorry for perturbing, er . . . disturbing you.' And for all Elsa's fussing, protesting she was sorry about the spill and he should stay a little longer, he wasn't disturbing her at all . . . she could do nothing but let him leave.

His heart beating like fury, Abel took refuge at home, in his orchid glade; he lay down right there on the floor, in the midst of them, without turning on the light, to fill himself with the seren-ity of his plants' presence, this field of living petals and damp leaves, the way you gulp down a pill, resolutely, an anti-anxiety or sleeping pill, tightrope-walker out on a wire, surrounded by the void.

Mila

35

said the fox

On Bastille Day in Vallé, the festivities began a little before eight o'clock. At first it was just the musicians warming up on the stage erected in the main square, as every year, outside the Ici Tout Est Mieux bar and the bakery on the corner.

As every year, the ensemble kicked off with the classics – 'Les Champs-Elysées', 'Aline', 'Capri c'est fini' – to loosen up their fingers and voices and to accompany the Vallois residents clustered at tables all over the square, as well as those sitting on the ground, all tucking in to fortifying repasts – roast chicken and frites, merguez sausage with mustard, mussels, kebab wraps – to line stomachs in preparation for forthcoming intoxication, the joy of those unmissable occasions that come round like clockwork. Their joy by right. You couldn't change such habits, they were what kept the walls standing. The July stars would start to show around ten o'clock, at the same time as the fireworks, and then all of these sparks would feed the common fervour, a high mass.

Just after twenty past ten, a young man emerged from rue Raymond-Aron, on the west side of the square. No-one paid him much attention, so many people were moving around, in excitement, chatting to friends, doing a little dancing ... Even so, people started to turn and look for he was majestically mounted on a horse. And people were thinking this must be part of the celebrations. The young man dismounted at the corner of the square, not stopping to tether him,

his fine white horse,

... and, having emerged from rue Raymond-Aron and alighted on the ground, the young man walked towards the nearest table, paused a few seconds, then cocked a gun that he had been holding down by his hip and that no-one had noticed, all being so busy in their humming, their revelling, it was the national holiday. He shot in the head a guy sitting at one of the flimsy wooden picnic tables set out all over the square, rows and rows, and the people sitting there were neighbours or friends or hardly knew each other at all.

The guy, who had his back to the young gunman, didn't see it coming and fell face-down over his plate. There was an instant of petrification in this corner of the square, while in the good-natured chaos on the other side, everyone else went on with what they'd been so fully enjoying: eating, laughing, dancing, talking at the tops of their voices. You have to admit: a gunshot does sound rather like the snap of a firecracker. Then the young man raised his gun to his shoulder and aimed at the head of a woman who turned to stone, frozen to the spot, her mouth stretched into a wide Munch 'Scream'. Bang.

Then he aimed at the woman sitting next to her,

at her head too,

and he had only been there thirty seconds so far.

After Mila had left for Paris in her friend Jérôme's car driven by Thomas, She and He, her parents, had stayed put on the pavement watching the car disappear, waving goodbye in semaphore to their daughter, and both felt a little stupid there, a little lonely even, so unused were they to rolling with the unexpected.

They went to Brittany with their daughter every year, in mid-July and over the same dates, and everything ran as if on autopilot. Now here they were in their house in Vallé, in the middle of the day without their child, without any plan. They could have left within the hour, barely deviating from their original intention, but they could also make a swift about-turn and open a bottle of very good wine, one of those kept for special occasions in the little cellar under the stairs, uncork it and make love rough and ready there in the kitchen, and why not?

She and He weren't yet fifty. They had conceived Mila, who wasn't yet called Mila, on the cusp of their thirties, having met five years earlier in the Paris Métro when She had been jostled by someone running past, had dropped her things on the ground, and while waiting for the same train He had helped her gather said things and enquired of Her: 'Are you alright?' 'Yes, thank you,' she had replied. It was the 1970s, the two young people had rapidly abandoned formality; playing streetwise, She had proposed a coffee, she thought he had lovely eyes and a real sweetness; He had smiled, they'd gone for that coffee.

They had had many coffees and completed their degrees, modern literature for Her, alongside the national music conservatoire, business for Him, studies which had led both to Paris – He being from Brittany and She from Charente-Maritime – then dispatched them to their encounter in the Métro, like that, fortuitously.

Neither had any particular connection to Vallé nor to anywhere in that region, but He was then hired by E.D.F. for a job in Orléans, it was a good position and he had accepted. She had followed him, so they had found a little house in Vallé, a town *with so much charm* (as She had exclaimed, on their first visit) and 18,000 inhabitants, on the banks of the Loire river, half an hour east of Orléans, and it had seemed the natural place for them.

She had given birth to their only daughter in the Orléans hospital in 1982. She and He had soon agreed on a girl's name, should the baby be a girl, but on the day of the birth, He had suddenly changed his mind. 'Actually I'd like to call her . . . You know? From that book you dropped in the Métro when we met . . .' She had nothing against a change of mind and, yes, she did remember that collection of poetry she'd been holding when she was jostled, it was a pretty name, and besides, without quite being able to express it, She was moved by this unexpectedly romantic notion on His part, just as the contractions were becoming real torture, He who wanted to link the name of his daughter, not yet born but almost, to her parents' accidental encounter, to build into his daughter's name a secret mechanism, a love letter hidden in a false-bottomed drawer, with love not for his daughter who he knew was coming their way at full tilt, but love for the literature and music student he'd never dreamed of encountering and who had come to rule as queen of his ordinary life, of his every whim and, yes, over his ill-prepared heart.

Mila who wasn't yet Mila had copped a name whose fortuitous origin she never found out, because She and He never told her that story. They might have told it later on, or not, impossible to know . . . Some secrets thrill like beacons in the mind, because they will never be shared.

Here is something Mila *had* wondered: out of the 36,000 *communes* in France, why did her parents have to choose this one? The town where one of the vanishingly rare mass killings by an individual ever seen in the country, even in Europe, in the twentieth century, was to take place. This got her thinking about the arbitrary choices we are constantly making, like a troupe of odd-shaped pieces from a vast wilderness of a jigsaw puzzle. The very essence of the absurd implacability of news.

Which had led Mila the artist to make contingency a central theme of her artistic practice for the last nearly twenty years.

Contingency: the possibility that something may happen or may not happen, that a being exists or may not exist.

Abel

36

your humble servants, we

Elsa reminded him of the mother of that graceful, troubled little girl, Abel thought. On the occasion of her nth rush to hospital, a clever shrink who had been following the girl's case from the beginning had proposed a theory. A rare syndrome with an unpronounceable name: when a parent harms their child subtly, by gradual poisoning, for example, nothing visible, in order to attract compassion and attention for themselves by way of the child's needs. So as to appear the shattered and devoted parent of a sick child. The shrink had described to Abel the one element that had sounded the alarm for him. When the girl was back in hospital, the ever-beautiful and tearful mother had insisted that on top of this she had just been burgled and had herself discovered the thief in flagrante in the middle of the night, that her husband was away and she had narrowly escaped being attacked. Her tale had seemed over-complicated, and bizarre given that her daughter was just then in a critical state, having lost consciousness after a fit.

The mother was overdoing it.

Everything about her was overdone.

So many bad things were happening to her, and yet she was so cool, so elegant. As if dressed up for death.

The shrink had also admitted to Abel that he had been troubled by her, he had wanted to rescue her, he had started thinking about her, and often.

Then the shrink had dropped the bomb: 'It's called Münch-hausen's Syndrome by Proxy. This is the first time I've seen it in real life, outside my textbooks, or outside a novel, indeed ... It is rare. Or it may not be that rare, but we don't tend to pick it up,' he had added, looking resigned and rather glum.

The little girl had been removed from her parents.

A year later, Abel had checked on her and she was in fine form, she'd had no further health problems. The mother was still detained. The juvenile division had opened her file again; the inquiry had not been closed. There was in particular a suspicion of a prior homicide, for this woman had had another child, before the girl, one who had died shortly after birth – of Sudden Infant Death Syndrome. In the light shed retrospectively on her person-ality and her difficulties, the investigators were evaluating the possibility of an infanticide that had gone undetected. Abel would be called as a witness at the trial.

Even if he was still suspended, he wondered. Or if he were sacked?

When he had learned of the turn the case was taking, he had been confused. Shaken. The case was no longer his responsibility, but he kept up with it, kept one eye on its progress. He had not seen the mother again.

Her first child, the newborn, had been a boy, he found out. Died at twenty-two days. Back at home, Abel had thrown the orchid he'd christened with that woman's name, a glorious flower, into the rubbish.

Why had Elsa made him think of the little girl's mother, he wondered, before sinking, finally, finally, into sleep.

Mila

37

Make bold to ask you

The wolves making merry in the hunting museum had not yet made their debut in the press. This was not as planned. Mila went to put a rocket under her journalist contact at the *Parisien*, and to ask her assistants to post more on their false Twitter and Instagram accounts to get the news moving. It had to get out fast. Everything had been minutely planned, nobody was going to derail her machine. It was already time for her to unleash her next set piece, as programmed, that night. She had decided to 'release' her *tableaux vivants* so fast that viewers would hardly be able to keep up. A journey in three stages, like those of a deep-sea dive, each deeper than the one before. A privation of oxygen that forces you to concentrate in order to see. Mila was thinking of the Millais painting she had discovered at the Tate Britain gallery when she was living in London. Ophelia drowning in the midst of a savagely poetic natural world. The morbid prettiness of this very English painting had struck Mila, who was only wandering through the gallery. Art galleries made excellent public squares for a flaneur in search of fresh food for thought. It was right that they were open to all, like parks, places of free movement where you could have a coffee with a colleague or eat a sandwich while reading a book. Even lie down for a short siesta.

In the painting Ophelia is singing hymns while awaiting her death, poor resolute Ophelia, holding tight to her bedraggled flowers. Her long hair that seems to catch among the reeds. Her face already that of a corpse on an autopsy table, mouth slack and eyes half-closed, an icy blue.

Blue where the light has been trapped.

Millais's work had inspired Mila's 2017 'Drownings' series. Although she would never admit to a homage. Mila gave no interviews and never answered questions. She occasionally sent out press releases which were brief, factual texts distributed via intermediaries. For this series on drowning, she had put bathtubs in various public places around Britain, in London, Manchester, Cardiff and Reading. Bodies (very lifelike dummies) had been submerged in them, their skins tattooed all over with passages from Shakespeare's plays. Enucleated, their eye sockets had been filled with real flowers sewn in place – water flowers: lotuses and waterlilies.

> Till that her garments, heavy with their drink,
> Pull'd the poor wretch from her melodious lay
> To muddy death.

Mila had wanted the studio Masson rented for her in Paris, close to the Saint Georges church, to be completely empty and lit only by the twilight that reached through its bay windows. She had imagined the studio as a womb she could escape to. She would not sleep there at night but would rest there during the day, so she had a tent installed in the middle of the room and in it a mattress and cushions. Using a pocket projector she beamed onto the canvas overhead not stars but photographs of her 'scenes': the horse freaking out in the Pompidou library, her wolves getting sozzled to the sound of cannon fire. She had taken hundreds of shots. She was seeking her own reality in them, in the shifting detail of her three-dimensional paintings. She felt her images' impact traversing and entrancing her. It was more powerful than drugs. She let her C.D. of the White Stripes' album 'De Stijl' play, at top volume, right into her head via a Discman saved from the Nineties; she was staring at the images of her work going round like a carousel, getting drunk on the harmonies of her snaps, their major and minor scales, their grammar; this was her work, she was more than Mila, she was soaring above herself.

Mila put up a tent in every studio she occupied. A womb within a womb where she communed with the hyper-coloured prints from her installations. She was inspired by Tracey Emin's piece 'Everyone I Have Ever Slept with 1963–95'. Emin had erected a small blue tent, inside which she had appliquéd the names of all the people she had slept with in her life to date. But slept with in the literal sense. As well as her lovers', those named included her grandmother, who she used to like sleeping with, and her foetuses.

Mila was considering her statement, the text she would send out via all the networks. It would go out when the third and final tableau was complete. At last she was going to take the stage. She had never spoken as directly as this, never before said 'I'. She had never explained herself, never boasted or apologised. She disappeared within her works; she felt she was both everywhere and nowhere. As if the art never truly belonged to her. Her pieces were enough in themselves, they carried no *explanations*. But she had come to the end, even if no-one knew that yet; this triptych would be her final creation, there would be no Mila after this. So she had to speak before falling silent. And for the first time she had to name: she must choose a name for the baptism. All her works had been named by the press or by art-world critics, never by her. The way it works for serial killers, who are saddled with names dreamed up by the police or by journalists: the Golden State Killer, the Boston Strangler, the Butcher of Rostov . . . The victims too were sometimes given nicknames, like the Black Dahlia. Some killers chose their own names, like Jack the Ripper, but then they ran the risk of communicating directly with their pursuers.

Her creations' names had always seemed to share a single sensibility: 'Fires', 'Martyrs', 'Drownings', 'Clocks', 'Scarves' . . . Always plural, even though each series was essentially a single whole, and always a simple, generic, descriptive word. These words had grown into an army. In the cocoons of her tents, in osmosis with the photographs taken at her installations, Mila had given them other names, secret, private names. 'Scarves', so-titled by a journalist, was her first work – a work of art that hardly knew it was one. She wasn't anonymous, then, just unknown. She would become Mila after that. It had been an impulse, an emotional outlet, it was nothing. She had been nothing but animus. And she had felt strangely powerful all of a sudden. She was trying to remember who she had been in those days and how 'Scarves' had come about.

The White Stripes' album 'De Stijl' was released in the United States in June 2000. It had revolutionised music. That was a month before the Vallé massacre.

Camille

38

what your name may be

Camille Pierrat looked at herself in her bathroom mirror. She had just blow-dried her hair so as to induce some movement into it, a fantasia of waves intended to appear natural. She appraised the result, without much conviction. She had brushed a shadow over her eyelids and applied a touch of sheen to her lips. She turned her face to the right then the left, sucked her cheeks in a little, made a kiss of her mouth and looked up at herself from a lower tilt, eyes peering upwards as if pleading, like a cat in heat, she thought.

Camille never wore make-up to work. She generally put her hair in a ponytail, not too high (girly/prissy) or too low (business exec style) but at middle height. Neutral, she felt. She rinsed her face in freezing-cold water, as if to chill the wrinkles venturing around it, and added rough dabs of a supermarket moisturiser to avoid tightness after the cold water. And she was ready.

But today she wasn't going to work. And she was cross. Camille had no time for people who took pride in their own craziness, or who cast their moorings to the four winds when they could really have kept their ship together and handled the rapids. Nor did she enjoy chasing after people, or being stood up. Over the last few days, Abel Bac had managed to cross every one of her red lines. He had ditched her yesterday evening at the Carolus as abruptly as if he'd seen a ghost. Without explanation.

He had not thanked her for coming all the way to his apartment to check on him and bring him information. Bac was normally a bit of a brute, but he was polite. She wasn't after pleases and thank yous, she was no fisher for compliments, but still he could take a break from standing her up all the time, as if she didn't count, or worse, as if she wasn't really there at all. He was clearly a bit off-track and not thinking straight. His hand had been bandaged, as if he had been in a fight. She had not asked about it, but she was no idiot. And Bac had been on Tinder! What a hoot! The guy didn't even know how to download an app. He was still using a paper map of Paris.

Yet now, all of a sudden, he had signed up to Tinder? She didn't buy his bullshit. Perhaps he was pulling a fast one on her, telling her porkies to put her off the scent? It was a very long shot, but Camille had the ridiculous idea that Bac was mixed up in the nonsense going on in the art galleries. Which was impossible, of course. Bac was about as conversant with art and that whole mare's nest as she was with the titty dancers at the Plaisir Pigalle.

Today Camille had a date with an old pal from her police college class who was now at the B.E.F.T.I., the online fraud brigade. She got on alright with him. She had warmed to him when they were studying together. The guy was no daredevil, but he was good for a laugh, he liked to dress up, kind of English-gent style, steered away from the herd, knew how to put on a party and was particularly sharp on legal issues. She had always thought he was a bit lost at the college, with the rest of them; she'd have bet on his going for public prosecutor, he would have aced that. And done it with class. They were meeting for lunch and he had suggested an Italian canteen in Barbès, with some cutesy hipster name, somewhere in those narrow

Barbès streets that were torn between vegan yoga and the wholesalers' offcuts markets, streets seething with fast-moving life, a chaotic culture clash. She wasn't unhappy to be seeing him, they hadn't caught up for over a year, and then she'd called a few days ago to ask him for a favour.

Hence Camille had put on make-up.

39

The horse

Camille had been ill at ease since Bac had got himself suspended from the force. She couldn't seem to let go of the business. His absence infected her mental space, and everything else was just distraction. Yet how furious she had been when he had aired her after the night when they had got it on a bit. That had weighed on her for a good while. It was almost like she had tried to rape him. She had gone for it because she had sensed an openness, and she was not a social outcast either, she wasn't one to ask a guy twice. In a song Camille caught on the car radio, a chick with a pretty-pretty voice had sung, sentimentally, that she had *lost her kisses*, and that had made sense to her. To lose your kisses like you lose your keys or you lose track of time. Camille had felt something like that, something sharp, when Abel Bac had snubbed her. She had sought Bac's approval, his eye. His acceptance. He wasn't the sexiest or the most fun among the guys she worked with. But he was Bac. There was no-one else like him. Full of passions soaking through the silence. She wanted to understand him through and through.

At the restaurant, they ordered burrata with raisins and blue rapeseed vinegar; her buddy chose it, seemed to know the place well. Then they had spiced sardine bruschetta with rocket flowers, and it looked as if he thought that was plenty. Camille was already fancying a Maccy D's, but she kept shtum. They trotted out the required courtesies: how's work, recent big cases, latest pronouncement from the Ministry of the Interior on *police violence*, and back over a few memories from the college, *Shit, do you remember the night when hahaha* . . . Camille thought he was ageing well, he was looking good, then she told him so and instantly regretted it, his halo of confidence swelled so alarmingly over the starched bistro tablecloth; yes, actually, he confirmed that at his end things were going well. He had wind of a knockout promotion, not to say too much, whereas she, for her part, did not wax lyrical about her life, things weren't going too badly, but there was no great excitement thus far, and then his own satisfaction with his slick little Italian bistro, which he seemed practically to own, was becoming tiresome. After the sardines and before coffee they got onto the suicide of a kid from their class, which had made it into the *Parisien* a few months earlier. This dashed Camille's mood, the guy hadn't been particularly ambitious, that wasn't his style, he was more of a decent bloke, with a solid backbone to him, you might say, and some real moral fibre, and the fact he had made a last supper off the contents of his standard-issue pistol was not very cheering, she wouldn't lie. Then they'd abruptly swung over to a fresh subject because suicide was quite a downer for dessert. In short, they made it to the limoncello via a nicely judged social slalom (not too much, not too little) and could move on to serious things.

'O.K., I did what you wanted. And you owe me one for another time. But can I ask you something, Camille: why are you trying to get info about your colleague on the sly? Doesn't look very legit from here.'

40

an animal with brains enough

No, it wasn't legit, you weren't meant to go investigating each other, that was a very clear red line. If there was a rotten apple, it was sorted internally. You did not go building cases against one another. Camille had called her friend because she knew he had kept up a close friendship with a colleague at the police inspectorate. She hadn't been able to let it go. Now it was too late: Camille had broken the rules, she had gone nosing around in Bac's dirty washing. She felt sullied. Worse, she was now indebted to her accomplice – a bad place to be. She wished she could forget what she had heard, wind the whole film back and be able to show up head held high at the Carolus, to give Bac stick without any reservations. She could hardly go asking Bac out of the blue: 'Actually, mate, who are you really?'

Camille was bloody well placed to know that no-one was who they claimed to be. That was the baseline. How many chicks had she interrogated who still hadn't recovered from getting their teeth punched out by a guy they'd been living with for years, though no-one could have predicted it. *But there's no way, he would never do such a thing.* Yeah, right, now he's really screwed your looks, my dear. Worth facing the facts – we'd all do better that way. The perfect guys whose hard drives were happy-hour highways to Paedo World. Not to mention those who killed their better halves and whose neighbours never noticed, suspected or heard anything at all. *He had a clean slate until now, blah blah* ... There were times when Camille felt like screaming at them: 'But nobody has no past, bloody hell, unless they're a fucking pot plant!' She'd interrogated guys with double lives, ten telephones and five women. Teenagers who'd done their classmate in to see if it was anything like on T.V. In a way, that was why the criminal trials were so grim: the supermarket-style bright-lights display of all that was sordid. Nothing went untouched, truly *nada*, the kids' whole lives were rolled out and sold cheap. Every one of their texts and mails was read, their accounts were plucked bare, their notebooks and chequebooks, their comings and goings, their guilty pleasures and unmentionable obsessions were revealed, their prescriptions scrutinised and their brands of condoms and lubes held up for all to see. Criminal trials flayed people alive, defendants as much as victims; even their friends and family were stripped bare. The man who couldn't get it up anymore and the woman who practically wet herself every time – it was all good for filling in the picture. The picture of all the fucking lowlifes without any pasts, then.

Only a solid democracy would require so much time be spent checking out every poor sod who admitted on day one to killing his wife. But why did he do it? How did he do it? Which way did he drag her through the garden – by the arms or the feet? And why did he bury her head under a budding rosebush and not under the hyacinths? We insist on precision, insist on knowing the exact instant of the turning point as if we could have been there in the room with him and closer still, right inside his head, in his arm when it tensed up to strangle her. We immerse ourselves in the shadows, but we reject all grey areas. What we want is spotlights to sweep through those horrifying corners. How many hammer blows to her skull? Did he rape her before or after she stopped breathing?

We demand to know what they're like: the dying person's eyes and the eyes of their killer.

We want their colour, we want to breathe their irises, to taste the dilation of their pupils.

To comprehend means to take with us. To incorporate into ourselves.

Abel Bac had been suspended in the wake of a one-off and extremely well-informed anonymous telephone call to the force, disclosing that this officer, whose career and service record were thus far faultless and irreproachable, had not been registered at birth under this name and had therefore knowingly concealed his true identity.

'So French! We do love a good snitch!' Camille's pal from police college had chuckled.

Camille had not cracked a smile. She went pale.

He had gone to a lot of trouble to dig up this info, he made clear. There was a good deal of the hot potato about this case, he added, as if to underline the scale of the favour he had done her and the precious time he had wasted for her sake.

'But – shit! He should never have been able to sign up to the police without providing his complete background, it doesn't make any sense,' Camille protested.

'Have you known him long, your Abel Bac?'

'That's nothing to do with it. You can't sign up to police college with some made-up story about who you are. I've signed up, so have you. You just can't do it.'

'You gotta believe they're seriously entertaining that possibility, cos they did their due diligence, no question about that, before they sacked your colleague.'

'But he wasn't sacked! He's been sus-pend-ed!'

'They must be in the process of running their checks. But somewhere along the line they've smelled a rat. Either they've found some kind of gaff, or his new name's a cover for something really bad in his past. If you want my opinion, I reckon he's up shit creek. Your bosses too, actually; this is not the kind of thing you want popping up in the papers ... In the current climate, terrorism everywhere, paranoia about attacks, you have to think: a cop in the henhouse, with access to everything, and he's not the man he said he was ...'

'You're way out of line. Bac is straight as a die. There's no competition – he's the squarest guy in the force. Never a minor dodge or a fix, not once has he been rude about a suspect, or tried to influence a case.'

'There you go, he's a sly one.'

At that Camille had ordered another limoncello. And the maître d' had brought her one on the house.

In ordinary times, Camille did not use her days off for snooping behind her friends' backs. Generally, she preferred to get some exercise, swimming at the pool in Ménilmontant or running around the Buttes-Chaumont park. She also loved going to the cinema by herself, and watching two or three films in a row. She savoured the experience of going into a dark theatre in the middle of the day, when the sky was high and blue outside over the busy people, the perennial humours, of afternoons in Paris, and then emerging after the last session into a darkness that had fallen without her, stuffed with lights and images. Subjecting herself to the strangeness of different films' clashing atmospheres and then the genuine shock of the real world awaiting her after the last credits.

After her Italian lunch, she felt somewhat stunned, on edge.

She thought about going back in to do some work, regain a bit of control and shrug off her uncertainty. Then, suddenly, she could see herself all made up in her figure-hugging shirt, and she hated herself. Her old classmate had done all the digging, so she had the facts she was after: where Abel Bac was born, when, in which town. So it was Vallé. Never heard of the dump. Actually, no, it did ring a bell, in fact.

Like an old news flash.

Abel

41

Replied,

On July 14, 2000, in the morning, Abel, who wasn't called Abel yet, had opened his eyes much too early, long before his alarm. He had no need even to check the position of the hands, he knew it must be between four-thirty and five in the morning. He knew it because he was intimately familiar with the hours of darkness, familiar with their particularities, their texture, their silences. Between four and five o'clock, the opacity of the silence at the night's nadir was just beginning to fray, a distant car engine hummed, the church bells seemed to ring more shrilly, the animals' waking welled up from the town's rural flank and, paradoxically, the streetlights' extinguishing sent an electric charge rippling through Vallé from top to bottom of the town. It was dawn.

Motionless in his single bed, Abel was watching for the slightest foreign sensation that might come to fill his insomnia, to help him pass the time, as they say. The summer would be a long one, identical to all the other summers he had spent here, in Vallé, pinned between his mother and the wall, cornered by the simplicity of his mother and tormented by the breath of the world for which he could not produce the right ticket.

In his insomniac hours, he imagined being a rock, he went over all his granitic hardness; he was living but petrified, only his mind could caper about, unchained and cruel; impossible to cage that or reduce it to calm. While his body obeyed its confinement, so obedient that he could trace the outline of every one of his muscles, could go over all the humps and dips, his mind was chasing over the fields of who he was, over what he had done and the little he dreamed of doing.

Two weeks earlier, he had got his baccalaureate. He had passed it on his first try and topped that off with a distinction. His mother was happy. She had always worried, not about Abel himself, who wasn't yet called Abel, but about their kind of people who tended to live in the poorer parts of towns. She had bought a bottle of champagne to celebrate the occasion. She'd never tasted champagne in her life before, not even at her own wedding, for she had not married. That his baccalaureate was the vocational 'bac pro' made no difference; to his mother a bac was a bac and it was more than she had ever managed, for she had left school at sixteen and been a cleaner most of her life, except for the period when she'd met Abel's father, when she'd been a waitress in a crêperie called Chez la Mère Muc and had fallen pregnant, but the bloke had not stuck around for long.

Abel, who wasn't yet called Abel, had done his vocational bac in production engineering (with free-machining for his specialism). As had his friends and as, too, had Juliette, the only girl in the class. Only one of them had failed, but he had missed classes for part of the year, and he was a bit crazy, the others said, a few marbles short. It was true and not true, Abel decided that morning, that Éric was crazy. He sometimes behaved quite oddly, but Abel often hung out with him, they got on well, and everything considered, Éric was good fun, he was canny. He knew a lot of history, all about the two world wars, the major battles, Napoleon, that kind of thing. The truth was he was more interesting than Abel's other classmates. And Abel knew that if Éric hadn't passed his bac, it wasn't because he was stupider than the others but because he hadn't shown up for all the exams, that was all. So he had been eliminated.

Abel had drunk the champagne with his mother the evening of the results, not the whole bottle, but they had toasted his achievement and she had wanted to talk to him, as if you have to talk at the few solemn occasions that mark the shape of a life, so his mother must have thought. Abel had already had champagne, several times, because it sometimes happened that the lycée pro boys would slip into parties thrown by the posh kids at Lycée Paul-Bert, the lycée in upper Vallé, and they were something else, quite a different scene . . . But Abel had not told his mother about that, neither that evening nor any other. To be invited to those parties, you had to have some kind of connection. Sports could do it, the youth club too, and the church was another option. Abel didn't go to church, but some of his classmates, including Éric, had been going since Sunday School. Éric had been very involved and through Sunday School he had met some of the kids from Paul-Bert, so occasionally he'd be invited to the parties. And he would bring Abel and others from their class along with him. It was true too that Éric was better-looking than the rest of them combined, so that must have helped, with the posh girls at Paul-Bert. Even though Éric wasn't very sociable, and he was a bit screwy.

People said he didn't wash, that he cut his arms with an Opinel knife, that his mum was a religious nut and a gossip. Abel used to bump into her, you couldn't carry on past because she would not stop calling you to come and talk, and her hair was a strange, wild shade of blonde. His mother used to see her often, because she used to help out with cleaning the church. His mother used to say of Éric's: 'Can that woman talk!' She was called

Marie-Josèphe, Éric's mother. Marie-Jo. She must have come to her faith belatedly, hence her extra dedication.

That morning, when Abel lay in bed listening to the hours go by before he got up, was the morning of July 14.

Every year in Vallé they held a fete in the market square to celebrate Bastille Day, the national holiday. It would begin around eight o'clock, a local band sponsored by the town hall would play classic French songs like 'La Salsa du Démon' and Eddy Mitchell's heavier rock tracks. People would stand around eating sausages and frites, the young people who hadn't gone away sun-seeking would start getting smashed quite early and were generally dancing even before the sun went down. There would be little French flags stuck on the tables, and blue, white and red crêpe-paper garlands pinned to the streetlights. At around ten o'clock, the music would stop so the crowd could enjoy the fireworks launched from Rantal fort, the highest point in the town. The mayor of Vallé, a debonair local right-winger with the looks of a cuddly grandad, had held his post for more than twenty years and he was not stingy with the pyrotechnics budget. He was well liked. They would finish with the biggest bangs and then, after the fireworks, it was back to the music, with a turn to more dancy hits, Ricky Martin and Madonna, and by then everyone would be in their groove. It was a nice occasion.

Abel, who wasn't Abel yet, went every year, to meet his friends, and he too would drink the warm beer which you had to gulp fast so that drunkenness could take charge. The year before he had flirted with a girl from Paul-Bert, they had danced, she had had an incredibly lithe body and he had been a little overwhelmed, not knowing quite how to take the thing forward. But the second the fireworks went off Abel had taken the plunge, as it were, and had snogged her properly, with tongues and for a long time. He had even dared to touch her breasts in the darkness, the girl had been jubilant, her name was Johanna, she was a first-year like him but doing literature at Paul-Bert. After that night they hadn't really seen each other again. There had certainly not been any further snogs.

That year, Abel had done a lot of wanking to visions of Johanna, to his vivid recollection of how she danced the lambada; his imaginings of everything he could have done with her were endless. Perhaps he would see Johanna again, that evening at the Bastille Day fete, she'd be a year older and that much more ardent – or perhaps he would find another Johanna. There were not so many parties, either, in this part of the world, so Bastille Day was special. His mother never came. It wasn't her thing, she was reserved, *she didn't get involved*, as she used to say. In the evenings, practically every evening of her life, she used to watch television or listen to the radio. That was her entertainment. She sometimes went to have dinner with a girlfriend, unpretentiously, eating in their kitchen. As much as Abel preferred to pursue his quest for a Johanna alone or to knock back beers and bad fizz with his friends who had just graduated, he was upset that he had never really asked his mother to come too, never demanded that she come out, come with him to enjoy herself, the whole town was having fun that night, it was the eve of summer proper, the beginning of the long holidays. The whole town. Abel was eighteen, it wasn't long before he'd be off and out, full throttle, he was itching to go abroad with a rucksack, to take random trains, to go in search of new languages and new people, so it would be nice to go to the celebrations together, with his mother, he thought, for once.

Abel and Mila

42

Sirs, you yourselves

. . . and he'd only been there thirty seconds, the young man with his gun. Blood in the plates: yet more red for Bastille Day.

Calmly, the young man lifts his gun to his shoulder and aims at heads – bang, bang, bang, with no more emotion than at a fun-fair stand where the prize is a teddy.

Men, women, children, without discrimination. He takes down those nearest to him, those who happen to be easily within range.

Then all at once the crowd awakens, enraged, explodes from its torpor, and some of them leap towards the killer. He's not a young man now, he is the killer, the murderer, he is the horror raining down without warning,

into the heart of the festivities, the cheer

the way a shot fired into the passenger seat of a car hits more than a hundred decibels, deafening

some leap towards the killer to stop the torrent of death.

Then a body confronts the young killer and grips his arms, to make them drop the gun, both figures are clinging to the weapon and nobody around them knows what to grab, arms plunge into a cauldron of confusion and one last shot is fired – bang. Now it's the young killer who falls, his gun turned against him. People are screaming. A wail rises to the sky as with shaking hands the crowd holds close the mortal injuries of those shot down,

just when,
as the terrified horse whinnies,
from the fort that overlooks the town,
known as the Rantal fort,
up shoot like shrieking flowers,
like psychedelic orchids,
the Bastille Day fireworks.

Mila

43

may read my name

After July 14, 2000, there were weeks and weeks that took on the same colour for Mila. A grey or blue. A blur, with some shading, bumps, textures, but no flash.

It was unreal: they were dead, She and He, and Mila realised she had not known them all that well. They had never reached the moment when children grown into adults change gear, all of a sudden, and see their parents as they are: ordinary people amid a vast crowd, who have made many questionable choices, taken good and bad decisions. And Mila at the last frontier of childhood, seventeen years old, would have needed a few more years before seeing her parents as other than She and He. A solicitor she did not know, her parents' friend and their chosen locum should something happen, had taken the bull by the horns. They had been provident by nature, and death is a bureaucratic thing. Mila had signed everything, in the places the solicitor told her to, without reading, without seeing anything beside the greys and blues before her eyes that stood in for the world. The Vallé house had been put up for sale and was swiftly sold. Mila kept nothing from that house; everything was given away, sorted or sold off by other people, volunteers, nice people who wanted to help; clothes, crockery, furniture, the pathetic trinkets of She and He, physical reminders of the traces of their lives which Mila could not face, not now. Bewildered as she was by what had been done to her parents' heads, to their faces, to their poor bodies.

'Nothing.'

'Are you sure?'

'Nothing. I don't want anything.'

'There are the photo albums.'

'Bin them.'

Her parents had no personal diaries or old love letters; there were no false-bottomed drawers with mysteries to plumb; they were in death as they had been alive: honest people without secrets. The mystery now lay in the manner of their killing, but they could play no part in its resolution. The solicitor made a fair attempt at arousing Mila's interest, at warning her, shaking her, before she ditched the lot. But he made no headway. It was as if a fire were burning in her, and all the things they had left behind them were flares, sparks from that fire. She had even refused to go inside the house after the massacre – for that's what it was: a massacre. Not being eighteen yet but a minor, Mila had been gathered up, like a wilful cork about to float away downstream, by a friend of her mother's, a woman she had never met who lived in Paris, in a two-bedroom apartment in the 15th arrondissement.

The friend's name was Carole, she had known Mila's mother since forever, from when they'd both been at university. They had not seen much of each other as adults, but their bond had stayed firm. They would call each other every month, to chat freely and keep up with the passing time. They never forgot to send each other postcards from their holidays, from Mykonos, Cairo and the Aveyron; each remained a place of potential refuge for the other, a bolthole.

And Carole did exactly what was needed, which was nothing. She allowed Mila to curl up until the worst of her pain loosened its grip. She became the refuge that had never been explicitly discussed with her friend, the place of safety in the event of storms that we think of as hypothetical, a nice idea; she became not her friend's refuge but her friend's daughter's, and it was almost the same thing. Like the invisible vows so powerfully present in the air between people choosing each other: 'We don't meet often, but you know, you could call me in the middle of the night to bury a body and I'd be right there at your side.' It was something like that: she'd been called in the middle of the day, in the middle of a rotten tooth that needed a crown – Carole was a dentist – to help bury the bodies, in a manner of speaking.

That's all Mila was now: in transit.

Her disbelief was over, she had not wept, she was beyond or somewhere short of tears, in a lost, grey-blue zone, a garden of paralysis, all she could do was listen to herself breathe, she spent hours following the waves of her breath, bubbles of air as if wired to her veins, and she thought of She and He not breathing any-more, and how she had never thought of that, that they were beings that breathed.

Mila would not go on to do medicine. She would not sleep with Fyodor again, to improve on their fumbling experiment. She had attended none of the silent marches, she had not spoken to the press, she had not read the newspapers. She had her parents cremated, left the urns at the funeral parlour and told nobody apart from the solicitor and Carole, who, for better or worse, had become her temporary guardian, as if Mila were a young plant uprooted by a gale which she was to try, against the odds, to get growing straight once more.

Mila, who wasn't yet Mila, who was now becoming Mila, waited, breathing in little gulps the scent fading out of her mother's scarf.

The one thing, the only one, she had kept.

44

My shoer round my heel hath writ the same

Carole, Mila's mother's friend, had read everything, she had examined everything and looked at everything. The briefest article that appeared was straightaway perused in mute horror, then reread with more composure, then reread over and over, to extract some new information, a detail, a fresh angle. All the big national papers had immediately sent their crime reporters to camp in Vallé, to dig in, to find out. 'The Vallé Massacre', 'The Bastille Day Slaughter', 'The Bloody Ball', 'The Fete from Hell' . . . There had been a lot of ink splashed about, a lot of gory headlines. Carole kept it all at her clinic, so that Mila would not come across it, kept – perhaps – for later, for Mila, who might one day want to know, but she realised deep down that she was collecting all these cuttings mainly for herself, because she could not seem to turn her mind to anything else. She also felt the morbid excitement of having a role in this disaster: she had been the friend of one of the victims, and now she had made herself the guardian of this tall, rather unlikeable adolescent, whom, moreover, she had never seen before except in the photographs her friend had sent, especially in the beginning, photographs of a smiling baby, then a mischievous little girl, as children often appear in photographs. Later there had been fewer pictures, because she and her friend used to speak and meet mainly to talk about themselves, to capture in this friendship the girls they had been and the women they were becoming, not to coo over children, houses and holidays; because their friendship was, in fact, rather streamlined and unburdened by petty unkindness, such as that of showing off one's good fortune.

And Carole had to consider, before the invasion by this scowling seventeen-year-old of her nicely done-up apartment in the 15th with balcony and lift:

'True, but who would bother to be nice, in her shoes?'

45

The fox excus'd himself

Mila reread her text, her statement. For the tenth time. She wanted rhythm, transparency. Simplicity. It had to flow. She was very tense. Tonight she would direct her final installation, the last act of her creation, the grand finale; there could not be a single technical problem or glitch. Everything was planned, the gallery was working with her in full confidence, all the physical elements had been gathered and stored in large lorries, including the key pieces which a small team of pros had 'borrowed' just a little illegally. She had a meeting with her assistants in half an hour. She was afraid. She did not like blood.

Statement by the artist Mila

La Vita Nova

Some of you have been wondering for years who I am. Who is Mila?

I say some of you, for I'm no fool, despite what some would claim; I am aware that my notoriety is considerable within a small circle.

I am the author of the recent performances in three Parisian art galleries.

How good it feels, for once, to say: Yes, it was me.

And this piece is called La Vita Nova.

In this title, those who enjoy a bit of literature will of course recognise an homage to Dante, to his first work, La Vita Nuova. *Everyone knows Dante's* Inferno, *it's become a cliché, an empty expression, a mere cultural marker; but we ignore this first collection of historic lines which he assembled upon the death of the woman he loved. It is a trail of remembrance, of the skins of memories that we patch back together, necessarily, to make them fit our reality, or at least the flavour and colour of it. Memory is a fabrication like any other, a work of art.*

La Vita Nova *is MY memory. It is what brought Mila about. It is what I lost and what I gained in a single day.*

I know you will be annoyed with me, as usual. And as usual I am teasing you.

You will say that I tricked the galleries, that I thought in my arrogance I could do anything I wished, that Mila is so full of herself – so morbid, such a sell-out, so fake, revolting, hollow.

But I have always done everything I wished, be in no doubt about that. I do not seek your love.

And today I am no longer for sale.

A hint, even so, because I do like you; you have kept me warm even in the muddled flood of your indignation, so I can reveal to you: a painting is an artifice in which we hide our heart. My nocturnal triptych is not a true work of art; it is a message, a poem addressed to a man who has no knowledge of it. A man who ceased to grow – just as I did – on the day of his trauma. I wanted revenge, I wanted him to be guilty and to suffer, because we always require a guilty party. But in constructing my revenge like a sophisticated suit tailored to him, I made a mistake.

He is the friend I have spent my life hoping to meet. Now it is too late.

A day – as a great French literary critic explained at one of his magisterial lectures – a day can be the fulcrum of a life.

It is not mathematical, the middle; it is hard to know the exact date of our own death (short of anticipating it long before bringing it about oneself), but one day will be the middle of our life. We realise it's the middle, effectively, without need of two equal halves, for what we have been until that point, what we have built, must end in order to turn into something else.

Precisely so as not to suffer a living death.

Therefore we must embrace that slope, that far side of the hill. In my case, no doubt, becoming once more that person who is not Mila. I shall see – it will be a brand-new life.

I wish you joy, you band of bastards.
With affection,

Mila

The text would do. It couldn't be too long; evasive but not abstruse; simple. She wasn't writing it so they would understand, she was doing it for herself, and for him. The need for certain words to be said and to say goodbye in the first person.

After the third performance, Masson would shop her and everyone. He would have to. She would have loved to see his face, old Jérôme! And then the critics would sprinkle her actions with meaning or madness. Her final work. But that would no longer matter. She would be far away. She had no-one to answer to.

Except Abel Bac, perhaps.

The gentle stone in her shoe.

*Somewhere in the Police
Headquarters*

46

for want of knowledge

'You are who? Could you repeat your name, please?'

'I am the Director of the Musée d'Orsay.'

'A police car is on its way. Don't hang up. I'm transferring your call.'

When, at the Information and Command centre for the Paris police, one of the many centres taking emergency incident calls across France, the operator took her break that night, she nodded to her colleague Omar, who was also a smoker. It was a long-running ritual between them. Julie supplied the chocolate and Omar a thermos of coffee. And every three hours, they would go down the four flights of stairs from their studio at the police H.Q. into the street, to have a cigarette break and release the tension built up across the series of calls.

To get some air.

One of their shared frustrations arose from never knowing what happened next to their callers. Did it turn out alright in the end? Was the person taken into custody? Was the situation now under control? Omar really struggled with these thoughts. He had once said to Julie: 'It's as if you were forced to read a book, knowing you'll never find out how it ends.' Calls requiring an intervention were the minority. Seven or eight calls out of ten might be trivial: people wanting some information or making prank calls, also people who'd lost the plot, older people, people who were alone, in crisis, desperate, lots of calls from people who couldn't stand their neighbours' noise anymore, a few informers too, the odd racist accusation, people at the end of their tethers, on tranqs . . . You had to decide very quickly: emergency or not, needing intervention or not. Then, potentially, provide the caller with another number to call for assistance.

The computers knackered your eyes. Each officer at the centre had three live screens, one for research, another with a map showing patrol vehicles' and callers' locations, and another one for when they had to fill out a Pegasus form, this being the info sheet they sent to the operator who would link up with the nearest police patrol's radio.

When Julie and Omar were on their break, they would revisit the evening's calls. It was their debrief. A little excitement sparked from recounting the standout calls; it was a tacit rivalry between them. 'Just now I had a guy who . . .' 'And you won't believe it, but I got this crazy lady who started off by saying . . .'

Some nights, there wasn't a single one to giggle about, misery upon misery. Last week, Omar'd had a would-be suicide on the line and he was still rattled by it.

The other frustration the pair shared was being treated at times like call-centre staff, when they were professional peace-keepers. But they weren't going there this evening.

Tonight Julie had hit the jackpot, and she was desperate to tell Omar about the call she had handled from the Musée d'Orsay's director.

At first she had thought it was a prank, one of those weirdo calls they received all too often. The woman on the phone was in a panic and moderately incoherent. Julie asked if she was calling about a robbery – what she thought she had heard, as the woman was talking at top speed. Julie had eventually managed to piece together that some kind of artistic experiment had gone wrong inside the gallery, and they needed the police right away. She had filled in her Pegasus and sent a patrol over, then tried to untangle her caller's confused statements.

'What was it that went wrong? Are there injured people inside the gallery?' Omar said.

'I didn't get it at all. She was telling me about a famous artist, but also there were T.V. screens and flowers and fireworks. I tried to get her to focus and, yes, I did ask if there was anyone injured, and she said: "I don't know but there are bits of human bodies." '

'No way – *bits of bodies*?' Omar repeated, angling his thermos over his colleague's cup to top up her coffee, doubtless subconsciously to prolong their break, so she wouldn't stop talking, because they were having a nice time, they deserved some respite, and he'd have liked some more detail on this call from the hysterical gallery boss, she had got him interested now, even if they never did find out how this one ended, and Omar thought Julie had tonight's prize for the oddest call in the bag.

Mila

47

Me, sir, my parents

Mila was eighteen and she was surviving, forging a life for herself rather like that of a goldfish won at a funfair. She fed by picking up edible and ready-to-eat things in Carole's fridge. She went round in circles. She would go from her bed to the sofa to the armchair and back to bed: day over. Her mind was hard at work, blocking memories from coming to the surface. This in itself – the attempt to think about nothing – was an exhausting exercise in vigilance. She put on the same jeans, the same shirt and the same jumper every morning, until Carole snuck them away to run them through the machine at a high temperature, at which point she would, without objection, fall back on another pair of jeans. Mila did not do her hair, she did not wash and she did not cry. She did not answer the house phone (which caused problems for Carole, who had practical matters to manage while being reduced to very partial communications by her A.W.O.L. adolescent), she did not watch television nor listen to the radio, and she didn't read any books.

The only imagery she could not control was the production of her dreams. Mila dreamed. She dreamed about Marina Abramović covered in blood and food, a knife between her legs, she dreamed about fireworks exploding in her eardrums, she dreamed of heads cut off, of bodies in agony and of missed trains. She missed a lot of trains in her dreams. She would run, she put heart and soul into it, but she missed them. The train always went without her. Sometimes Mila would wake up sweating, her eyes spattered, and then she knew that at some point in her sleep she had been crying.

She did not want to hear her parents' names, Carole understood: they were She and He. They were dead. Carole took care of this entity with the commitment of a new goldfish-owner. She fed it, washed it when it smelled, found the process boring and was no more bothered than that; she wasn't about to flush Mila down the toilet. That's how it was.

So Carole took on a lot of work, she filled her work diary, and in the evenings she went out more often and later than she used to before inheriting her ward. She could no longer invite friends to her apartment – that would have been disturbing and mortifying for all concerned – so Carole went out to eat and to the theatre, and she stayed over with her lovers. Mila had forced her to become less of a homebody and to appreciate and take advantage of the chance she had to enjoy the sights outside the fishbowl.

This primitive situation lasted about a year. One morning, Mila went outside.

Carole had already left for work. So Mila explored her neighbourhood, the 15th, as if it were an undiscovered country. Paris.

Mila was living in Paris. She had not really noticed. She knew, but it had been a fact without substance. In the street, she cadged a cigarette from somebody. She had no money. She could not get a coffee at one of the busy café terraces that stretched into the streets all around, but she almost wanted to. And then she had to get back, for she was beginning to feel giddy, it was a lot all at once, this crash back into the world.

But she had no key to Carole's apartment. She stopped someone in the street and asked them to help her, she needed to find the phone number of a dentist's clinic and then to call it. She told her good Samaritan that she had a problem and needed to call her mother. The kindly person looked up the dentist's name in the phone booth directory, called using his own card and told Carole on the other end:

'Madame, your daughter is here. She seems a little lost.'

These words hit Carole like a punch to the solar plexus. She controlled herself and said yes, as if this were quite normal.

She could not just step out in the middle of her appointments, so she asked if Mila felt able to come all the way to her clinic. 'Take the bus,' she told her. 'Dodge the fare, I'll pay if you get a fine.' And Mila had managed to cross Paris.

That afternoon was a busy one for Carole, so she suggested that Mila either take her keys and go back to the apartment or that she wait in the office until Carole had finished work. In the bare minimum of words, Mila indicated that she would wait in the office.

'There are some magazines, if you like.'

After sitting in an armchair for a good hour without moving, Mila suddenly felt like rummaging. She opened the drawers, went through all the shelves and looked into every corner, like an unschooled ferret.

And she found them – all the press cuttings.

Everything about the Vallé massacre.

Mila stuffed it all into a bag and left, without a word.

48

did not educate

When she realised that Mila had gone, Carole had slightly panicked. She called her own landline at home, in the hope Mila
would have got back and might deign to pick up, but of course it
rang into a void. She thought about calling the police to register
a concerning disappearance, but that would have been excessive.
Mila was a grown-up, she was free to move around as she wished.
Besides, the other set of keys she had given her had gone too. Perhaps Mila had simply gone back to the apartment? Carole decided
she really should call in some help. She had neither the time nor
the skills to guide this young adult out of her petrification. Now,
after Carole had waited so long and done nothing, Mila might
well end up throwing herself under a bus.

That day, in that moment, Carole blamed herself – for waiting.
For waiting for it to be over.

For feeding her goldfish while looking the other way.

Back home, climbing the stairs to her floor, Carole repeated to
herself like a thought talisman: 'Let her be there, let her be there,
let her be there . . .' She wasn't addressing anyone in particular;
Carole was an atheist and uninterested in these things, but all
the same.

And Mila was there.

Half-dressed and covered in blackish smudges, she was there.

In the middle of the living room.

At first Carole felt a rush of relief, then she took a look around her apartment, which she had had completely redecorated (paintwork, wallpaper *and* tiles) only two years earlier by the go-to home decor firm Leroy Merlin.

Now all the walls and floors were covered in newspaper. Using lord knew what kind of gluey substance, Mila had stuck newspaper pages onto every surface, including the sofa and the tables, and the poor-quality ink had leached into everything. You could easily imagine that a team of chimney sweeps had staged a wild sabbath in her apartment. Grey dust was everywhere, even filling the air. And Mila was covered in ink.

'Are you alright?' Carole had asked, in alarm.

'Yes,' Mila had said calmly, almost tamely.

'How about we go out for dinner?' As she made this suggestion, Carole was thinking lightning-fast: you had to behave as normally as possible at the most abnormal times.

'O.K.,' Mila said casually. 'I'd better get dressed.'

While Mila was off getting dressed, Carole contemplated the devastation with horror. All her walls wrecked. The appalling front-page photographs presented like a grotesque kaleidoscopic collage. And then she noticed a strange sensation, that she had to root out and drag into the light in order to examine and identify it.

What was it?

Well, in a way, yes, in some way, Carole felt it was *beautiful*.

49

So poor

The day Mila papered Carole's living room with the cuttings that described her parents' death, subsumed among all the other deaths, and agreed to go out for dinner, was a turning point. Not that Mila became chatty or friendly, but without further turmoil she put an end to her life as a goldfish. And Carole called in a cleaning company which took three whole days to restore the apartment to rights, during which time she and Mila stayed in a hotel nearby. Mila did not apologise and it cost Carole a small fortune; the company specialised in heavy-duty cleaning and often worked on crime scenes.

Mila now took showers, got dressed and went out. She still wore only jeans and T-shirts, but she washed them herself. She would put away things she used or moved in the apartment. Sometimes Carole even felt as though no-one else was living there, or that it was a very hazy entity, like a ghost in a country house. Mila would disappear for entire days. Carole had no idea what she got up to. But she did come back in the evenings, or sometimes in the middle of the night. The point was, she was alive. So Carole made no attempt to get involved.

She noticed that Mila had started to see other people. She accepted a few invitations from her old friends at the lycée. *She went to some parties.* It was in these terms that Carole described it to one of her friends, who often enquired about her protégée.

'She's going to some parties.'

These were magical words. Carole could equally have said: 'She's just enrolled at university.' For Carole, Mila was back on her feet.

She almost gave up worrying about coming home to find Mila had killed herself. (For a while, she had removed a number of objects from her apartment that could have been repurposed as lethal weapons.)

Carole did not call Mila *Mila . . .*

She used her given first name, the one Mila's father had suggested at the last minute in the maternity ward, in a burst of romantic feeling between She and He. Nor did Carole know the Russians, or much else about the life of the young woman who had tumbled into hers. As we have said, she and her friend, Mila's mother, had had lots of other things to talk about when they spoke. People often assume that parents love to talk about their children.

Before pinning them up like paper garlands or votive offerings, Mila had read all of the articles she had found hidden in her guardian's office. She had stuffed her mind with them.

And then she had felt that most powerful thing, something she had lost sight of: anger. This anger now drove her out of bed in the morning, out of her isolation and out of Carole's apartment. And she would walk, endlessly, through Paris, without a map and without knowing the territory, in an attempt to shake off her anger, the way a drenched dog shakes itself to shed the water in its coat. And she had begun to *want to do*. She wanted to write her anger on the walls, on her skin, she wanted to spit out her anger and use the spit to draw with, she wanted to give form to her anger and make a show of it. It was during this period that she got herself arrested.

Out on her night-time missions, Mila had become interested in five statues. They were the bust of Apollinaire sculpted by Picasso which stood in the little garden beside the Saint Germain church, César's centaur on the rue de Sèvres, the bust of Dalida in Montmartre (giving her breasts a rub was, they said, a potent guarantee of good luck) and the lion at Denfert-Rochereau. It was at the fifth statue – the Joan of Arc on the place des Pyramides – that things had gone wrong.

Mila had drawn, or rather rolled out, some nice long straight lines on the statues with the help of some red duct tape (she had discovered this very thick and super-durable tape in a hardware store); these 'drawn features' ran all over the statues and spilled out onto the ground like shadows thrown by fires or bloody fault-lines. Next she had knotted a broad scarf around each statue's neck (she made the scarves out of fabric scraps picked up for a song at the Saint-Pierre market), and finally she had added blood dripping from their ears with the help of a tin of crimson paint. They looked wild. Mila was pleased.

But it didn't work out for Joan of Arc. Mila screwed up. She didn't work quickly enough and a police patrol had apprehended her and taken her to the police station. Landed with a summons to immediate trial and charged with defacement of public prop-erty, she had automatically thought to call Jérôme Masson, one of the Russians, who had just passed his bar exams. He had duly shown up to assist as her counsel. Mila had emerged with a fine and a warning. She did not mention it to Carole.

She was not yet called Mila.

Two weeks later, a wildly excited Jérôme had called Mila to say that a rather prestigious journalist had written an article about the defacement of the statues. Pictures had been taken by passersby before the council had been able to clean up the craziness, and the journalist had collected the images. He covered cultural occasions for *Le Monde*, and he lived on the square with the Dalida statue, whose desecration he had seen first-hand. His piece began with that shock, and then he elaborated, with much imagination and speculation, upon the act he had witnessed and what he had gone on to discover about the other statues' disfigurements. He proposed a politically engaged reading, and suggested ingenious associations between the Centaur, the Lion, Apollinaire and Dalida. He went after connections, meanings and symbols. The poet and the singer had both been tormented souls who had died violently. He imagined that the Centaur, this man-horse, was a projection of the poet as warrior, and that the Lion was a mythological lioness; the journalist spun a whole story around them. And his article ended with a mystery: who, therefore, was the after-hours artist whose fury had transfigured these statues?

Mila thought it funny, but Jérôme was really buzzing. This was more exciting than his pupillage at the law firm; this felt like being part of a smuggling operation, at the heart of a happening. They were young, still.

Jérôme said to her: 'You have to claim your action.' He had used that word, *action*. Mila had found this a bit silly. She had not said a word about her intentions, about what she had done. Jérôme insisted.

'Send a response to the paper!'

'What for?'

'To explain yourself.'

'I don't have to explain myself.'

'Just to say what you did, just that.'

'I won't put my name to it, either.'

'Precisely – you won't sign it – or you could use a pseudonym. As an extension of your action!'

Once more that word, *action*.

What Jérôme did not know, and nobody would find out, was that the scarves around the statues' necks – around Apollinaire's, Dalida's, the Centaur's and the Lion's necks – were impregnated with Chanel No. 5. That's what had cost her the most, far more than the fabric offcuts, the paint and the rolls of tape: her mother's perfume.

'You can simply sign yourself as "Mila"! That's you, while also not you, right, Mila?'

Camille

50

a hole was

Camille Pierrat had gone to see a journalist who covered the courts and with whom she had an understanding. They respected each other. Each appreciated the other's work, within its realm of action and its boundaries, and they did each other favours and exchanged the odd, under-the-radar warning when a case was hotting up, before the pack got wind of it. The journalist kept the police officer abreast of awkward news before it got out, and the police officer kept the cream of her more interesting cases for the journalist. And sometimes, they came to a mutual understanding on a leak that would suit both parties. It was unofficial, fair enough and untraceable. As far as possible, Camille preferred to meet her in person rather than speak on the telephone. You never controlled a telephone call, it could always be recorded. Besides, there were things only articulated when you were breathing the same air and looking each other in the eye, when you could tell that the other person wasn't up to any monkey business but trading fair and square.

The journalist had joined the profession long before Camille had even considered joining the police college; she was an old bird of the old school, every inch a traditionalist, knew the game like the back of her hand and had seen more criminal trials than any ordinary hack could stand and still sleep at night; moreover, Camille had always enjoyed her articles. She thought her friend wrote well, better than the other journos, and had one day realised that what she liked in her friend's writing was the fairness, her refusal to pass judgment. She told the story and did not badmouth the police, the defendants or the victims. In a way, she made the wretched less vile. And Camille respected that.

Camille went to meet her in the café below her office. Not the one all her colleagues went to – no thanks, discretion was the name of their game – but a tucked-away little dive bar run by Koreans who knew their style, because she needed someone to tell her about Vallé.

'What's got you onto this old news, Camille?' That was the journalist's first question, once she had ordered a green tea and some nougats. 'Too early for pastis,' she had clarified, without missing a beat. She was no fool, Camille thought. She knew Camille wouldn't go nosing round a backstory for no reason, especially not when the case was twenty years old.

The journalist began her tale. 'Vallé was THE major story, in full Technicolor. It stole all the headlines for a good while. And we weren't used to that – it was too big, like something out of a film. Vallé was the no-news hick town stuck between the countryside proper and the outer suburbs, half-posh, half-working class. You had all the ingredients for major devastation: about a dozen dead, ordinary people, good citizens, couples, even a child, shot at point-blank range by a young man – in fact he was a teenager – right out in the street. Bullets to the head, not a word of warning. Apparently he was shooting at random. And all on Bastille Day. Can you imagine? It's the small-town fete, same as ever, everyone eating sausages and waiting for the fireworks. And remember, the whole town is there, all in the square, the one time in the year – it's like a reconciliation. Symbolic. The proles' kids trying it on with the rich kids. It's the national holiday – solid as rock. And we're in the heartland of France. But then: carnage. Everyone got stuck in, all the media, it was as big as little Grégory. It was news that touched the whole French nation: the emergence of a legend. Mass shootings like that are extremely rare in France. It's an American thing. We were still reeling from the Columbine massacre which happened the year before, in 1999, in Colorado. There it was two teenage losers who killed thirteen people in their high school. Spectacular. Well, Vallé was of that order, literally done like a show, a production in a public square, atrocity by way of theatre. And with the horrendous sense of the lack of motivation, of deaths due simply to bad luck.

'The Vallé killer was a boy from the town's vocational lycée, in his final year, a kid with no prior history, bit of a misfit but much like all boys his age. A good-looking kid with a taste for the dark side. He hadn't been spotted as difficult; well, no more than just that. But that year, a fortnight before the massacre, he flunked his bac. That's the only fact worth noting. He wasn't a poor student, but he must have begun to come unstuck because he missed some exams and they failed him.'

'What was his name?'

'Éric something. I only remember his first name. An ordinary name for an ordinary kid. An average four-letter name. Éric lived with his mother, his stepfather and his stepfather's son. It must have been complicated at home for him, his mother had him very young, like at sixteen, doubtless in some unsavoury circs. And not much fun either. Long story short, she found herself a fresh baby-father later on, remarried, and turned into a fully fledged born-again churchaholic. Trying to make amends somehow, perhaps? In any case, she can't have made home life easy, making her offspring pay for her own past mistakes. That's what came out in the witness statements. Not fundamentally a nasty woman, but wrapped up in herself and with a razor-sharp tongue on her. That's what people said, and also that she never talked about her son. Never. As if she were ignoring him. He was there, but not for her. She was in denial about him. One of those people who provide the colour in a backwater town's mythology, in its folktales. Everyone knew her and had their story about her, everyone said: 'I remember one day, she went and ... and she said ...' And people dusted off their anecdotes, their penny's-worth, their hot goss. Everyone had a piece of the story, like a puzzle in black and white, but in fact no-one really knew her,

'no-one.

'You see?'

Pierrat said she did see.

'So we've got to the festivities, it's about half-nine and everyone's stuffing their faces. The party's hotting up, in a friendly way. Then this kid, Éric, shows up at the square. Sit tight. He shows up perched on top of a white horse, like an Apocalyptic horseman.

'But at this point, people aren't paying too much attention, there are people in fancy dress, the odd fire-breather, circus acts ... hell, it's carnival. So the kid gets there, riding in like an emperor on his horse, cool as a cucumber, via one of the streets off the square. Almost discreetly. He dismounts and he's got a gun. And he gets on with the job. He shoulders, aims and fires.

'He killed seven people there in the square. Quite randomly. The people nearest to him. It only took five minutes.

'Then, all at once, the crowd fought back. The shock faded and people jumped on him, and in the middle of the mayhem and the fighting, they managed to turn the gun around, in fact to turn the gun on their attacker, and they killed him. It's barely believable but there are a few photos from the scene. People didn't have mobile phones to make videos like they do now. But it was a party night, I remember it very well; there was a woman with a camera who was taking pictures of the festivities for the local rag, and she was right beside him. So she snapped away, she took dozens of pictures of the slaughter. They got into the press – gutter stuff.'

'Why do you say, "I remember it very well"? Sounds like you were there,' Camille said.

'I followed the trial, for *Libération*. It was one of the first that I covered. The atmosphere in the court was indescribable. As if the whole town was in there to mourn and call for justice. But there was no-one to hang, because the guy was dead.'

'So who was on trial?'

'There was something of a muddle over responsibilities. Buck-passing. There was the kid who'd procured the weapon, a little local dealer from the next-door shithole, a shallow character; and there was also a boy who was suspected of having known and not told anyone. A friend from school who he might have confided in. A rough draft of a letter addressed to the friend was found. It was enigmatic, but there were some who thought it outlined what the killer was planning. He was a young kid, same age as the killer.

'I remember the friend's face: a good-looking young guy, quite as lost as his bestie the killer.

'When the massacre happened, he was in the front row, this kid accused of knowing the plan, sitting at the same picnic table as some people who were shot. There were people who thought that couldn't be happenstance – that the killer wanted his friend to be there. They thought it was evidence of some kind of collusion, or a declaration of love. People are crazy.

'So this young guy is there, sat on the accused bench in a trial that's looking for a guilty party, no matter who, and his own mother got a bullet in the brain, right in front of him. Just like that, in a blind spot. And this is the kid they haul up to face the judge! It's insane. But there had to be someone on trial, some sacrificial scapegoat. The hearing went badly. The journalists' reports were red-hot. The inquiry was wrapped up, quick and dirty. People were screaming in the public gallery when they showed the photos, the images were blurry, they were . . . Well . . .

'. . . they were like abstract paintings.

'Picture it: we were trying a poor young kid who'd just lost his mother and clearly had nothing to do with the whole mess. He was only mates with the killer. I was furious. I can still feel the horror when I think back to it.'

'How long did they go down for?'

'Sod all. The local dealer must have got a few months for trafficking, I don't remember, but he clearly had no clue what his client was planning. He can't have been more than about eighteen either. He was selling weed on the weekends in nightclubs, and a bit of coke. He'd sold this gun, probably nicked from his uncle's wardrobe, for next to nothing. He was no receiver, hardly a big fish.'

'And the other guy?'

'He got nothing at all, thankfully. He was acquitted. It was crazy that he'd got mixed up in the case, and everyone knew it, it was clear from the start. At his hearing they made him describe what he saw. He was the silent type, which didn't help, almost stand-offish, but then he talked, and it was as if he was reliving the whole massacre . . .

'. . . and he talked about his mother. He said he'd caught his mother's eye before she was shot. And he said something like: "I'm the one who asked her to come out for Bastille Day. She

never used to come. But I insisted. Because I'd just got my bac."
Camille, that was one of the very few occasions when I cried in
court. It was torture. And then, the kid started to shake and he
fell over: it was a major panic attack, he was gasping like he was
drowning, it was so loud, and he was carried out of the court.
Completely heartbreaking.

'Seems the fireworks went off just at that moment. Just when
people were being shot. Suddenly there were rockets and flares in
the sky. You have to remember the poor pyrotechnist sitting miles
up above had no idea about his timing.

'This Éric's story was really just the everyday story of an
unhappy kid. He was a grim introvert, and he wanted everyone
to know he rejected them. Fascinated by gruesome things, fire-
arms, historic wars, he'd done some creepy drawings which were
displayed at the trial. Not a happy youngster. And then there
was the letter he wrote to his friend – it was more like a morbid
poem. He was nothing but a child whose mother didn't love him.
He never found his place. That's all. Because he wasn't wanted.
It's as old as Time. And it went so wrong. If you knew the number
of cases I've looked into where we've had to drop the idea of
understanding the motive. Where expert shrinks have been con-
tradicting each other . . . Why do people do what they do? The
answer's in books, not in life.'

'What about his mother, and his stepfather . . . What did they
say at the trial?'

'Oh, yes, I was forgetting the main point: they were dead. Spit-
spot. The kid had already nuked them before he went to the
Bastille Day party. In fact, he began with them – and he did them
with a hammer, not the gun.

'When he left his place, as well as taking the gun, he took a
backpack with three things in it, among them his toothbrush. No

joke. As if there could be some next step, a possible future. There's no future for the damned.'

'Fuck me, the whole thing beggars belief. And I don't remember it at all – how did that happen? I mean, I was little when it happened, but even so. It's true the name of the town, Vallé, that did ring a bell . . . it had a ring to it.'

'It's old news, and besides, each news story pushes out the last: I can honestly vouch for that, I've been at this gig forever. But what's intriguing about the news – and there's not one story that bucks the trend – is if you were to put it all in a novel, everyone would say it was too much.'

'Real life is unbearable.'

51

their entire estate

Before parting, the two women sat for some time in silence. The café owner cleared their table; the journalist had hardly touched her tea. Perhaps it was now pastis o'clock. Camille said she ought to go, and thanked her friend for taking the time to fill her in. Then, suddenly struck by an idea, she asked: 'What was the name of Éric's friend, the one who got his letter and ended up in court?'

'Hang on, I'm trying to remember, it's coming back to me . . . The first name was quite a rare one, it stood out . . . No, I don't remember anymore. Would you like me to dig it out?'

'No, don't worry. I'll find it.'

After paying for their drinks, Camille was putting her jacket on and halfway out of her chair when the journalist asked brightly, for the second time:

'Why are you genning up on this old story, Camille?'

Camille's movements slowed, as if she were buying time to consider whether she should answer or not. Whether there was even anything to answer. She did not speak. Perhaps she would have said something in the end, but the journalist pipped her to the post.

'It has to do with what's going on in the art galleries, doesn't it?'

It wasn't a question. Not really. Camille smiled sadly. 'I didn't say a word.'

Elsa and Abel

52

My friend, the wolf, however, taught at college

Elsa knew things were getting out of hand with Abel. She had not anticipated this, it just did not happen to her anymore. She had always been fully in control, even when what she did suggested the opposite. She liked to work in a controlled nosedive. She had noticed that often people found her responses strange. But the fact that she noticed this marked the fine line separating her from lunacy, because mad people never themselves notice when their responses seem strange. Elsa, Elsa . . . it was pretty if you said it aloud. An anagram of 'sale'. And she relished it when Abel said her name. Her rusty old name. Buried deep. The music silenced along with the dead.

All of them were simple four-letter names: Abel, Éric, Elsa, Mila. They were almost the same. She had never understood why people could not choose their own names. Parents chose because they were forced to, because the registrar was waiting, so, as with the umbilical cord, they had to make the cut, had to cheat; the best names meant something like *good luck*, otherwise they hid some kind of trap.

And then, when you wanted to ask, the parents were no longer there to explain. They had gone.

For her part, Elsa chose to be Mila.

After the abrupt departure of Abel – her prey, her discovery, her only friend – there in her ridiculous studio she knocked back the rest of the rum, serving herself in his mug so she could rest her lips where his had been. Around her there was nothing that added up to a real life. Everything was fake, except him. How could she have gone so wrong? He was the only angel, and she had made him an enemy. She waited for a sign from him, a move. This was all she could think of. She thought of nothing but him.

Abel Bac – brother – impossible lover. Because they could have loved each other, couldn't they? Bonded by the same fable and the same deaths. Two faces of a coin. Heads and tails.

Everything could have been different.

Everything should have been different.

Abel could not remember, but they had met before, she and he – in Vallé. He had not pieced the whole story back together and disinterred the fossils, as she had done. She was just a tiny dot floating somewhere in his memory, stored in the shadows with the forgettable anecdotes. And yet they had spoken and she remembered his name from then – which wasn't Abel but a fine, unusual name. They had acted in harmony: had become Abel and Mila, in order to survive.

To survive the night of Bastille Day.

She would open the door and go down the steps, the few steps. Her whole life since her parents' death had been a kind of MacGuffin. What about Abel's? Did he dream about the fire-works? Did he think every day about what happened? The difference was that he had been at the heart of the shooting, he had seen it happen. She, Mila, had been far away, in Paris, excluded from the most important story of her life. All she could do was imagine it, and recreate it.

She had been so furious with him – for being there, and doing nothing. For being that weak creature without words, for breaking down in court. She had hated him. She had chosen him to be a witness to her last work in order finally to massacre him in his turn, to punish him.

Now she was not so sure. In her head it was coming apart. She could not go back – this had shaped her entire life: you can never go back, you can't rewind the film. She could not go back to that Bastille Day morning and pack her bags and get in the car, the white Renault 21, with her parents, and go to Brittany and eat the petrol station biscuits. She could not save them, She and He. How many years would she need to accept this? How many lives?

The problem was this insidious feeling she had with Abel, which overtook her completely and which she did not recognise at all: she felt good.

She would open the door and go down the few steps. She would not look in the mirror. Her face would take her nowhere now.

Now, this was all that mattered: she had a viewer, her ideal viewer. Abel looked at her, even if he did not yet see her. But can a viewer understand all that has been done for him? And how he is loved?

53

could read it were it even Greek

Abel could hear a noise, a scrabbling at his wooden door, a presence on the other side, already he could smell the surge of her fragrance. He had that feeling which is so disturbing when you're in its grip: the profound conviction that you have already experienced what you're in the midst of experiencing. A sentence, a scent, a whole series of tiny moments are familiar, but you cannot remember how they end. It's a scene you will be observing from above or at a distance, like someone watching a play they already know by heart. Abel was reliving Elsa's inopportune presence.

That presence of Elsa at his door, in the middle of the night, when she was drunk and got the wrong floor. Which seemed to have happened a generation ago, though it was only a few days earlier.

Again he felt the throbbing pain above his eyes, the flashes across his brow, the headache; there was a drawerful of paracetamol packets in his tiny kitchen, for the orchids and himself, but however he re-ran the film of the actions he had to accomplish – get up from the sofa, move his body to the drawer, take one 1,000 mg pill, pour water into a glass, drink it down in one go and wait for the relief – he was stuck, because he sensed her at his door, Elsa, and the stupid logic of his movements might make her run away.

It seemed counter-intuitive, but he did not want her to go.

Abel was an organised, forward-thinking man. He was

capable of seeing beyond the immediate context, of imagining what was hidden in its folds. Abel knew he was a good policeman because his perceptions were so little polluted by emotions or prejudices. Ordinarily.

But just now he was unable to draw a mental map for his movements: no path or compass, no confidence, no intuition; he was truly alone.

She would end up knocking at the door. He did not move a muscle, he was sitting on the sofa in the dark, surrounded by his orchids; everything breathed better in the dark, he, his plants and Elsa too, doubtless, she would enjoy resting in the darkness. He'd like to show her the photographs of the stuffed and clothed wolves in the museum, wolves made up like an Aesop fable. He had studied the fables at the lycée with the teacher he liked, Madame Colombier. It was part of the French curriculum for that year's baccalaureate. That was something he had allowed to crumble from his memory, but however much we clear out, all we're doing is archiving the memories on shelves we imagine – wrongly – to be out of reach. Of course, it's all in there. He still vividly remembered a word Madame Colombier had used, a mysterious word that Abel, who wasn't yet called Abel, had held on to, the way you decide to hold close something you like, something pretty you want to collect and make your own. The word was 'anthropomorphic'. Madame Colombier had explained that this was the fabulist La Fontaine's preferred approach, using animals to talk about humans, that *anthropos* meant human and *morphē* was form. In Greek, if he remembered correctly. So the animals took on the appearance of people. Like the museum's wolves, drinking champagne and replaying a Bastille Day fete – in point of fact a very specific Bastille Day. Abel Bac knew exactly which one. Fuck, fuck.

*

He remembered Madame Colombier explaining that you had to look for the words hidden inside words, and that had been a kind of lightning bolt; when he had realised that this word *anthropomorphic*, an unfathomable and rather hostile word, was hiding simple words like human and form, he had felt stronger, less lost. So words could be puzzles, images could be puzzles, and Abel liked puzzles. Because as long as you had not lost any pieces over the years, they always ended up fitting together.

And everyone had now accepted, without need for further enquiry, that a crow could hold a cheese in its beak. And, Abel thought, Elsa would say: 'Then why not have shit in a tin can, or nature uttering a cry of anguish?'

Elsa who was still there, not budging, outside his door. He had never invited anyone into his home, he had almost invited Camille, but he could not do it, no-one came to his place.

He did not want to have to explain the superabundance of his houseplants, that would be worse than undressing in front of someone, but Elsa would end up knocking, wouldn't she? He really did have to make a decision.

He waited, eyes closed, his right arm extended to stroke one orchid's petals with a fingertip, the way you gently, unthinkingly, muss a kitten's fur, to enjoy its warmth and its wildness.

And Elsa banged at his door.

54

The wolf

Suddenly throwing the door open, Abel gave Elsa a fright and she took a step back; but perhaps she really was frightened because she had drunk too much, because coming to see him was not in her script, because she had dropped the controls in order to live something else, to surprise herself. Elsa did not let anyone surprise her now, not since changing her name. It was her job to create the boom, and the fallout. She asked if she could come in for a drink.

'I've no alcohol here.'

'So invite me to drink something else.'

'I don't invite people into my home.'

'Abel, let me come in.'

Elsa was barefoot, she had come down to his floor without shoes, and as Abel was not moving, she lit a cigarette, adding that it was fine, she had plenty of time. Elsa's mouth inhaling the smoke, Elsa's eyes which had not left his, Elsa's feet bare on the landing floor. Abel told her it was forbidden to smoke in the common areas, and Elsa smiled.

'You'll set off the fire alarm,' he said.

'There is no alarm in this old firetrap, Abel. Give me an interesting reason not to come in, otherwise I'm sleeping on your doorstep.'

'You're annoying me.'

'Why?'

'I mentioned when we went to the Pompidou Centre together that I have plants at home . . .'

'Yes.'

'Orchids.'

'Yes.'

'I have a lot of them. I mean they're all over the apartment. Actually, to be precise, I have ninety-four . . .'

'That's nice,' Elsa said, continuing to smoke and tapping out her ash on the landing without concern.

'It bothers me.'

'What bothers you?'

'To have to show them to people.'

'You've never, *ever* had anyone else in your apartment?'

'No.'

'What do you do about sleeping with someone?'

'I go to her place.'

'True, you bring a hot prospect back to yours and she thinks she's landed at the florist's counter, that could be stressful.'

'Good night, Elsa,' he said, and tried to close the door.

'It's O.K., Abel, do let me come in. There's nothing to worry about with me, right? You know that, don't you? Look at me.'

'Or perhaps there's everything.'

'*Touché*. What were you up to?'

'I was going . . . I need to use some headlice shampoo.'

'Is your head itchy?'

'Yes.'

'Show me where.'

'Dammit, everywhere, Elsa.'

'Me too, Abel, I'm itchy too. Perhaps you gave them to me? So let's do the shampoo together,' Elsa said as she castled with Abel, making a mockery of his roadblock; her cigarette almost finished, she nudged him, dodged around, stepped into his spot, and checkmate,

with a sprinkling of ash over him,
she was in.

55

to flattery weak

Elsa turned on the light, decisively. She was inside. *At last I am in your home.* Then she froze, stunned. It was a small room; she could have danced three steps one way then three the other and hit both walls. She gathered it all in, looking right, left and up; she observed. She took in all she saw, the way the gaze becomes a collector, becomes breathing, how it inhales, swells and fills, she saw Abel whole. Dazzled by the bright light, he was still behind her, waiting, there was nothing to say, he waited for her to undergo atomisation by the bonfire of his flowers, for her to feast on the violets and mauves, to confront the yellows and whites, to be dizzied by the splotches and tears that the petals shrieked, for her to catch onto the mouths, wings and gulfs formed by their sepals, myriads of lunatic heads, of ovaries pressed forward, of genitalia readied, immodest and wild, his flowers . . .

. . . the violent blues, the tentacular roots, the perverted reds, the shy pinks.

Elsa turned to him, her face a wreck, on the verge of tears. Now she was gazing at him, as if, Abel thought, Elsa were seeing him for the first time. Her lips were trembling. Then, sure of himself, confident of his effect like a practised sculptor, Abel asked: 'Beautiful, right?'

Elsa groped for the words, almost spoke then stopped. At last she answered:

'I have never seen the like of it, Abel. Never.'

'Come with me,' Elsa said, taking Abel by the hand and leading him to the bathroom, where the open door shed a glassy blueish light. He stayed standing there in the tiny room and his body, so displayed, looked almost as if it were caged. She said, 'I'm coming back.' And she brought a chair in with her, which she wedged up against the basin.

'Sit here, Abel.'

Abel sat, he complied, he obeyed. He had shown her his flowers, she could do as she would with him.

Elsa unbuttoned his shirt, slowly, unhurriedly, and each button that slipped out of its hole revealed the naked torso of the police officer in limbo, vulnerable.

At the last button, he shivered, as if a cold gust had blown over him without warning.

Now Elsa lifted his shirt over one shoulder, then the other, leaning over him . . .

. . . and leaning over, the tips of her loose hair brushed against his face, the way the bead curtain at the door of an old dwelling may suddenly shiver without human presence. Now he moved only to allow her to work, and breathed in the scent of her intruding hair, which dusted the air with fresh pine resin. Further away, as if from the depths of a stage set, from her throat, rose the singing body-blow of the rum. Now, from his new distance, Abel could taste Elsa's fragrance. She tugged on the sleeves and got rid of his shirt altogether, tossing it in a ball to the ground, and Abel couldn't believe it.

'Calm down, Abel, and tip your head back.'

He let his head drop back and his skin recoiled at the cold, hard touch of the porcelain against his neck. In this position, he thought, she could cut off his head, or break his neck, he was completely at her mercy. Elsa rolled up her sleeves and turned on the taps – both at the same time, hard. She waited for warmth, the perfect temperature, then she dipped Abel's face right under the water. He closed his eyes and she dug her nails into his hair, she went chasing right down to his scalp, every strand, driving her fingertips right into the depths of the chaos of his hair. She pulled and stroked, gripped and released her fingers. Abel could hear life outside, drenched as if heard from the bottom of an aquarium, the gouts of water pouring periodically into his ears susurrating around him, only interrupted now and then by a booming torrent that saved him from floating away altogether. Elsa wiped away the water dripping into his eyes, and it trickled down his neck and onto his chest. He was not cold.

She turned the water off and set him upright. He was dizzy and kept his eyes closed. He heard the top of the bottle click off and felt the viscous liquid spread over his head. Elsa gathered it all, kneading and penetrating, hair by hair, resolute and taut, sparing nothing, she possessed, she took over, impassioned, filled with that calm voracity, a lover's greed.

'You can open your eyes, Abel.'

She gave him a little shake, handed him a towel.

'It's my turn now.'

'What?'

'For you to wash my hair.'

And Elsa took off her men's pyjama top, too big and too blue for her.

Underneath she was naked.

She sat down and tilted her head back, making her throat stand out in a precious arch, like a path.

'Now, come here, Abel.'

And Abel went.

Camille

56

Approach'd

Bac, I've tried calling you so many times. It's quite urgent. I have news for you, things to tell you. It's a bugger to keep getting your answerphone. Call me.

Bac, I'm a bit worried. Perhaps it's not my place. But you did ask me to fill you in, and now it's snowballing, you know. My head's spinning. I would really like to talk to you. Not just leave you voicemails, so I'm just, well, I'm talking to myself now, see? A bit fucked off. Call me.

This is my eighteenth voicemail, Bac, I mean, hell, you are fucking me around. And your mailbox has been full for days, so I'm stuck with these stupid S.M.S. voicemails and I can't even swear at you properly. What are you – some kind of fucking *ghost*? *Call me.*

Bac, this is the last time I do you a favour, I promise, what do you take me for? You ask me to dig up info for you, *gratis*, in my spare time, like I'm your hired help. Is that it? Good old Pierrat, Your Dirty Work Done, No Questions Asked – that's me. Call me.

Bac, I swear, I'm sending a patrol up to yours on place Clichy with orders to bust your window if you don't show some sign of life. Nothing fucking doing. What the hell are you up to? What's your game? You're dug in with some chick from Tinder, right? Call me anyway. I've sent the patrol over, you would've wanted it. Bastard.

O.K., I didn't send the patrol. But I promise, this time tomorrow, if you've not bothered to call, I'm pressing the button, no sweat.

Do you know how long I've been trying to get hold of you, you son of a bitch? It's been twenty-four hours! I went past your place, no lights on, where the fuck are you?

No, I won't let go, no, *I will not let go*. See, I'm the kind of person who doesn't drop a case. What are you? Who are you? Have they voodoo-ed you? Have you vanished into thin air? Where the hell are you? Why've you disappeared? Do *you* know what's going on? No, you don't, cos you're in the shit, my friend, deep deep shit, brother, you're beyond fucked, I found out. Call me – just call.

Abel, I've found out that's not your name. I'm sorry. You are the strangest guy I know. But I do know you a little by now ... I know I know you. Back me up. Even if this isn't your name, I don't give a fuck, you can't lie about who you are, not for this long. I don't believe them. I'm not sleeping anymore either. You know what it's like, insomnia. It's your fault. I don't feel like jacking it in. Call.

Where the bloody hell are you?!! I've looked *everywhere*.

Bac, it's me again. It's me, Camille. You know that evening, when we kissed, and you turned me down. Shit. I was so hurt. You snapped me in two, like a twig. Yes, you rejected me. You practically pushed me off, as if you found me disgusting. I didn't dream it, I wouldn't have kissed you if I'd thought you didn't feel something. I don't understand. You've never said anything. You never mentioned it. Do you know how hard that is? How much I've thought about it? No, you don't. You don't know the nights I sat up thinking about it, knowing there's nothing between us, and I still had to get out of bed, tweety tweet little birds, do the job, hup-to, because someone has to do it, cos no-one lives your life for you. Because no-one else suffers for you, Bac. This is genuine bullshit. When you suffer, you're totally alone, when you've gone to shit, and then that's it, you have to get up again. Cos the weirdo here is you. It isn't me. You just float on, easy. You don't give, you're above it all. Now they're all talking about you, and you're the one being watched from above. The rest of us are just melting into the background. I'm the background – is that it? Can't you see me??! Call me back, please. Please.

Bac, I know about Vallé. I know *everything*.

Is that why you're stuck on this story with the horse? I don't get it, Bac. I didn't see anything. I'm out of the picture.

Your mother died that night, on Bastille Day. She was with you at the celebrations. She was shot by the psychopath. I've got it. And you – what happened to you? The nutjob in the art galleries who set up that party of stuffed vampire-wolves has something to do with it, right? Something to do with what happened in Vallé? Is that person working for you – or trying to reach you? You can't just disappear, I also need to understand. I need to. Has someone got it in for you? Do you want my help? I'm afraid for you, Bac. For me too.

I'm just your average girl next door, is that how it is? I'm a decent girl, and that's why I'm here. But that isn't true, Bac.

It wasn't your fault. I don't know what you've been through, but it does look like a real shitstorm. Your mate was the killer, right? You were friends with the guy who zapped everyone, and you didn't know he was going to do it. You were innocent. But you wound up facing the judge. Is that why you decided to become a policeman? I've pieces of the puzzle, but not all of them. I don't have you.

Who on earth chooses such a strange name when they want a new identity? *Abel Bac*? Where did you dig that up? Sorry, I keep on sending audio messages to you. Cos I can't seem to do anything else. I feel like someone spiked me. I've had twenty-two coffees, you idiot.

This is my last message, Bac. If you don't reply I'll stop. You're driving me crazy. I've never in my life talked so much to someone who's made me feel so alone. Go fuck yourself.

Bac? Shit, Bac? This is urgent. It's red-hot! There's been a third art gallery break-in – at the Musée d'Orsay. I shouldn't even be telling you. I could be in some deep shit. I will defo be in the shit. I've been called to the scene. I'm on the way there. This time there's a body, Bac.

to verify the boast

The forensic experts were hard at work at the crime scene, comb-ing through, noting down and gathering every element that could harbour some D.N.A. The area had been cordoned off. The 3rd district crime squad had picked up the case, as its territory covered the left bank. Even though the Pompidou and the hunting museum were not within their ops field, for the Orsay, it was over to them. The gallery's director, who had now popped a Xanax, had been taken to rue Bastion to give her statement. Camille knew they would have spotted her because she had gone snooping on the other side of the line. She had got the intel for herself on what was going down in the art galleries, and it had gone higher: someone had shopped her. She knew they had sent her here because she would be obliged to answer for herself. Why was she interested in a case that was nothing to do with her? How did she know to show up ahead of everyone else? Well, they should clock her now. She had been working completely in the dark for ages. While hanging around the police-taped areas, she had stopped in front of a painting – something for her to focus on. It had caught her attention as she went by. Two legs spread wide, a woman's geni-tals, slit open, hairy, serene. Simply there. Her first thought was that she had never seen her own vagina as clearly. That it was quite fascinating to see it like this, with all the little features. Then she thought that if she went down on a woman, this was precisely what she would see, in super-close-up. And then that she wouldn't know quite where to begin, whereas for herself, she could help, she knew how to guide someone. But was her self-knowledge a general thing, after all, abstract? And then she reflected that there was no head in the painting. It was a headless body. And that got her thinking about the murderers who tried to cut the heads off their bodies to get rid of them. The heads were always a problem. She turned to the explanatory blurb. *The Origin of the World.* You don't say, old chum.

Camille was taking in the art because she could not bear to look at what was unfolding in the hall behind her. It was unsettling. It's not every day you find yourself strolling around an art gallery *qua* crime scene. She had to stop staring at this headless vagina which had her mesmerised. She wanted to cry. She had put herself in a really bad position with her boss. Not only had she dropped the work on her own desk in order to chase Abel Bac like a woman possessed, on top of that she had been snooping way out of her own territory. She was *persona non grata.* She felt humiliated. Bac gave her nothing. Why was she doing all this for him? She knew perfectly well why, if she could just stop lying to herself. Because she never stopped thinking about him, she was obsessed. And she hadn't recovered from his rejection.

Because she was in love with him.

The Musée d'Orsay was once a major railway station. When you stood in its main concourse, you could still imagine the crowds that must have gathered there, waiting for their trains. The families and people on their own caught in that curious tension between stillness and being on the verge of movement, typical of travellers on the point of departure. Some places are more liable to the imprint of the past, and the Orsay was altogether haunted.

An X on the psychological map, a hotspot for arrivals and leave-takings, a crossroads; it had been clever to turn it into an art gallery, ambiguous corral of memory. A building whose purpose changes has to be reinvented, it has to demonstrate canny new angles. At the Orsay it was gratifying how visitors now entered from the highest point, and the old station opened up beneath their feet: no longer at constant risk of being run over, they were now poised to reap where they liked. You could take in the whole field in a single gaze, then go down the staircase on the right or the one on the left, there was no obligation either way. It was an adventure.

Entering high up that particular evening, broaching the concourse of the former Orsay station turned art gallery by order of the President – how often, in their terror of being dwarfed by their role, these men liked to gift themselves a little metempsychosis by lending their name to a new-born museum . . . So, that evening, on entering the concourse of the former station at its highest point, all you could see at first was a great bed of flowers. The strange impression created by this artificial landscape. It instantly called to mind Van Gogh's poppies; the golden hair, brash blue skies and over-decoration of Klimt; and perhaps also Frida Kahlo's hair. There, the Musée d'Orsay was dressed to the nines – an embroidered, powdered and painted gallery, almost sequinned with the thousands of flowers. The floor of the gallery was so thickly covered that the whole space was growing and trembling. Hundreds of blue, white and red flowers, all surrounded by dozens of mirrors, opening windows onto infinity. It would have tickled him, that former President of the Republic. Orchids. It's disturbing how beautiful flowers are. You forget.

Shocking like a field of umbrellas or a forest of lamps. The unpleasant sensation of a twisted version of nature complemented by irrepressible delight. From the ceiling's vault large screens were hanging, solidly suspended by an ingenious cable system, screens showing a light show against a night sky on a loop. The same video on every screen, a few minutes' delay between each one.

The gorgeous red! The beautiful blue! Fireworks banged and popped, exploding relentlessly but noiselessly. No sound. Depriving the vast concourse of the bangers' noise, so like that of bullets shot from a firearm. It's funny when you watch a firework without the sound: you still hear the noise. The bangs are inside you. A phantom noise, like the sensation in an amputated limb.

At the back of the hall, focal point of the nave, the great gilded clock – one of the last relics of the old station – dominated the scene like a wary full moon. It was a third eye from which was suspended a bouquet of arms and legs.

Scaffolding was on the way, to allow experts to examine them close up, before removing them. For the moment, the guardians of the peace were using the long open corridors that snaked around the vaulted ceiling to reach the clock and avoid stepping on the flowers, their heads and shoulders covered in gold confetti pumped out by snow-blowers neatly stationed around the concourse. It was almost impossible to move about without risking contamination to the crime scene, in this hijacked art gallery; that said, the people who had gathered there now seemed, in spite of themselves, to be caught in it, pinned between the grotesque and the sublime.

Abel and Elsa

58

For which four teeth he lost

She was here, on him, riding him, her wet hair stuck to her shoulders, and her breasts, her breasts which seemed to offer no apology for anything. How could anyone have such free breasts? She was here, on him, almost naked, and he wasn't itchy anymore. It wasn't so much the act – a penetration can be so banal, so banal the bodies' trading – no, it was his whole skin being covered with bruises, pummelled by her bones, the beautiful bones under her skin. It was like having a train run over him, but on an old colour T.V. It was his pelvis in her hollows, her knees in his eyes, her mouth swallowing the blood in gulps straight from the pump of his lungs. It was a tearing apart of skins to see what violence was brewing underneath; it was a surrendering to the danger, mouth wide open, once and for all.

Elsa's voice in his ear as she collapsed over his hips, butter into butter, the sticky warmth pooling over, her voice distinctly saying: 'You know, Abel, I wanted you.'

And her eyes signalling, while she fucked him every which way, her eyes saying I am not who you think.

Elsa's eyes. That is what sex needs: mystery. Otherwise it's a car park.

Afterwards, Abel cut and ran. Awakened from his stupor, he had taken fright, put his clothes back on and left, and she ran after him . . . Elsa ran after him, she tripped him up in the stairwell, but, merciful lord, who honestly does that? He careened down the stairs on his arse, on his head, it hurt like hell. And she was shouting: 'You can't just walk out like that! Come back! Come back, Abel! You don't get to decide!' And lights began to come on in neighbours' windows, doors opened and mouths began to jabber. The shame, and at the same time he felt as though he were drowning in a freezing-cold fountain and he'd never been more awake. That harpy had contaminated his whole apartment, every one of his plants. The flowers were screaming.

It was all over now, he had nothing left.

How light he felt, suddenly.

So he ran, to see if he could still run, if his body was still his own, he vanished down the rue de Douai, there were café terraces on every side, he sensed that he could power right through them, flay himself on their wine glasses and leave this skin to God or to the night.

Camille

59

the high-raised hoof came down

The Director of the Musée d'Orsay had spelled it all out for them. The goings-on in the art galleries over the last week were all part of a plan. They were the work of one woman – one *artist*. She tried to explain it to the police the way their teacher would have, but you could tell she thought they were thick. Well, maybe not thick, more maybe a bunch of nice but somewhat dim pupils. It was rather unpleasant.

Camille Pierrat headed off. There was nothing further for her to do there that evening. She had a hearing the next day at the police inspectorate as part of the inquiry into Abel Bac. Well, that was just a few hours away, now. And this was a super-sized shitstorm. She would have liked to say a few things about it to Abel, but he had never called her back. He had left her to carry the can. Camille walked a roundabout route home, via the embankment paths along the Seine. It was a clear night and her shoulders were covered with gold confetti.

Their suspect was a world-renowned artist known as Mila. Even Camille had heard of her, and her exploits. She had suspended human figures all over Paris a few years back. The buzz had reached even *her* ears, like a small river.

It's a performance. Well, it was to be a performance, we gave her carte blanche, it was planned months ago. Several of the

*galleries agreed to take part, but it was all completely
non-official.*

Why?

Why what?

Why non-official?

*That was part of the performance. We were meant to claim
we'd had break-ins – you know – breaking and entering? She
described it as an action piece, to take place right inside the galleries at night. Like a raid. The artist was to reappropriate the
gallery space, illegally. Anyway, we accepted. There were run-
throughs. The whole performance was storyboarded. But we
weren't allowed to watch, we had to let her work with her own
crews.*

And you were happy to hand over the keys to your gallery, to
this public institution, to someone like this, for her to do whatever she fancied in there?

*It was Mila – she's one of the most shown, most sought-after
artists in the world. And everything was planned down to the
last millimetre. She was offering to create an art event that would
be . . . audacious, completely new. It was as if she were using
the institutions like brand-new frames for her creation. Like a
reversed pathway, you know?*

No, I don't know.

*As if she were using the galleries as her raw materials. It was
an intriguing opportunity. Besides, as I told you, I had backing
from the Minister for Culture. I didn't just wake up one morning
and O.K. it all myself, you know. Have you called the minister?*

That's in hand.

*We were all keen, the Pompidou, the hunting museum and us.
And Pinault. We must have had dozens of meetings in preparation. We even put some budget towards the installations.*

And was the dismembered body a part of your plan?

Of course not. It's horrendous. I've told you a hundred times. I don't understand this madness. Are you sure it's a real body? Mila often works with models that look more real than real life. It's one of her leitmotifs.

Yes, we are sure it's a human body. It was removed from your clock, madame.

Point is, she's a world-renowned artist! If the Pope asked to stay at your house one night, would you shut the door in his face?

When did you meet this Mila?

Am I a suspect here? I understand the seriousness of the situation, but I've already answered all these questions from your colleagues. From every angle you can imagine. I'm exhausted.

Please simply answer my question. Have you met Mila?

I have never met Mila. No-one has met her.

So how did you hold the preparatory meetings for this project?

Everything went via her agent, well, he's actually her lawyer, Monsieur Masson. He has represented her since her career began. She is never personally present in art-world circles. The power she channels comes from her anonymity and the mystery that surrounds her. Have you contacted Masson?

Precisely what aspects of this performance were part of the plan?

All of it! The flowers, the fireworks on the screens, the confetti-guns ... Well, to be precise, the flowers were going to be lilies, irises and roses, not orchids. She changed that element without warning us. So yes, it was all planned, but not this horror.

What was it meant to show?

She could tell you. Find her and ask! The performances were to be like paintings, one in each of the galleries; a triptych, a three-part painting . . .

What exactly was the point?

Excuse me?

What was the point of all of this?

Well . . . it's art.

Right, then, madame, let's start all over again.

Abel, Elsa and Camille

60

with such a blow

This is the story of a man sealed shut. We often have insight about others, very rarely about ourselves. When Abel, who wasn't yet called Abel, had been acquitted of the charges levelled against him, he had not resolved to breathe. Because that didn't come to him. He'd been living between one breath and the next since the night when he had seen his mother shot down like a dog by a young man he liked, whom he perhaps even envied. Because Abel perceived no mystery in himself. He wanted to get his bac, kiss a girl or more than one (would have been alright), travel, then find a decent job. That was not what he saw in Éric. Some encounters challenge us right there and then, offering no option of greater distance or experience. Some sensibilities raise the intensity, act unpredictably, give a brand-new tint to the oxygen we breathe. And we sense that they don't do it on purpose. We move closer to them, ever so slightly, as if to hint, to steal a little of their heat, to live in their slipstream. Éric was that kind of person, and Abel would have rather liked to be him.

Abel had never managed to start breathing again. He felt as though what had happened was too big for him; his own pain and incomprehension outstripped the realm of his skills. It was too much.

He had allowed himself to be led. By social workers, legal guardians and lawyers, to whom he offered no more than his muteness and his obedience. The only thing he had decided alone, by and for himself, was to change his name. All he knew was that he wanted to cut Vallé out of himself, and he could no longer like this name which had been plastered all over the press, in every mouth, chewed over and over again. Being a killer's friend, being someone who saw his mother die. Not himself being a killer, for when a handful of people had at last leaped at Éric, moving as one, with one great cry, throwing themselves on his gun to stop the carnage, he, Abel, had been standing there, frozen in horror. He had been standing opposite Éric, his mother had collapsed on the ground, and he had not moved again.

Because of Éric's letter, he had been suspected of complicity. They had assumed he had had some hand in the planning. He, the unshifting, the genuine, the admirer. The last time he had talked about all of this had been in court. Concluding hours of torture answering questions about the months preceding that Bastille Day. He had tried, although his answers had held no meaning for him. He had obeyed the police officers; he had always been a good pupil. He became a plague-child. He did not see his graduating classmates nor his teachers again, did not see Johanna or Madame Colombier who had taught him what anthropomorphic meant. He was prosecuted and made a ward of the court, then dumped in a housing unit for young men, most of them delinquents, he had a bed in a dorm, a bedside table, a blanket, two sets of sheets and a court-appointed counsel who came to see him and who, it must be said, took his life in hand, almost like a sister: preparing for his trial, putting his dead mother's affairs in order (she had not had many affairs to sort out, had his mother), especially her funeral. At first Abel had been frightened because he could not pay this woman, and when he confessed this to her, she explained that she was appointed by the court and therefore paid by the State. Abel could not get his head around this; he was afraid he would be in debt, for, as his mother used to say in a voice buttressed by popular wisdom, 'my son, the rich are those who have no debts'.

It was she, his State-supplied counsel, whom he had asked if he could change his name and how to go about it. She had recommended he pursue this after his trial and promised she would help. By the standards of State judicial systems, his trial had come around quickly: a year and a half after that July 14. He had found it a long wait, but she, his counsel, told him that, considering the scale of the case, this was very quick and he was lucky. Abel who wasn't yet Abel had no opinion.

He was afraid of going to prison, without understanding why they might want to lock him up. His interviews with the police had been a muddled porridge, a lava of words, exhaustion and terror. Fear of saying things wrong, of doing them wrong. He had tried to be honest given that it was difficult to respond only with facts. That was what he had attempted. Yes, he had received a letter from Éric a few days before the celebrations. Yes, he had been surprised that Éric had written to him, he had never done that before, nor had Abel, either. They did not write to each other. That was all.

What he had tried to explain to the people interrogating him was that the letter had arrived and his mother had at first put it to one side. Why? Had she forgotten it or mislaid it? But Abel did not pick up the post, no post ever came for him. It was, entirely logically, his mother and she alone who emptied the letterbox. She had not given him that letter. That Bastille Day, when Abel had pressed her to come with him, and returned to the subject several times that day, his mother had unexpectedly said: 'Actually, a letter came for you the other day.' This was so unheard-of that for a moment Abel had thought: perhaps it's from my father.

His father whom he had never met, whose name he did not even know. He had been filled with this hope when his mother said he had received a letter.

Then his mother had said: 'I must dig it out, I'll give it to you in a minute.' The day had gone by, Abel thinking about his letter, but oddly he had not dared badger his mother to give it to him. Why not? He had no answer to this. That's how it was. She had agreed to come to the festivities, and a little before they went out together, in their best clothes, she had given him the letter. He had not wanted to read it in front of her, he had said he needed to use the toilet before they left, and then, locked in the loo, he had opened it. He had straight away checked the signature and, seeing *Éric*, he had been disappointed, then unnerved. Not excessively unnerved; it was more as though a distant warning light went on in his head to indicate 'This is odd, isn't it?' But it had stayed in the background. There was no emergency.

How can you tell what's going to change your life? They were funny, these police people, trying every imaginable angle on the story of his letter. Yes, of course he had thought, 'That's strange,' but only for a millisecond, he had not been that bothered. He was just disappointed as he had so hoped for something else. He had skimmed the letter, because his mother was waiting and he was only meant to have gone for a piss, not understood much of its garble, then automatically tucked it in his trouser pocket and left.

The psychologists who had assessed him for the trial had made a big deal out of this. *He kept the letter with him, in his pocket. It was symbolic, a meaningful gesture. As if it was a love letter.*

After the trial he never saw a shrink again. He had gone

through the steps to change his name, with his lawyer's help. 'Why that name?' she had asked. He had replied, 'Because.' She had been paid by the State, and Abel Bac had joined the army, all fresh and clean with his brand-new I.D. card.

There were two things he never told anyone. The first was that, before he died, Éric had smiled at him. And his smile had been beautiful. The second thing was that his new name had not been randomly chosen: he had read it on a stone commemorating Jews deported during the war, in a square in Montmartre. Abel Bac was the name of a dead child.

61

As laid him bleeding

To the officers of the D.P.J. 3, Maître Jérôme Masson told all there was to tell, no arm-twisting required. He dished the dirt like a pro.

When he was woken in the middle of the night by three officers who crowded the screen of his intercom, police armbands to the fore, his first thought was that Mila had died.

Both his children were in bed, his wife had been woken like him by the repeated assaults on the buzzer, so he knew where his loved ones were. (He had been to check only an hour before, as he did every night, that his children were breathing, an unalterable ritual. Whenever he found one of them too deeply asleep, he would shake them until the signs of life grew strong and unmistakeable.)

Hence his first thought at the irruption of the law and order forces into his home, after dark, was this: Mila was dead. Deep down, he had felt the unleashing of a brutal flood of anguish and, concomitantly (bizarre as it might seem), a potential relief. How could he be relieved at the loss of someone he had lived alongside since forever? He was her closest friend and her public face, he knew her intimately, he protected her. Together they had earned a lot of money. Jérôme had a life apart from her, and other clients, of course, but she was not a client. She was a treasure and, yes, something else that was more like a burden. If she died, he could at last say everything. Even his wife did not know who Mila was or how they had begun to work together. Now he could enjoy the questions, the probing and comments; he could enjoy it alone, no longer share the crown. He could create their story, polish it and make it so perfect that he too would believe it wholeheartedly. He would be the narrator and one of the protagonists – the only one alive.

Mila was not dead, at least not to the knowledge of the three policemen standing in his entrance hall, but she was the object of a live police search. The first thing Masson told them, for now he could disclose it, was that she had disappeared. He didn't know where she was, he could no longer reach her on the telephone, and he was worried. He dressed and went with them. As if he had been waiting for this moment. For the first time, Mila's performances had not unfolded according to their plans and he had been sidelined. He had even been that day to the studio where she was meant to be living. He had not found her there, nor any trace of recent occupation. Clearly, she was not sleeping there, even though a tent had been erected in the middle of the main room. He did not know where Mila was living and she was no longer answering his calls. They had been speaking on the telephone every day, but now not only had she cut off communications, she had lied to him.

He hadn't seen her for two months, not since her arrival in Paris, in fact. When he had met her at the Gare du Nord, emerging from the Eurostar, she had been wearing sunglasses and carrying a tiny handbag. All her belongings had been transported from London by his team. He had given her the keys to her new studio, they had had lunch together in a private room at the Dôme, like a pair of lovers; the table had been reserved under a false name – they had used many pseudonyms over time, to book hotels, exhibitions, concerts and restaurants ... In her Berlin performance known as the Dark Rooms, for which Mila had comprehensively graffitied the toilets in some film theatres, she had slipped their false names into the texts covering the walls, like a hidden trail. He alone had known.

At the Dôme, they had gone over the details of her new performance, which she was calling *La Vita Nova*. A little pompous, in his opinion, but he had not said so. He was not involved in her decisions, her obsessions. After this lunch, they would no longer be meeting in person, except in an emergency, but they were meant to speak every day. He was handling the arrangements with the three art galleries, with Pinault for the fake burglary, and with some suppliers of raw materials (wholesale florists, mainly), and he was to keep her updated. As usual.

Before their reunion in Paris, he hadn't seen her face-to-face for about a year, and, seeing her again, he had thought her a great deal changed. For one thing, she had grown much thinner. Her hair seemed blonder than he remembered, longer too. But this wasn't what had made Masson uneasy. It was the whole look of her that he did not recognise. It had taken him a little while to put words to the impression she made: she had seemed vulnerable.

Against all his expectations, Masson had found her very beautiful. Although there had been no frisson between them since a brief flirtation at the lycée. He looked at her, that day in Paris, like a stranger. Or like a lover he had lived with until their parting and was only now meeting again, suddenly, after years of separation. And her attractiveness struck him, painfully, for he had ended up losing sight of it, it had dissipated over time. We tend not to see people after a while, when we live right alongside them.

When they caught a taxi together from the Gare du Nord to the Dôme, Mila had not talked but sat looking out of the window, without removing her sunglasses, like a woman going to meet her past. Their lunch had been pleasant and lacklustre; Mila was sweet, subdued, hardly there. Neither mocking nor brusque – she was the antithesis of how he knew her. The only aspect remaining of her old self was her sense of humour, which she deployed as universally as ever, about everything and nothing.

This should have rung alarm bells, this is what he kept on thinking in the officers' car as they drove rapidly to the police station.

Alarm bells should have rung, for, as they'd sat down to lunch, she had pushed up her sunglasses (now they were alone in the Dôme's private room), had stared at him and said:

'Jérôme, I want you to stop calling me Mila. I would like you to use my real name from now on.'

Masson had been caught off-guard. He had not called Mila anything but Mila since the lycée, but he had never forgotten her name. So, trusty and solid as ever, he had answered, smiling:

'Certainly. As you wish, Elsa.'

on the ground

'Alright, move on, please, there's nothing to see here, you bunch of donkeys! Off you go! Everybody back home, please, shoo! Close those doors, let's all get back to bed and there's no need to call the police!'

Elsa's strident tone had managed to convince the inhabitants of Abel's building (who decided en masse: *she's gone hysterical*) to go back to their lives without making a fuss, after they had all come out to listen, doors ajar, to the altercation taking place in their stairwell between a man and a woman.

When there's a spot of bother in the air, coming out to watch is a dodgy business that swings between voyeurism and bravery, the sick curiosity (*something's going to the dogs somewhere, I fancy knowing more*) sometimes turning into last-minute heroism (*this is going very wrong, I gotta step in*). Abel Bac and Camille Pierrat could have spoken at some length on the subject, thanks to their considerable experience of questioning witnesses confronted with precisely this dilemma. The witnesses could turn out to be active or passive (the great nest to be untangled in a split second when choosing between *I ought to step in*, *I have to step in* and *I am stepping in*). Some witnesses shouldered a lifetime of guilt for *not* having intervened. Camille was not always gentle when they debriefed after such an occasion – 'Bastard hears a chick getting her head kicked in right next door and the fat fuck only turns up the volume on his T.V.!' – but Abel did not pass judgment. 'How could you know how you would respond when it hasn't happened to you?' was the gist of his reply to Camille. For it was never quite that simple in Abel's take on it, though he was no orator. And Elsa, who had become Mila, would have told the other two if she'd been there for the conversation: that's *kairos*. She would have explained it something like this: Kairos is the Greek god of the opportune act. Before is too soon, after is too late. You have to jump or act at time T. Otherwise you risk living with the hesitation or the missed opportunity for the rest of your life. Camille would then have remarked that Kairos was also the name of the national employment agency's web portal and that the French authorities had a fucking strange sense of humour. And Abel would not have said anything then, because he would have let the two forceful women talk and fill the space.

But Elsa, Camille and Abel will never go for a coffee together and discuss the choice of whether to act or not, and that's a pity, when you come to think of it.

Elsa was losing track. She still had headlice lotion on her head, hair in her eyes and tears in them too, she was hardly dressed, she'd had no shoes on in the first place when she had gone to drop in on Abel, and Abel had taken off. What on earth? She didn't have long, and with the mayhem she had touched off at the Orsay, it was a matter of hours. Masson would be cornered and he would tell everything, he was finally going to tell everyone who Mila was. Masson did not know her address here, in Abel's building; for the first time she had personally rented the tiny attic studio on the top floor, and yesterday she had chucked her mobile in the bin. Still, she had no time to lose. The police would be hacking her personal accounts and it would not be long before they followed the trail back to her little hideout on place Clichy.

At first she had looked for an apartment in the neighbourhood, to be close to him, to spy on him and observe his reactions as her performance of *La Vita Nova* played out. She wanted to be the spider watching the fly struggle in her web. But it had not felt sufficiently . . . organic. She wanted to be close enough to touch Abel. She wanted to step into his life. So one day she had approached one of the students living up top and had offered her a large sum of money as well as an alternative pad, so she would move out and let Elsa move in. The girl had not needed much persuading and had even left her few odd bits of furniture and chipped crockery as a bonus.

The perfect stage set.

Elsa wondered if they had already got somewhere with the body parts. She would have liked to be a fly on the gallery wall and to contemplate her work as well as witness the chaos. The intoxication of this torment.

She went back to Abel's place; his door had been left wide open when he had fled with her in pursuit. She went inside and looked at everything, to photo-fix it all on her senses, for she would not be returning. She inhaled his movements in that air, the slightest displacements of the animal in its cage. Next she went to fetch what she had planned to give him, her leaving present, and she came back to put it in the middle of his living room. She did not pick up the fallen chair in the bathroom, did not mop up the water that had run along the grooves between the tiles all the way to the bedroom parquet; under her breath, she said goodbye.

Then, out loud, she said: 'I hope you will understand.'

63

full low

After so many detours to put off getting home, Camille was lost. She felt reinvigorated by the walk, restored from walking down random roads she did not know. She thought about Abel and his regular night-time walks, that was something he had told her, that he had often mentioned, in little anecdotal comments.

That he had *shared* with her, his nocturnal walks.

She had imagined it as a kind of tiring, pointless exercise, much as she felt about jogging and those fruitcakes she saw running through Paris, glassy-eyed, their bodies rake-thin, hurdling exhaust pipes and the chill misery of excessively early mornings. Perhaps she had got it wrong. That was not something she often admitted. Abel had confided that what upset him on his walks was when he did not manage to get lost. How it felt so good to get lost. Tonight Camille understood, and she went on walking, absolutely lost. With the powerful sense that she might never find her way again. And then the details around her began to be beautiful: a little mosaic monster by Space Invader smiled at her, a cat on a balcony leaned out at her approach, a vast tag made of collaged white paper letters screamed an anti-femicide slogan, an empty bottle of fizz had been left on the ground and a Bic biro stuck in its neck, like a single flower.

Every bar full of night owls that she passed beckoned her for a last glass or to seek out further adventure; the I.G.P.N. and her morning summons now seemed trivial, as if for someone other than herself, for Officer Pierrat.

She looked at the time on her mobile: the night was almost over, it was ten past five. It began to ring, which gave her such a shock that she let it slip and drop to the ground. She quickly retrieved it, it could be Abel, but on the other end was a colleague from D.P.J. 3.

'Yep?'

'Pierrat? Your voice sounds weird.'

'No, actually you gave me a shock when you called. Made me jump.'

'Sorry. You asked me to let you know if I found out anything more about the Musée d'Orsay case.'

'Go on, I'm listening.'

'Are we clear that, if anyone asks, you know NOTHING?'

'Of course.'

'O.K. I'm doing this for you, you know?'

'Spit it out, then!'

'I've some pretty solid info on the body, or rather the body *parts* . . . One of the legs is from a young woman, another is a man's leg, there's a female arm from an older person, and so on. In other words, it's a mish-mash . . .'

'But how many people are dead then?'

'Actually, it's not so bad, seems they've all been dead for quite some time . . . I mean, the owners of all the limbs . . .'

'I don't understand.'

'It's something of an open secret in Paris, perhaps you've heard about it? Maybe when the forensics are chatting on the side . . . About the medical school . . .?'

'No, I still don't get it.'

'The medical school is also a centre for the donation of bodies for medicine and science . . . Well, naturally it's become a lovely well-stocked shop of horrors over the last few years. Hard to get your head round it, a real horror film: there's this vast cache of dismembered cadavers rotting away there and no-one's lifting a finger to sort them out. Not enough fridges, no real record-keeping of the bodies' provenance . . . I've heard there are rooms where you find yourself stepping on heads and organs all over the floor. It's the Nazis' mad laboratory.'

'In the middle of Paris?'

'Yup. A slaughterhouse on the rue des Saints-Pères, in the 6th. This is going to end up all over the press, it's just a question of time. There's already been quite a bit written about it, people working there trying to blow the whistle. Anyway, to go back to our case of the *artists* at the Orsay . . .'

'The body bits all come from there – from the medical faculty?'

'Yes. We received intel that it was broken into the night before, but they took a while to call the police because the situation's quite embarrassing. They didn't have any security system, the boys got in by smashing the doors with a bog-standard crowbar. What's worse, the staff couldn't even tell what had been taken or even if anything *had* been stolen, it's such a pit in there. Such a bloody graveyard, I should say. Like: "Right, let's count all the heads to see if one's missing . . ." Can you imagine? Anyway, our thieving comedians must have thought they fancied a touch of the morbid, a little corpse for decoration. Well, they'd only to go and help themselves from the shelves of the medical faculty! Almost as easy as going to the butcher's. Gross, the whole thing.'

'Not comedians . . . It's *her* – this Mila. *She*'s the one who had only to help herself. Artist, my arse.'

'Yes. And all those decent chopped-up people who donated their bodies, they can't have dreamed they'd end up strung like hams from a clock in an art gallery . . . If all this gets out, it's going to be a media carnival. Well, one important thing is we're no longer looking at a homicide. That's something. And I didn't tell you *anything*.'

'Thanks, I owe you one.'

'Yeah . . . And Pierrat, don't let them hassle you.'

Camille fell into a seat at the next brasserie she came to and bummed a cigarette from a young guy finishing his drink and his night out beside her. She never smoked, except in emergencies. This time it came from her belly, a need for nicotine, to let her shoulders loosen. She ordered a coffee, lost in translation in the cool interference of that grey hour when the late-to-bed and the early-risers clash and kiss, and she digested the info. Now, she could admit to herself, it was her right, it wouldn't bring bad luck: for a moment at the Orsay, yes, for a second, she had wondered deep down if that suspended body, how to articulate it, might not by chance have belonged, in part, to Abel Bac. There . . . it was said . . . it was out. With Bac unreachable for twenty-four hours, the five thousand messages she had left him, his mobile off and still off, without any signal, the absence of lights in his apartment – she had pictured a very bad scene.

And Camille's fears had overtaken everything else, everything she had learned about Bac. She didn't give a toss that he had lied, that his past was full of bodies and secrets, she did not blame him. By what right could she possibly blame him? The only thing she feared was that he might disappear.

Abel Bac was a black hole, she knew it already, though she struggled to admit it, the thing was, she thought about him all the time. She raised her little white coffee cup as if to make a toast, thought about the people who had donated their bodies to medicine, such a fuck-up, and said aloud: 'To your health, boys.'

64

My brother, said the fox

She made it home, feeling better after her very strong espresso at the brasserie, and the sun was rising now. She had come straight back, no more detours, suddenly desperate for peace and quiet, to stop getting lost, to wash the night off and go to bed, if only to sleep for a couple of hours, but happy to stop thinking for those two hours and recharge her depleted batteries, ready to go and confront the I.G.P.N. She had not even tried to call Bac one more time, what good would that do, she knew he was alive, had both his arms and his legs, somewhere, and that thought was a powerful consolation.

Camille tapped in her door code, pushed the heavy door inwards, crossed the courtyard, took the staircase on the right. She totted up the aches: in her ribs, thighs, lower back and shoulders, she was wrung dry, first floor, second, she started untying her scarf, unzipped her anorak, wondered (it was one of those myriad micro-thoughts that are constantly passing through us without fallout or connection) if she would make herself another coffee or just lie down in her clothes and not lose a moment's unwinding, she was still all fired up, a fire she would like to wash off, let vanish down the plughole like the swirl of a poor-quality dye leaching away, she felt for the keys in her pocket and was about to take them out when she saw him

... him there ... A crumpled, huddled figure on her mat.
Like a bundle of laundry thoughtlessly tossed onto the doorstep.
A punch in the heart.
Abel Bac.

65

this shows how just

'Pierrat, I was waiting for you here. I'm sorry. I don't have a mobile now,' Abel said, getting to his feet.

'Are you on drugs or something? You look wasted.'

'No, no.'

'How long have you been on my mat?'

'I really don't know.'

'O.K., never mind, come in. Did you see any of my neighbours?'

'I don't think so. I fell asleep.'

'Go run your head under the cold tap. You look as if you've been at a punk ash rave.'

'Elsa told me I looked like a painting by some Norwegian, Munch. Do you know Munch?'

'Err – yes. Elsa? Yes, I know of Munch. Sure you haven't taken anything? Do you know how many messages I left for you? You really are an idiot.'

Camille wondered who Elsa was, all five senses on high alert now, as Bac seemed to be inhabiting some other planet. He looked gaunt, his clothes disordered, his eyes sunken in their sockets. Since this wasn't the first time he had visited Camille at home, Abel made his own way to the bathroom to run his head under the tap. Still following instructions, then. And at that Camille thought: Shit, it's a sty in there, my dirty bras and knickers everywhere. At critical moments, it's often the tiniest, most trivial details that surface and overwhelm everything else. She said nothing. Abel managed to string together some practical moves: he turned on the water and dunked his whole head in the basin, into the icy water, which ran down his neck and into his eyes, now he was reliving that moment a few hours before with Elsa, Elsa's hands deep in his hair. His stomach twisted, hard. He called through, asking if he could borrow her toothbrush. Camille answered yes, straight away, probably she'd have agreed to anything he asked, even while thinking it was all so intimate suddenly. Bac brushing his teeth with her toothbrush, like the morning after a night together, when you might as well use the same toothbrush and share deodorant, when it's even a little exciting to return to these small, private, anodyne gestures after fucking without restraint. And of them all, sharing a toothbrush would always be the weirdest.

Abel was calm, wiped out, distant, even alien. He drank on autopilot the coffee Camille made him. Coffee, that keystone of exchange, civilisation's reflex, its antidote. He would have to talk to her, he'd have to let himself open up, but what to tell her? How to tell it? How do things get told? Camille waited for it to come out, for something to begin. Her colleague did not seem altogether present but rather levitating over her breakfast-bar stool, like an accomplished yogi. She rummaged in a kitchen drawer for a pack of cigarettes and lit one.

'Do you smoke?' Abel said, drawn from his daze by this pragmatic detail.

'No,' she answered, exhaling the smoke.

Camille was losing patience. She got in first. 'I'm going to tell you what went on last night, while you were lord knows where. Did you listen to any of my messages?' Abel shook his head. So

Claire Berest

Camille plunged in: the I.G.P.N. after her arse because of him; the break-in at the Musée d'Orsay which wasn't one because it was all organised by a screwy diva artist; the body parts nicked from the medical faculty; the flowers, the fireworks, her panic . . . It all came out too quickly and Abel couldn't follow, now Camille felt like landing a smart one-two on his nose, but she kept her cool and went back over everything step by step, trying to impart some sense to the whole story. And, doing so, she recognised her own joy: he was here, in front of her, in her home; he had come here, looking for her, he had waited for her. Taken refuge with her.

Camille recounted every moment of her night. The Musée d'Orsay transformed into a phantasmagorical forest, the motifs of the fireworks and the blue, white and red, recurring everywhere like in the scene at the hunting museum, the gold confetti-blowers filling the air in the hall with hundreds of thousands of glinting fireflies, even Courbet's painting of the woman's vagina. And Abel came back to life, his Abel face returned to him, he shrugged off his fright and was now listening to his partner with objectivity and agility, like a detective; he became a detective once more, he took all the elements on board, sat up straight on his stool and leaned towards her. He was here.

He asked to see her photographs from the scene. She handed him her mobile, full of pictures from the gallery. 'The images there don't do the scene justice,' she explained, 'but the actual effect is incredible. It's as if the gallery was turned into a landscape, a kind of weird forest . . . It's hard to explain.'

'The flowers,' Bac said, 'are they orchids?'

'Yes. But they were dyed, as far as I could tell. The work that must have entailed, can you imagine? What was the point?' Finally Camille showed him her shots of the human limbs hanging from the clock. She relayed the info gathered by her pal at

D.P.J. 3, the body parts stolen from the medical school, but she said nothing to Abel about her fears for him.

Together they went back over the facts from the beginning, the three art performances, the three galleries. And Camille caught a hint of their debriefings, when they had worked together, the spark, the sense of competition, how they complemented each other, she had missed him so much.

She also told him about Mila. This artist who was actually very well known and had instigated all these happenings, in full complicity with the galleries themselves – 'And with the Minister for Culture, if you please!' (She was tempted to add *and with taxpayers' money*, but you couldn't really blame the bankers this time.) It had all been a trick; Mila had created the impression of a series of burglaries. They had all been in cahoots, even Pinault. Right up to the bodies that appeared in the Orsay – that's where it had gone off the rails.

'Do you know about Mila? It's a pseudonym; no-one knows what she looks like. Have you heard about her art before?'

'No,' Abel said.

'Sure? Even when there was that big media fuss about her in Paris, with fake bodies, well, models, that were hung from public buildings. Doesn't ring a bell?'

'No, Pierrat, I don't remember that.'

In fact, Abel remembered it perfectly and he also remembered that name very well indeed: *Mila*. He had seen the bodies hanging from the Saint-Jacques tower during one of his night walks, the firemen had been in the process of taking them down. He had been fascinated, had stayed all night to watch them work. But he did not want to tell Pierrat. He had no wish for complicity. He felt a warning chill climb gently but surely up his spine like a clammy reptile.

Camille saw that Abel was growing distant again. He was there but far away, and there with them was the elephant in her kitchen: Vallé. She had to tell him that she knew about his tragedy, she knew why he had been suspended. The anonymous call about his identity. But that might mean losing him again just when she had got him back. So she strung this moment out, giving all the details she could muster, carefully reinforcing the connection between them, to minimise the risk of breaking it. He went on examining the pictures from the Orsay, the flowers, the thousands of blue, white and red flowers. Camille thought: Go on, Bac, talk to me now.

They were sunk in silence. Camille lit another cigarette. And saw on her hands and sweater the last of the gold sequins still clinging, and before her Bac's cautious face bent over the images, apparently in the midst of decoding something, as if he were trying to translate a text written in a tongue he hardly knew. She said:

'Our team went and woke this Mila's lawyer, with a bang as you can imagine, and they won't let him go until he's spat it all out. But they don't know where *she* is. Even her lawyer doesn't know. The chick has vanished.'

Abel looked up at Camille, he was staring so hard at her that she felt embarrassed. By some effect of the shadows in this room barely lit by the incipient dawn, her colleague's blue eyes looked very black.

Abel said: 'I know where she is.'

66

What once was taught me by a fox of wit –

'What d'you mean, you know where she is?' Camille squawked.

'I have to go,' Abel announced.

He told her like this: *I have to go, Pierrat.* At this Camille yelped: 'No, absolutely not! You're not vanishing somewhere and ditching me again!' And the floodgates flew open: 'I know about everything! I know where you grew up, I know what happened in Vallé, I know all of it, do you realise? You have to stop this not replying! Stop this shit of ignoring me, this looking right through me, as if I'm not worth stopping to see!'

Abel hardly started at the mention of Vallé, his native town and his nightmare. He stood and made as if to leave, and Camille, with all her police officer's strength, held on to his arm. He twisted away, but she was hanging on tight. He pushed her and she pushed back. She blocked him. This would be resolved in pure hand-to-hand. She readied her fists. Abel smiled. 'You want to box with me?'

The tension receded.

'I know where Mila is, I know who she is. I have to get there before she gets away. Let me out.'

'I'm coming with you.'

'I have to handle this alone. It's *my* story.'

'This is non-negotiable. Where is she? And how do you know where she is?'

'Don't say I'm mad. I think she's in my building on place Clichy. I think she's living on the floor above mine.'

'It's that Elsa, is it, who thinks you're a Munch? We'll take my car. It's outside.'

Camille drove. At this hour by car, they'd be at the apartment in ten minutes. Bizarrely, she did not doubt what Abel had said. She believed him. They were together again.

He told her about this neighbour whom he had not encountered before, who lived in a studio on the top floor. Whom he had not stopped bumping into over the past week, since he was suspended. And whom he had, in a way, become friendly with. He had told her about himself, she was funny, quite separate from the rest of his life. He told Camille how she had been completely plastered and tried to get into his apartment and that was how they had met. Also that he had been going out of his mind since being sent home, that he could not understand what was happening, and this girl's nuttiness had felt so welcome, so natural. He tried to tell Camille . . . he had never said so much in one go before. Camille drove, her eyes on the road, but she took in everything he said, all the pauses as he chose the right words, to keep them like tattoos on her body. Go on, Bac, keep on talking, she thought, don't stop. And Abel described how they had gone to the Pompidou Centre together, how looking back it was really peculiar that she had come with him like that, a stranger, but she had a certain knack, he said, of making everything seem inevitable. Necessary. 'She told me some stories and it made me feel better.' It was incomprehensible, now he thought about it, how this girl had got close to him. 'She even recommended a restaurant for me to take a woman to that I was meeting from Tinder.' With Camille right there, the absurdity melted into logic. 'It was as if she knew me, I can't explain it, Camille. As if she had put a spell on me.'

This was breaking Camille's heart, cracking her in two, but she concentrated on the road. Good girl.

They were almost there. She needed a parking space. Short of a space, double-parking and she'd flash her police badge, couldn't be helped. 'If I go back over our conversations, I think she mentioned my profession, the other night, the fact I was a police officer, but at that point I hadn't yet told her. We were talking about Munch, in fact, and she was saying I could have investigated him. But it was only later that she asked what my job was. It's her, it's Mila.'

'What was your role – were you to be part of her performance? Something like the horse in the Pompidou and all that carry-on?'

'She explained that to me: the concept of performance art. She said she was writing a history of art thesis. It was all about that for her.'

'Had you ever seen her before? Take your time. Didn't this woman remind you of anyone at all?'

'No. And I generally remember faces.'

'Why would this artist have decided to, er, include you in her work?'

'Everything she created, her whole visual set-up – I don't know what to call it – the whole thing, it told the story of what happened to me in Vallé when I was eighteen. On Bastille Day . . .'

'So you are actually her performance. Only you have no audience.'

They reached his building and Camille parked hurriedly. Abel leaped up the stairs, his colleague at his heels, a new Don Quixote with his Sancho Panza. Abel raced straight up to the top floor, to Elsa's room. Her door was unlocked. He opened it. The room was bare.

The armchair and bed were still there, but all the rest, the knick-knacks, the crockery and clothes, had been tossed into a cardboard box, the way theatre props are bundled away. Dust danced in the shaft cast by the skylight. The window was rattling in the wind and the view over Paris in broad daylight was rather spectacular, Camille thought.

Abel was silent. He stepped outside again, Camille still following behind. They walked down two flights, to his place. Camille thought: *I shall at last see inside Bac's place.*

They went inside together, in silence. On the floor sat a little plant pot prettily tied up with ribbon and cellophane, with a card attached. It was an orchid. Abel opened the card, read it and closed it again.

'Is it from her? What did she put?'

Abel held the card out to Camille, who, as she in turn read its brief message, felt emotion swell inside her throat.

'But why would she give you an orchid before she left, Abel? What does it mean?'

67

Which on thy jaws this animal hath writ –

'Why? Because of this, Camille!'

Abel had shouted, suddenly she did not know this man, his arms describing a sweep around the apartment, as if to show her something.

'This what, Abel?' Camille asked softly.

'All my plants of course! She's given me an orchid to add to my collection!'

'What plants do you mean? What collection?' Camille said, suddenly horribly afraid.

'Here! All around us, you can see there are orchids all over the place! Everywhere! Here, here, here!' Abel shouted, pointing into his apartment.

Camille felt the emotion that had choked her on reading Mila's message a moment ago jump another octave. A speck of a tear fell from one eye as she said:

'But Abel, I don't, I don't see anything in this room. I don't understand . . . There's *nothing* here!'

And Camille again looked around, frightened, trying to see what her friend was looking at. There were indeed terracotta pots scattered about, filled with water, flowerpots without flowers. Abel stiffened, breathing faster and faster, he was struggling to speak, he muttered, 'But I can see them.' And he seized Camille's hands, for he was swaying.

Epilogue

68

'All unknown things the wise mistrust.'

When the nurse brought his medication, he handed Abel a letter that had come that morning. Abel had had a few visits since he had been admitted, mainly from Camille, but he had received no post. He thanked the nurse. Of course he was nicely floating with all his meds, he had lost track of the days, but he knew.

He knew it was from Her.

So he did not hurry to open the letter. Lying on the bed in his little sickroom – he was lucky to have a room to himself and even his own bathroom – he gazed at it. He would wait for the right moment to open it. He did not know when the right moment would arrive.

When Abel read the letter, he would discover that Elsa felt bad about tormenting him. In it, she tried not to justify her actions but to tell him her own story, the story that had led her all the way to him. She admitted it was she who had made the anonymous call to the police that had led to his suspension. For Abel, that moment seemed an eternity ago. In her letter she wrote at some length about the word 'inform' and its shameful connotations, and about this first hostile move towards him which had enabled the rolling wave of her performance. She wrote that he must have guessed by now that it was her. But that there should not be anything left unsaid between them.

She made some jokes in the letter, which was just like her.

Caustic as ever. She also told him how, in order to plot this last piece, for the first time in her life she had plunged back into her high-school years, going through her early memories with a fine-toothed comb to trace how she might have acted differently, to recall what she had seen and what she had missed. Only then had she realised that she had met Éric at a party a few years before that Bastille Day, that she had forgotten his name but could still remember his face. Because it's true he was good-looking, right? She had even been attracted to him, or at least spotted him, it was a party, the loud music was doing its thing, and there was this young man just a little different from the others and she had chatted with him. Can you believe it, Abel? I spoke to him at that party! But despite her efforts, she had never been able to recall what they had said to each other that evening.

On the other hand, she remembered very well what she and he, Abel Bac, had said the first time they had met. It was a year before that July 14. I couldn't remember your face, which is odd, but I remembered your name, the one you buried along with Bastille Day in Vallé.

They had been summoned to the same lycée on the same day to take their oral exam for the bac. As they came out of the exam hall, there had been just the two of them standing in the courtyard, both still tense but relieved, and they had spontaneously begun talking. You asked if I had a cigarette, but I didn't smoke. And I thought perhaps that was an excuse to talk to me. Which made me happy.

They had laughed when they realised they must have been examined on the same text. Pure luck!

Do you remember, Abel? Look well among your memories. That girl was me.

They had both been faced with Aesop's fable of 'The Fox, the

Wolf and the Horse', in La Fontaine's text. And the two kids, as they were then, had playfully compared their respective interpretations, particularly of the last line.

You didn't agree with the moral of the tale, Abel. You didn't understand why wisdom should be wary of the unknown. But I said that the fable shows you can't trust anyone, even and especially those who appear closest to us.

Within this letter, Abel Bac would find Elsa's words. But just then it was too painful to read.

So he left the envelope on the night table in his sickroom, carefully letting it lie there, next to his orchid.

Author's Acknowledgements

My thanks to Albéric de Gayardou, Laura Serkine, Émilie François, Olivier Jacquemond, Claire de Vismes and Virginie Hagelauer.

Thank you, Isa, Anne, Pierre and Lélia Berest.

Thank you, Manuel Carcassonne, Alice d'Andigné, Paloma Grossi, Vanessa Retureau, Charlotte Brossier, Héloïse Rachet, Maÿlis Vauterin, Thomas Guillaume, Nicolas Haddou, Raphaëlle Liebaert and all the family at Editions Stock who look after and support me.

To my Frida and to Juliette.